Also by Bruce Crown

Chronic Passions
Forlorn Passions
How Dim the Promised Land

Originally published in hardcover by Vintage Copenhagen Publications in August 2016
First trade paperback edition: August 2017
Reissued: December 2017, August 2018

Vintage Copenhagen Publications is a division of AP Publications. The AP Publications name and logo are a trademark of AP Publications.

The publisher is not responsible for websites (or their content) that are not owned by the publisher.

The Copenhagen Speakers Group may provide authors for speaking events. To find out more, please contact speakers@vintagecopenhagenpublications.com.

A catalogue record for this book is available at *Library and Archives Canada*:
395 Wellington St,
Ottawa, ON
K1A 0N4

Cataloguing in Publication Data available upon request.

Crown, Bruce, 1989—
The Romantic and The Vile / Bruce Crown
FICTION / Drama
FICTION / Literary
Toronto : AP Publications, 2016.

Printed in Canada, the United States of America, and the EU.

978-0-9918883-6-8 (Softcover)
978-0-9958492-2-8 (Hardback)
978-0-9918883-7-5 (eBook)

Cover Painting: Van Gogh, Close up of *Wheat Field with Cypresses;* 1889; The Metropolitan Museum of Art

BRUCE CROWN

THE ROMANTIC AND THE VILE

Für Lilli

Ethereal sunbeams never disappear; they are as eternal as its seeking rays.

So in a voice, so in a shapeless flame
Angels affect us oft, and worshipp'd be;
Still when, to where thou wert, I came…

John Donne, *Air and Angels*

PREFACE

Writing a novel is physically exhausting. The reader always fails to see, until they finally have nothing better to do than read the bloodied soul of the writer's creation, the artist writing out, word by word, expression by expression, the consistency of a person's demeanour and the predictable range of their reactions. An old gentleman would never forget to stand upon a lady's entry, or would he? What if sufficient build-up had been established such that a woman on his mind causes his body to fail. Is it more symbolic for a narrative when the gentleman *forgets* to stand, or is every one of his having stood, and continuing to stand save that one time, diminished by the momentary lapse in his range?

Images are even more complicated; the writer imagines the aroma of petrichor and the sound of a woman's footsteps. But those footsteps and that aroma are not the same imagined… even the woman differs from reader to reader. Ergo the arduous road continues, of reading and rereading in silence how people behave and react to each other. The reader sees none of this and feels none of this. The laborious task of the reader manifests in scanning the words line by line, page by page, into the writer's deliberate orchestra where the final movement of his symphony is either too satisfying or not satisfying enough. For the reader, sometimes words are an emptiness without anything in them and sometimes they are the emptiness of the universe that houses everything in it. Prisoners of their own minds, neither writer nor reader can ever know when and where the next section of the narrative will walk through the mist of their subconscious, let itself in, and greet them.

The writer, only having words, understands their cutting nature. Their ability to deceive, to betray, to unite, and to love perplexes him; before he knows it there's a copious amount of them and each take their own direction. Suddenly, two or three simple ones decide to go the same way: a personal pronoun, a noun that can be taken as a verb, and a second personal singular pronoun moves under the surface of his skin up to his eyes that looks but rarely sees. The writer has written the words and the reader has now read them. Deep in us some of those words can alter our compositions and rewrite details about the person we think we are. Most people, knowing their nerves could not bear these alterations, rewrites, and edits are simultaneously aware that they must deal with their misuse when they are alone and see no meaning in them past their letters. These people put on their armour and take it off for no one until they forget they're wearing armour at all. How can the writer give the one thing that matters to him: those simple words, with the foreknowledge that if his beloved dons a lifetime armour, he will never get any of them back?

BC. August 2016.
Toronto.

THE ROMANTIC AND THE VILE

BOOK ONE

THE ROMANTIC

I
Côte d'Azur

Yachts sway above the deep blue waves of the French Riviera. Its waters are a veiling paradise that enjoy 300 days of sunshine per year; paradise for some, hell for most. It's the Mediterranean coastline that extends from the Italian border to the southeast corner of France but it's really an island. An existential island for journeying souls to unveil and repair themselves until they're fit to ascend its ledges and reach the apex of Paradise. Its clear turquoise water reflects the jonquil yellow sunlight over 115 kilometres of sandy coastline and beaches. Streets are filled with exotic sports cars and pretty women frolicking from designer boutique to designer spa, thanking Plutus for their lucky fortune and marching straight into the fourth circle of *the Inferno*.

Quaint little buildings coloured orange and crimson tower over the rocky edges of the meridian. From one door to the next, narrow alleys twist the thoughts of labourers, artists, bartenders, liars, thieves, politicians, and bankers alike.

Neil Meyollner and his wife Nora reside in a unique six-bedroom penthouse at *Le 21 Princesse Grace*, the most exclusive street in Monaco's Larvotto district. His wife had lost interest in the blue Versace silk curtains they'd bought the previous season and since they wanted to change the curtains for a third time this year, Neil decided to completely renovate the penthouse for his great love. He had already, for their fourth anniversary, bought the penthouse next door and tore down the separating wall to merge the two and create wardrobes for each of the 5 bedrooms. The previous renovation had left 476 square meters of living space and a 95 square meter terrace.

"I feel cramped, Neil," she'd said to him after returning from a girls' night out.

He abided to his love of unity then and he abided to his wife now; he would *always* abide, even if it meant their apartment would end up costing 120,000€ per square meter. Annually the pool, sauna, concierge, and private chauffeurs ran the cost of the place to 65,000€. But again he abided because unity is expensive.

We emerge through a circular unity from our mother's womb and seasonally precipitate our thoughts until the head of the snake reaches its tail in death. Born unwise and warm until we perish in cold ignorance among others. To reconcile the disunity we feel, we search for equal unity with another. But wisdom is not unity. Every narrative and epic is only a miscellany of letters arranged to form meaning. In ignorance we trade words like old merchants with language as our currency but exchange them with the foreknowledge that they will never mean to the other what they represent for us. If we are lucky we find another with equal ignorance and now we are doubly unwise, misting through our cloudy subconscious in vain hope that we will eventually find wisdom. But wisdom is not unity. We procreate, considering ourselves wise and united. In our "wisdom" we grow old and share our ignorance with our offspring so that we may unite through "wisdom." But only after we're dead do we finally understand that wisdom *cannot* be unity. In illusory unity we reflect on reciprocating the love of ignorance but united neither in wisdom nor in synthesis. Even in the presence of our so-chosen *soul mate* and the most intimate moments we may share with them we only dent upon the surface of both souls without so much as a thought or touch. Nothing we do is to synthesize wisdom but only to appear wise to ourselves. We are malevolent or benevolent for the same reason: to unite wisdom with power. Since power comes from money, everything we do is to perpetuate our power so that we may legitimately say we are wise, despite the fact that accumulating money does not equate wisdom, and thus we feel as ignorant as ever. Wisdom is the same in all humans in that there cannot be a synthesis of it except in illusion, indolence, and ignorance; but our sense of wisdom is equated to our self-proclaimed vision of power. The more money we have the more authentically we feel our wisdom. Neil was the wisest man in any given room and yet there was scarcely a power he would not relinquish for his wife.

Sacrifices are necessary in life but in love more often than not the preferred currency is souls. Neil had to rent out pieces of himself to make sure the renovation was perfect and in time for Nora's birthday. Until then they'd been staying at *the Grand-Hotel du Cap-Ferrat* half an hour away from their penthouse, a few floors above Edwin Voclain and his wife Holly.

Neil had opened *Couronne Asset Management* with Edwin just after they both graduated from Cambridge. Edwin had coasted through life and continued coasting along the Riviera. He thought he was naturally talented and had never given a second thought to his affluent upbringing. His father was an investment broker from Wall Street and his mother began working at the NASDAQ when she was twenty-one. Out of insecurity he always thought himself slightly smarter than Neil but that is how all great friendships are born. *CAM* was actually Neil's idea but he was a scholarship student, pouring people like Edwin their Italian espressos and Ardbeg scotches with nothing but his intellect and his Bic ballpoint tiding him towards the coast. On the surface Neil knew he wouldn't be where he was without Edwin and it was this that bothered him the most. That despite his brilliant ideas and resilience he still had to prostitute himself to the most ancient of Gods: money. It was Edwin's connections that gave them a leg-up on their competition; it was Edwin's indolent machismo that prospective clients loved to see; it was Edwin's ridiculously coloured suits bringing the team designer donuts that won their hearts. Never was it Neil's stoic glances at the accounting sheets or his motivational talks on how to increase everyone's vacation time *and* improve their exclusive client base.

Nora had been out partying with Edwin and Holly and Neil's early meeting was the perfect excuse to bow out. He got up carefully not to wake his wife and sat on the floor on the antique silk Persian Kermani rug at the foot of the bed. Reaching under the bed where he kept his phone he checked the market. Canadian uranium was down and the Euro was up just as he'd predicted. He could finally buy Nora that chopper she'd wanted. The sun was still rising over the water and he looked at the colours before tiptoeing out of the room and into the shower.

Empty bottles of GlenDronach and Monkey 47 covered the kitchen counter. The after party. Neil washed the glasses and left a tip for the maid.

He emailed Edwin lest he wasn't thinking of showing up; rich young Arab boys with too much of Daddy's money and not enough sense need that elitist and insolent charm only the ignorant can bring.

Heading to the office now. N. M.

The hotel's breakfast restaurant: La Véranda, offered an assortment of juices, drinks, and food. Neil ordered a fresh fruit salad with carrot juice and an espresso, and had the Baker's Basket of warm bread sent up to his wife with a note: *warm bread for my warm angel when she wakes up*. They say romance is dead.

Hiring the hotel's chauffeur service, he sat up front with his driver Alec and talked about various investment strategies. After glancing at the Coke can in the cup holder, he tried to tell him that saving even 1€ a day is better than spending it on a can of Coke. For some unknown reason Neil felt compelled to ask, "Alec can I ask you something?"

"Of course, sir."

"Call me Neil."

"Sure… Neil."

"Do you read?"

"Sir? … I mean Neil."

"Books I mean."

"When I have the time."

"What do you like?"

"I like Camões and Pessoa."

"Portuguese writers. They're passionate."

"They have some excellent copies at the *BOMO*."

"Where?"

"The book boutique."

"Oh?" Neil looked around as if expecting to see the store manifest in front of him.

"It's just around the corner on *Avenue du Port*. They have English books there. I don't know if they have them in Portuguese."

"Or a dual-language edition?"

"That would be perfect."

Driving past the *Banque Populaire Côte d'Azur* Neil's phone beeped.

"Excuse me, Alec."

"Of course, sir," he slowed behind a red light.

They cancelled for today. Partied hard last night and didn't want to come in this early. I rescheduled for next week. :)

EdWIN.

P.S. Calvin would be a good addition to the team. Let's hire him. The other guy was junk!

Neil read the message again.

"*Merci,* Alec. My meeting is cancelled. You can just let me off here."

"I can take you back if you like sir. To the book store perhaps."

"No. It's a fine day. I'd like to walk."

"Very well." They came to a stop in front of the *Hotel Novotel Monte Carlo*. "You should definitely check it out."

"I will. See you back at the hotel."

"Good day."

Neil watched Alec merge back into traffic and head towards the stadium.

It was 19 degrees and sunny as he expected but he felt hot. Taking off his jacket and untying his tie he had an affinity to head to the bookstore. Then he suddenly felt faint and collapsed on a bench nearby, facing Larvotto Beach.

"It's hot," he turned to the man sitting next to him smoking a pipe.

"Ja," the man returned in a German accent. "I come here every day. Quite nice."

"Yes."

Neil caught his breath but couldn't remember how to get to Avenue du Port. "Do you know how to get to the BOMO?"

"*Das was?*"

"The book store. It's on Avenue du Port."

"Avenue du Port. Head to Boulevard Rainier III. Then Rue des Agaves. Up the stairs at Rue de la Turbie and then a right at Rue Grimaldi before you see Avenue du Port."

"*Dankeschön.*"

"*Bitte.* You vant me to repeat it?"

"Nein. It should be straightforward. I have my phone too if all else fails."

"Ja ja."

Neil got up and nodded; the man flicked his Panama hat.

A woman carrying a crying baby brushed by Neil and he looked at the flushed face of the infant and wondered why it was crying. Without noticing he smiled even though the baby's eyes were swelled shut from the tears.

People sat along the sunlit streets among the cool breeze on benches and grass patches. Some kids kicked a football around. For a moment Neil went numb and immediately made sure to watch a single wave in the horizon and overwhelm himself with emotion. He couldn't *afford* to be numb; he wanted everything only for his wife and for no one else. He would crush a company or a man who dared not to treat his wife with the respect she deserved. Of course this was Neil and was no indication of Nora as a woman or person at all. She barely deserved Neil and had neither the intellect nor passion to comprehend the depths his soul would sink at the mere mention of her name.

"Was it a right at Grimaldi or left?" he whispered to himself and guessed right without realizing the serendipitous unraveling that was about to take hold of his life had made certain he would guess right. At a stoplight he gazed at a red crosswalk and feared stepping on it. Hopping on the white stripes of the pedestrian lanes he found the roundabout that connected Grimaldi to *Avenue du Port*. A kid who thought he was skipping joined him as if the red was lava and jumped from one white stripe to another and Neil smiled and waved.

His phone lit up: *Heading to lunch at Muse. Made dinner reservations at Caina. <3.*

He stopped at three-quarters across and looked at the green neon "Pharmacy" sign before a car swerved around him and he took a moment to respond to his darling wife.

Have fun. I don't know if I'll make it for lunch. Did you get my breakfast basket?

Waiting a couple of seconds he saw the "…" which meant she was typing a message but then it disappeared and no message came.

"*Bonsoir,*" an old man with a golden cane waved when Neil looked back down the street.

"Bonjour," Neil nodded and walked towards the BOMO. In the back of his mind he relegated the meeting with the Arab sheikhs or princes or whatever they were, wondering about what Edwin would do to charm them if they didn't drink. Edwin would always bring a nice bottle of Glenfiddich or GlenDronach; he was so predictable and that was what made him simultaneously dishonest and trustworthy.

"What book am I going to buy?" he thought to himself just before a truck turned left out of the way and he saw the blue logo for the BOMO.

Inside the smell of both new and used books meshed to create a new smell: knowledge combined with curiosity. A used book meant one of three things, either someone was passing on the knowledge someone else had retained, or the knowledge was not sufficient for them, or they were not sufficient enough for the knowledge. Occasionally a young brat in a beanie with designer brogues would glance up at Neil in disgust as if he were the representative of the establishment that had meticulously oppressed them, even though none of these so-called freethinking hipsters were actually oppressed. They'd oppressed themselves just to fight the same battles their parents had already fought, being too lazy and weak to take on the *actual* establishment. It was simpler to scowl in disgust at suits despite wearing casual luxury clothes designed by mediocre rappers. It was simpler to go on harrowing rants about franchise coffee houses despite religiously attending cafés that exclusively served them manual-pressed South American coffee at the same profit margin as the franchises they were supposed to be fighting.

It amused Neil. He found himself in the literary fiction section looking up and down the shelves for something that caught his eye. The wood glistened and felt coarse at the edges but glossy where the books stood tall. How much Ovid, Dante, Huxley, and Hafiz teach us about love and justice and loyalty and greed and death and still we've learnt nothing.

A woman, who like Neil, seemed lost among the infinitude of words and narratives, began her search on the opposite side of the shelf where he was looking. Naturally and pursuant and to the rules of literary romantic fiction the gap between them tightened until they were both eye to eye with Huxley's *the Genius and the Goddess.*

"That's a good one," she whispered to herself while she took it off the shelf and caressed the cover.

"*Pardon*?" Neil queried in French.

She turned the dust jacket towards him, "This is an excellent novel."

"Oh… Yes. You can't go wrong with Huxley."

"Are you looking for anything particular?" her gaze slipped into the distance behind them and then towards Neil's ring finger.

"Not really. I wanted something … what's the word… *engulfing* to read," and then he was compelled, driven even, to continue talking, "I travel a lot. Spend a lot of time on the road in cars and planes and live in hotel rooms which means…" he interrupted himself when he wondered *why* he'd said so much about himself to a stranger.

"This one is good. Would you like it?" she handed him the Huxley.

"The Huxley?" he looked at her up and down and then shook himself free from the prison of his marriage. He had been lying to himself when he thought and acted as if his relationship was perfect. He had deceived himself into believing that he had no choice, that he loved Nora more than anything else on this planet. His marriage… he thought, his marriage that had been tethering the thin string of infidelity for as long as he could remember. Neil was sure to an acceptable degree of certainty, that his beloved wife, whom he was over the moon for, was having an affair. That was of course no excuse to desire this woman or contemplate booking a flight somewhere, anywhere, where he wouldn't have to worry about return rates and stock increases and futures derivatives. This woman, this *stranger,* whom he'd shared more about his life than with Edwin and Nora combined in recent months, with her hand reaching out to him with *the Genius and the Goddess*, simply confronted him with the stark realities of his disappointing friendship and failing marriage. What stirred his heart more than this woman's desirability wasn't necessarily her light ash brown hair, her toned forearms, or her athletic body curved perfectly along the small of her back. No. It was ubiquitously opaque in the shadow of his now waning heart why he wanted her and looking past her grey irises it frightened him. His desire was neither sexual nor lustful. He hankered for a conversation with substance, a conversation that wasn't about where they would sit at *Caina* or whether the Hermès curtains would match the Persian rug they'd ordered.

"Yes. I think it's one of his best," she looked back at the shelf and touched the spine of a *Hesse*.

"*One* of his best. Certainly not his best," Neil chuckled.

"Oh? What's his best then?" without either of them being aware of the machinations of circumstance she had already beguiled him as if they were both frozen in time, unable to move forward or backward without the other.

Neil chuckled but then realized he couldn't really answer, "I… don't… know. Can I think about it?"

"Always."

From the outside perspective it had to be vague yet simple, why this austere man, despite the rules and traits demanded of someone like him to attain what he'd acquired: success, wealth, meaning, influence, would then reject the associative traits that accompanied them: ruthless, manipulative, adulterous, wicked. Neil wanted to believe that what amassed a complete person was in fact a chore life demanded of the self, and to avoid the existential crisis that it would never matter how wicked or noble or unfaithful or honourable he could be with impunity, he seemed bound to tie his existence to a conglomeration of pure motives and impersonal actions.

"Garbage," a man in a black-beanie chortled and threw a green book onto the shelf. Dust kicked up and it slipped through the edges of the wood and dropped in front of the woman.

"It's 20 degrees out… I'll never understand young people."

"You and me both," Neil looked back towards the man who had now disappeared into the Self-Help stacks.

The woman bent down to pick up the book at the same as Neil and they both chuckled. It was a regular Moleskine bound by its signature string.

"Is this someone's journal?" she opened the book to handwritten notes and sketches and her eyes widened.

Neil's gaze ventured onto the shelf where he saw the Oxford World Classics edition of *the Sorrows of Young Werther*.

"What is it?"

"It's…" she closed it and put it back on the shelf.

"Let me see it," he took it back off the shelf. The cover was worn from overuse and the pages were yellowed by time. He opened it to a pastel sketch of a butterfly on a flower. "Chair."

"What?"

"Reminds me of that chair in the museum."

"You're talking to yourself," she furrowed her brows.

"The chair in a modern art museum. They had to put a sign that said: *this is not part of the exhibit. This is a chair you can sit on.* People thought it was an art piece."

She laughed. "How does that relate?"

He turned the journal to its inner cover, "Look. There's an email. Someone left their journal here and people think it's a book for sale."

"Will you return it?"

Neil went through the varying scenarios in his head. Emailing the person and having to follow up to return their journal to them. He simply didn't have the time. With the meetings and the renovations and the helicopter purchase but the way she asked the question had guaranteed his assent. "I'll email *raphaeladler@umail.com.* We'll see what happens. These are someone's thoughts. They should have it back. Are you taking the Huxley?"

"Yes I am," she stood up and straightened her floral summer dress.

"I'll take the Goethe then. Would you like to walk out together?"

"Sure," they made their way to the counter.

"Hey," a dainty young woman in jeans and a blue polo greeted them, "Together or separate?"

"Togetherate," they said at the same time.

"Please. Allow me to purchase that for you," Neil smiled.

Her lips arched towards the sky.

"So that's one *Genius and the Goddess*," she looked at them, "*Sorrows of Young Werther*," and the journal stared back at her like an abyss, "Oh the green Moleskine as well? Three items total."

"No. That's not part of it; it's used," Neil returned, thinking the woman believed he wanted to buy a new journal.

"Yes of course. This is one of our most popular books."

"What? This is a book?" the woman in the floral dress pointed to the cover.

"This is someone's journal," Neil tapped the hardcover, "You haven't tried to return it?"

"Of course we have. Everyone who buys it donates it back after trying to return it to the owner. Sometimes they send it back in the mail. It's practically the mascot of the store by now."

"I'll buy it," at that moment Neil decided to actualize the meaning he'd been searching for.

His phone chirped while the cashier tallied up the price and Neil handed her his American Express Platinum card as he read the email.

Saw this. This is what Nora would love! The others are junk. ;) EdWIN.

The email included a link to a review of the *Eurocopter of Colibri* which had him wondering both why Edwin cared so much about what he was planning to buy his wife and how to bend the realities of his life so not to be bothered by the illusion of meaning in acquiring more objects.

A grey Vespa scooted past them when they exited.

"Thank you for the novel."

"*De rien.*"

"May I ask you for another favour?"

"Of course," Neil began walking towards Caina.

"I'd like to give you my number. Would you mind texting or calling me if you ever find the owner of that notebook? I'd like to meet him."

Neil took the book out of the bag and caressed the cover again, "Sure. I just realized. I don't even know your name."

She smirked, "Christina."

"My name's Neil. It's a pleasure."

"Nice to meet you, Neil."

"Your name sounds familiar. Have we met before?"

"I'd remember," she took a business card out of her leather purse and handed it to him.

Professor Christina Lindström. University of Stockholm. Classics and Literature.

"You're a literature professor? Should I call you doctor?"

"Please don't," she flagged down a taxi, "But get in touch if you find him."

"I will."

She nodded and a cab stopped in front of them.

He opened the door for her, "And what if I don't find him?"

"What do you mean?" she got in and greeted the driver.

"May I still get in touch?"

Her smile was the last thing he saw before she closed the door and the black-tinted window separated him from the look in her eyes.

On the walk back towards Caina, he received an email from one of the owners, Guido, informing him that his regular table, Table number 4 on the second terrace had been reserved specifically for Neil and his party. He walked across a red crosswalk and was almost hit by a dark blue Ferrari who then honked its high-pitched squeal and flipped him off. There was time to head back home to change and shower before meeting everyone else for lunch. Traversing the same route backwards he saw the old man sitting on a bench further out this time.

"It's too hot," he sat down next to him.

"*Ja ja*," he fanned himself three times with his Panama hat, "Oh. *Vat* did you buy?" he pointed to the blue BOMO bag.

Neil handed the books to the man.

"*Göthe und…*," he touched the cover of the journal, "You bought a journal?"

"Not exactly," Neil flipped through the pages and showed the man that it had been filled.

"Oh. You found *someone's* journal?" he put his Panama hat on and hid his eyes, "May I see?"

"Of course," Neil handed him the Moleskine.

He opened the book to a particular page and read a poem. Touching the words with the tip of his fingers suddenly he slammed the cover closed and handed Neil back the journal. "It's good," he flicked the brim of his hat, "Don't lose it," and with his long thin cane in hand, began walking away from the bench.

Neil watched him walk through a narrow street and disappear behind a streak of sky that shined between the houses. Opening the book to a random page he found it titled in a language he couldn't recognize.

Skjult Harmoni. Hidden Harmony.

Europeans do not understand North America but for the varying news outlets they read, most of which are in their own languages. Filled with their own cultural bias or lacklustre understanding, their analysis of the average North American lacks the most basic feeling. Simply because we can ride helicopters to our villas in the country or accumulate vast amounts of wealth and buy houses in Europe they think we care for nothing but money. The British especially, seeing their so-called brutish empire now long dead have only their incomprehensible accents to hold dear and berate the North American for not speaking *true* English. Yet it's another sign of status and of money. But North Americans don't care for money in the slightest. Most of us spend it the moment we acquire it whether in intelligence or not. Money is nothing to us but the idol and ideal of success. We are the true idealists. Of course we have set our ideal on the wrong idol, since the only true idol for a man ought to be his passion, and a passion cannot be money since it is tangible and sensible. Even Plato, who by the modern definition would be European, is contemptuous of people who believe the senses can yield knowledge. In other words, that something has to be graspable in order to be real. Doesn't the *Theaetetus* define such people as eu amousoi? Amusing enough, eu amousoi translates literally to "happily without the muses." What insipid lives these people must lead, without a divine inspiration that gives them an insight only a muse could bestow upon the lonely and melancholic.

Neil reread the words again and again and let them simmer in his mind, feeling for his wallet and then for Christina's card. How exact and personal the words, not a single one wasted and yet he was as ill informed about the subject as if he'd just learnt how to read. The Greek stood out as if they'd been written exactly for Neil Meyollner and no one else. He flipped through the pages to see if the thought continued but it didn't. Flipping back through the first few pages he saw three different signatures and on the facing page Raphael quoted *Paradise Lost*: "I sung of chaos and eternal night, Taught by the heavenly Muse to venture down the dark descent, and up to reascend...."

He felt ashamed and nosy reading someone else's thoughts. A journal is really an extension of the writer's mind and no one should be allowed to glimpse into another's thoughts. To curtain his shame he drafted a note to the email listed under the *if found.*

Dear Raphael Adler,

I came across and purchased your journal from the BOMO in Monaco and I'd like to return it to you. Please be kind enough to write me when you have the time.

Sincerely, Neil Meyollner.

He deleted *and purchased* as to not seem too forward and replaced the *Sincerely* with *Cordially* after considerable thought and sent the email. For a moment he hesitated and rued the email because he wanted to keep the book and read it. Reaching again for Christina's card he wrote her an email.

Dear Professor Lindström,

I have sent the email to our mutual mystery man and I regrettably read one of the passages in it. It is quite interesting.

Yours, Neil.

He sent that one immediately because he knew if he reread it he would erase the *Yours* and a part of him didn't want to.

When his phone chimed his breathing sped up, thinking it was either an email from Christina or Raphael.

Where are you?

R. <3

It was only his wife. She signed her emails to him with random letters that made up her name without any consistency or order. It was, he thought, an act of rebellion since he never allowed himself to be anything less than utterly cordial, even to his wife of eleven years.

On my way, darling.

Love, Neil Meyollner.

While he walked back to the hotel he looked out into the sea and felt as if he were seeing it for the first time. The baby blue of the waves fawned over the fair yellow of the sand and kissed them with their foamy lips. Somewhere down the horizon, as if God had arbitrarily picked a spot to dip his paintbrush into a different colour, the hues darkened into azure and then progressively cobalt and finally beyond the edge of perception turned into ultramarine.

Neil waved to Alec on his way in and shook the porter's hand. When he entered the suite he heard Edwin talking with Nora and went straight into his study. Listening to their voices for a moment he heard them speaking with such glee; they were so confident that their conversation was worth having that it often beguiled others almost as though their conversation had substance. Neil heard them speak about the previous night's gala; who was wearing what and from the matching sets of colours and clothes gossiped about the various affairs they thought were going on. Name-dropping was of course natural, who attended and what they'd said. Seeming by appearances that they knew everyone but themselves. Neil opened and read the investment reports and dozed off watching the numbers rise and fall before the markets closed until finally he caught the end of their conversation.

"King Farouk of Egypt outlawed red cars in his empire. Now of course his Bentley was red and so were his family's cars and his security detail's car. So cops wouldn't dare stop any red cars and whenever normal people saw a red car… they *knew*… their king was about. Why do you think he doesn't allow light-coloured ties? We live in Monaco for Christ's sake! Does he wear those ridiculous ties just like King Farouk drove the *only* red Bentley. … Or was it a Rolls?"

"There's no time for the queens when you're running an empire. There's no time for women when you're running an empire," he heard his wife saying.

"Empires are run by queens," Edwin laughed and slurped something.

"Empires are run *for* the queen," Neil entered. He noticed immediately that both the cretonne of the curtain and the furniture upholstery had been altered to match. Some of their paintings had been brought in, including their gold frames personally bought by Nora on a sojourn to Venice. Across the three walls she'd hung a Native American in the style of Gauguin, a woman and a rose by a John William Waterhouse student, and a landscape in classic Monet fashion. Carved mahogany tables matched the overlay of the kitchen and a wooden vase that sat between the sink and the island. It was then he noticed that the writing table in his study had been altered to match the lining of the kitchen island as well. The place had now retained a significant, minimal, and yet grand aura. The objects that surrounded the entire suite were the summation of Nora Meyollner's existence.

Edwin crossed his legs, unwrinkling his *Incotex* linen and cotton-blend jacquard suit woven with a subtle navy and black floral pattern.

"You missed out last night!" he bit the handle of his *Thom Browne* round-frame tortoiseshell acetate glasses.

"You had our paintings brought in," Neil addressed his wife as she set an espresso down in front of Edwin.

"Yes," her shallow-set aqua green eyes glanced at him, "Where were you?"

"At the BOMO."

"What's that?" Edwin queried as he sipped the espresso, noticing his pinkie wrapped around the cup and immediately raising it to point out.

"It's a book store. On Avenue du Port."

"You can read?" Edwin snorted to himself. On the surface only Edwin could laugh at a quip jabbing Neil's literacy. It was in their college years when he caught Neil listening to audiobooks on an old cassette Walkman. Wanting to sleep with a girl who had a penchant for only bedding *hipsters*, Edwin had, in their senior year, given up his designer polos and Gucci loafers for Converse All Stars and nerdy superhero tees. Neil's old Walkman was the perfect accessory to show Elaine how avant-garde he truly was without his Centurion card. Waiting for her Females First: Universal Gender-Equality lecture to end, Edwin had turned on the tape hoping for modern indie trash only available in cassette but was instead confronted by an audiobook of Ovid's *Metamorphoses*. Thinking himself quite clever, Edwin then told everyone that Neil couldn't actually read and instead listened to tapes of the assigned texts for class and somehow thought that compensated for his inferiorities.

"What'd you buy?" Nora queried, "Or didn't you buy anything?"

Something peculiar happened, "A new translation of an old Goethe." Neil didn't mention the journal.

"Sounds like proto-ironic junk!" Edwin knocked dust off his *Bottega Veneta* intrecciato leather loafers.

There was something so indolent rooted in Edwin. He was so childish that nearly everyone pitied his existence. Neil saw a silent nobility in his behaviours, but also saw something maternal in the looks him and Nora would exchange between sentences. He resented that she told him she didn't want kids despite treating Edwin like a child. The way she looked at him. He didn't mind when you thought he was a fool or naïve or still a child. Perhaps this was his game. The mask he'd been wearing all his life and now it'd been too long to know how to remove it, or being far too afraid to remove it lest he be unhappy with his true face. We die wearing our masks rather than with our faces and it is our masks people talk about, never the real us.

When Neil let the silence reign long enough Edwin's tactic had always been to go straight to business in order to provoke a reaction, "You going to back to the office today or should I move the meeting to later on this week?"

"Reschedule for next week. Tell them only *if* we can pencil them in."

"What do you mean?"

"I don't like irresponsible people. They came to Monte Carlo and probably got wasted at the casino the day before an important meeting. And I'm supposed to make them money?"

"You make money when they make money," Edwin's tacit smile was meant to invoke a sense of loyalty to money he thought Neil had.

"Hmmm," Neil ignored what he'd said and turned to Nora, "When's your reservation for Caina?"

"*Our* reservation is at eight. We have our table! If you mean for lunch we're going to *Muse*."

"Perfect," Neil smiled.

"I detect sarcasm," Edwin got up and hugged Nora, "I'm out. Later!" and tapped Neil on the shoulder and walked out. "See you at three."

"Did you like the basket?" Neil asked once Edwin had left and went to hug and kiss his wife.

She smooched him on the lips, "Yes. There's an Hermès chess set that would go perfectly with the table Neil. You *have* to see it! It's like they're from the same wood!"

He kissed her, "You want to play chess?"

"The pieces would complement the leather lining on the couches!"

"Sure. It's on Avenue de Monte-Carlo isn't it?"

"Yeah!" her smile lit up like the red leaves of autumn in perfect cohesion with her yellow midday dress, "I'm going to shower."

"Sure love," he kissed her again and sank into the maroon leather armchair in his study. The silence ensured he would hear Nora singing in the shower behind the ticking sound of the matte stainless steel and lacquered-fibreboard supported *Roche Bobois* wall clock. Through the window the sun lit up the journal on his desk. Among the eternal summer Neil decided to venture once again, into the invisible fall of another's mind.

II
The Birth of Hercules

NEIL OPENED THE BOOK TO a random page near the beginning.

Revolutionerende Kærlighed. Revolutionary Love.

There are of course, many kinds of love; I maintain no illusion about that. Every kind of love can be broken down into two kinds: pragmatic and conceptual. The pragmatic is bound by physical nature and everything it entails. A slave to desire and lust. To escape this brutish and short-lived love the pragmatic forms an organizational, institutionalized definition of love. In a word, the conceptual idea of that love that began as desire. Desire for companionship, family, camaraderie, and so on. In modern societies it is sometimes possible, easier even, to forget that feral and pragmatic love exists. Particularly *because* we are civilized, we demand that we ostracize such wild behaviour, however pragmatic and rational. Most of Europe and North America lives within the illusory concept of love they've crafted. Once we abolish the pragmatic, now itself a conception of a lower form, another snare arises. The prison of institutional love. Each religion, army, culture, country, city, gender, class, and field now acquires its own definition of love. This becomes the acceptable concept according to which category you belong. What religion are you and part of what army? Are you upper-class or lower? The modern man becomes a living history exhaling a perpetual exodus from other institution's conception of love. But these facts, individually coupled with the illusory universality of these institutions create a prison by which the conception of the institution becomes a warden.

The feral and pragmatic is senseless and stochastic, a set of uncorrelated and unrelated events happening because things happen. The conception, born of our ideas and alterable on a whim, has meaning and purpose. But things happen quicker than our ideas change. What happened that made sense *then* may suddenly cease to make sense. An eroding concept is like a person who attempts to reason by logic the plot or arc of a hallucination he's had after taking LSD. A similar indolence appears when institutions apply their "universal" concepts to individual cases without considering all the data. The concept being applied would be rational if the hallucination really existed. But it's an illusion, a fabricated vision. When the *conceptual* is the warden, we are imprisoned by a drug-addicted insomniac. There is no sleep and a presence of surrealism hovers over our existence *but* the warden retains his intellectual faculty and thought when he is not partaking in narcotics. If the *pragmatic* is the warden, we are ruled by an indolent fool who has not even the capacity to understand that drugs may bend reality. To rise against the concept is thus to court chaos. But chaos is the warden of the pragmatist, and to the civilized, imprisoned by chaos is less tolerable than imprisoned by concepts. The exodus from chaos happens through creating new concepts. Sometimes there is no chaos, no temporary prison transfer by the pragmatist's yellow bus to the conceptualist's blue one; we move from one concept to another. Concepts change in feeble attempts to actualize the idea of love. To savour the new prison takes time. Thus all revolutions, even political and economical, retain their *honeymoon phases*. People finally believe "Neil" the universality of their conceptions. The dawn after the revolution is forever the brightest of them all. The saturated elation of those colours as the magnificent sun rose over the horizon after the French Revolution, the ending of the Crusades, the American Revolution, or the Confederation of Canada. The honeymoon phase may last days or decades but it is nonetheless fated to wane on people's subconscious, and the feral reality begins to simmer once again. When reality settles people realize the concept was not actualized the last time and the new concepts are as oppressive as "Neil" the old. Now what? Change and adapt and *develop* the concepts for newer and better ones. Imprisoned again. The circle of life. Ad infinitum.

"NEIL!"

He looked up to find his wife standing over him in her summer luncheon dress. It was blue. *Lanvin,* and matched her red shoes and purse.

"I've been standing here for *five* minutes!"

"I'm sorry. Time is important."

"You look different," she sat down beside him on the armchair but slightly on his lap.

It wasn't that he looked too serious; Neil had always been intense. It was that his face looked like a calm lake before it rains and among the thousands of forming ripples waves begin to fuse, making it impossible to distinguish the lake from the rainwater. He was even more at ease with himself than usual and it frightened her. She thought either that he didn't love her anymore, which meant she'd lose her advantage over him, or that he'd lost interest in wanting to be elegant and stylish which meant her social standing would suffer. How would it look, she thought, and what would Edwin think, if he suddenly stopped wearing designer suits or stopped coming to important social events?

"What do you mean, darlin'?"

"I do hate it when you call me that."

It was only in moments of great elation and profound torment that Neil's southern American accent would manifest. This time, he didn't know which it was and immediately closed the journal.

"You keep a journal?"

"No. I'm returning it. It's someone else's."

"But you were reading it."

"No. … Well yes," he stood up, "I'll head to Hermès now. We're meeting at *Muse* right?"

"Yes." She was nearly overwhelmed by the permeating pang of guilt that was coursing her icy veins.

He walked towards the door when Nora sighed and asked, "Are you all right hon?"

In the elevator to the lobby Neil leafed through the book again and decided that there had to be some cohesion and to read it chronologically from then on. Passing through the dotted design of the lobby he slowed down in front of the event room calendar.

Lecture: Creation & Death in Ovid's Metamorphoses. Professor Christina Lindström.

Her credentials were intimidating and Neil made sure to mark down the date of the lecture in case he decided to attend. Initially he was unsure whether or not he'd appear but every possibility becomes a favourable probability with time.

There was no time for tomfoolery in his mind. He got to Hermès on Avenue de Monte-Carlo a few minutes later while toying with the idea of going to Christina's lecture or even emailing her and letting her know that he'd seen it and wondering if she'd invite him. He had the *Metamorphoses* on tape and thought about moving it from his penthouse to the hotel so he could listen to it and be amply prepared.

The window décor at Hermès was creative. Signature silk shawls were stretched to look like flying carpets in complementary colours and thin metal sculptures formed basic shapes behind them. It looked like some art commission. In a world globally connected by the Internet and social media, where conniving advertising executives patent their farts and sell you their scent in exchange for your priceless time, this designer window seemed to venture into the opposite of the gaudy and the deafening social noise. Instead it tried to venture into the innocence of the cloudless sky. When you followed the sculptures close enough and pretended they were connected to the carpets like manta rays, the deeper pursuit into the naiveté of the ocean's purity and ignorance of its deep, darkening truth manifested before your very eyes.

It was so hot that Neil had been sweating and even inside it wasn't as cool as he wanted it to be. "Some water or coffee sir?" an employee asked.

"Both, please. Thanks," he sat down on the Matières Conversation armchair and followed the lined oak frame and padded seat covered in the red Clémence Mobilier bull calfskin leather. The person returned with the espresso and the glass of water and after a few moments a sales woman approached, personifying the velvety softness of their signature shawls, "Are you looking for anything specific today Mister Meyollner?"

"My wife," he inadvertently tapped the journal in his jacket pocket, "Told me about a rather elegant chess set."

"Yes, of course," she smiled and instructed in one motion to another employee walking by to bring a box out. "If you'll come with me you can take a look at it. It's Javanese rosewood and mahogany and has a calfskin strap in taupe."

"No, I don't need to see it. Please wrap it up."

"Of course, sir. Mrs. Voclain just had the same one sent to her hotel room. Are you looking for anything else?"

Neil felt his face heat up, "May I get another glass of water please?"

"Sure," she signalled to an employee standing near a counter.

While waiting for the water Neil saw the tie designs behind the woman and a particular one caught his eye.

La Danse des Tigres. It was yellow and blue with facing rearing tigers. "I'll take this as well."

"Very well, sir. Shall we wrap them together?"

"Please."

The woman shuffled some boxes and wrapping paper, "Uhh, that's weird. We seem to be out of proper size wrapping paper and boxes. It's going to be a few minutes. Would you mind waiting? I can get you another espresso if you like."

The journal shook in his pocket, "It's not a problem. Something cold would be fantastic. I'll read here," he pointed to the chair.

"Sure. I'll have some cold juice brought out for you."

"Thank you." Neil sat down on a chair nearby.

Before the first entry Raphael had written the following: *The artist's demons are always slightly out of his reach, they must never be beaten or tamed but always tethered on his mind's leash.*

Neil turned the page.

Lingvistisk Oprør. Linguistic Rebellion.

How do we rebel against language? Not to conflate the term rebellion with simple syntax manipulation like getting rid of capitals because it denotes some elitist hierarchy of language. That is absurd. Rebellion in the following way: comprehending that banking laws are designed to destroy the person who is not part of the intricate capitalist cabal. However, there are capitalist moguls, some of whom have built the very system they now exploit, who understand the law to such a technical and refined degree that I can only bask in awe at some of their propaganda. How else do I explain the nature of selling off investor options to a friend who then with malicious purpose bankrupts a second company he's created?

Now all my investors lose their pensions and life savings, except my friend and I may split the pension and savings of my initial investors among ourselves with no penalty from the law. The company simply went bust. It was a bad business decision. I would need an elaborate understanding of the system before I could exploit it. To the same token, can language be understood to the same degree? A rebellion that aspires towards righteous insubordination and yearns to challenge preconceptions about ideas that can be conveyed with complex thoughts? A paradox emerges. An elite education is required to actualize the kind of rebellion imagined. How else would we rebel against preconceptions without first knowing what they are and without being experts in their presumptions? Infiltrating the elite institution for the purpose of rebellion and not being lost in excess and comfort is thus a crucial step.

Example: *had*. This word is a disease of the language. The past tense of *have*. To *have had* something. Something you possessed but no longer possess. If "had" were a person I would find him and kill him immediately and without hesitation. I loathe the word and every circumstance that demands its use. Possession demands dispossession. Therefore having something automatically means that with the passage of time you will have *had* it but do not *have* it any longer. At most everything bound by time fades upon death: youth, elegance, beauty. And as I am beginning to learn, even great and profound love.

The woman had walked up to Neil and set the bags down in front of him. He noticed them when he closed the book.

"Thank you," he waved in her direction.

"You're welcome. I didn't want to disturb you."

He nodded and walked towards the hotel.

Before getting into the elevator Neil looked once again at the event sign for the Ovid lecture and with an intellectual seriousness reconsidered his tacit admission to attend. In the elevator he thought about how he and Edwin now had the same chess-set despite the fact that although both were masterful manipulators, neither Holly nor her husband could even move a pawn across a board… then he thought of Nora. They hadn't played chess for close to a decade now, but then why did she want it? Neil liked nice things too but he wondered why some people would go to such extreme measures in an attempt to portray deep profoundness with shallow means. Did a chess set signify intelligence? Was it symbolic of a certain type of person who also understood how shallow surface appearances can be or was it only a surfeit of consumption and ignorance, especially in the case of 2000€ chess sets?

Holly and Nora were in the kitchen talking about a magazine article that distinguished *minimalist* interior design from *contemporary fresh designs*. Catching the end of the conversation Neil surmised that the distinction was that the latter was more focused on a summer home setting whereas the former wouldn't tolerate personal objects around the house. Holly, in contrast to her oldest friend Nora, was wearing a red dress accented by her matching yellow purse and Prada flats.

Neil looked at them as if he'd seen them for the first time in that bar in Cambridge.

"Those babes are smokin!" Edwin had bit his fist.

They were so alike that Neil sometimes disgusted himself by imagining being in bed with Holly and asked himself whether she'd be any different than his own wife. Whether, and even thinking it he shuddered and took off his sport coat in a useless attempt to cool himself in the dreadful heat, he would be able to tell the difference.

"Is the oven on, sweetie?" he looked at Nora.

"No, Neil," Holly answered.

Nora never talked in bed and rarely made a noise, it was her rhythmic breathing Neil loved. He would've enjoyed dialogue but had never made any attempt to change her. You love someone despite the things you might do different personally. What if they breathed in the same rhythm? What if Holly also never talked and instead only breathed in the air of squalor and lust and love?

He always took extra care to be frigid to Holly, as if punishing her and not his wife. Punishing failure in lieu of the years that had surmounted her existence, she had still yet to carve a personality for herself. This was also why it bothered him, not to a jealous extent, that Edloser got along so well with his own wife, as if they'd all failed to recognize that they were all the same person, not as a synthesis of human unity but because they had failed to become a person and were content with the surfaces and masks that concealed the emptiness beneath their faces.

The conqueror Hercules dwells within. Let nothing evil enter! was etched on a designer mat before the terrace.

"Where'd you get this from? It wasn't there before."

"It looked nice. Do you like it?" Nora and Holly turned around in their stools.

"Did you know Hercules went through here?" he turned to Nora looking at the mat.

"Who?"

"Hercules. The great hero? Mythical demigod?"

"No, Neil…" she rolled her eyes, "I had … no idea," she looked towards Holly as if to placate him.

"He went through Provence on his way from Spain to Italy," he wondered whether Hercules had gone through that long winding street he followed through the bars in the balcony. Even if the legend was true, the Cote d'Azur wasn't a part of Provence back then. The image froze in his mind and burned through him.

"So?"

"He fought off two giants at a nearby plain. That's where this comes from. Superstitious houses would write 'Hercules lives within. Let nothing evil enter here!'"

"I didn't know that, Neil. It's interesting," Holly walked up beside him and looked at the mat.

"… I guess," Nora swiped up and down on her uPad.

"I'm going to hop in the shower," towelling his drenched, sweaty body, he stared at himself in the bathroom mirror. At his thinning hair at only thirty-six and the few wrinkles that had begun to form on his forehead, "It's because you're always furrowing your eyebrows, Neil," Nora had said and recommended an anti-aging cream.

The water was as cold as possible but he began sweating almost as soon as he got out. Cool aftershave, summer antiperspirant. None of it chilled his body.

An email chirped on his laptop screen while he was getting dressed.

Delivery notification failure. Your email to "raphaeladler@umail.com" has failed to deliver. Either the recipient has reached the capacity of their inbox or has deactivated their account.

He analyzed each letter in Raphael's handwriting on that cover page to make sure he'd gotten the address right.

Drafting another email to Christina he wondered how best to bring up the fact that he wanted to attend her lecture without appearing too forward.

The email failed to deliver. Our mystery man's email has changed or is full… isn't that peculiar?

P.S. I saw that you'll be giving a lecture on Ovid next week.

Neil.

In his mind it seemed so simple. He hadn't made it clear that he wanted to see her but left those words between the lines… *linguistic rebellion*, he thought. Simply pointing out the fact that she'd be speaking meant that she could either ignore it or engage with the idea and either way Neil would have the advantage in the incoming interaction.

As a couple, Neil and Nora used to walk along the forested paths of Cambridge and stop at a creek and listen to the sound of dancing trees. They used to hold hands in the woods for fear of separating in nature. *N-to-the-Power-of-Two,* Edwin and Holly had nicknamed them. "A force of nature. … So strong."

In the kitchen he drank some cold milk while Nora and Holly debated about the superiority of designer leather.

"What do you think, Neil?" Holly swirled on the stool.

"About?" he gulped the rest of the milk.

"Hermès or Bottega?"

There was a mild silence where the temperature rose and Neil felt beads of sweat sticking to his Tom Ford shirt, "Aren't they the same?" he finally said knowing that his comment would aggravate the both of them.

"Be serious!" Nora rolled her eyes and made a derisive comment in German. She was from Triesen, Liechtenstein and had met Holly in Switzerland every winter in their adolescence.

The clock in his office ticked, "We're going to miss our reservation," Neil drank another glass of milk.

"Are you okay, Neil?" Holly looked at the glass in his hand.

"What do you—," he thought it was Nora who asked and his spine tingled and singed, "Yes. I'm fine."

"Maybe you're coming down with something," Nora put her fingers on his forehead.

"You know I don't get sick."

"Yeah… a regular Superman."

"And we all have our kryptonite," he looked at his wife.

* * *

Muse was located at *Le Méridien Beach Plaza* next to where Neil and Nora's apartment was being renovated. An elegant half-Greek, half-French gentleman who knew nearly everything there was to know about how to play with emotions ran the place with German precision. It was designed by Tristan Auer and the entire place ranged you up and down. Odd chairs and objects, such as a wooden sofa sculpture faced the water and the glasses were all different colours. To this day, Neil thought that there was some conspiracy going on with those glasses, they would always be perfectly placed pursuant to the patron's mood. Neil always got the blue or the black or the colourless one. The background of the place was obvious, everything played with your feelings because Muses were the guardians of the arts in classic mythology; they served as inspiration for artists then and served as inspirations for the rich to acquire more followers on social media now.

The breeze played with Holly's highlighted ash brown hair when Neil and Nora walked in, "We're siting by the water right?" she asked.

"Of course!" Edwin was already sitting and was leaning against one of the parallelogram-shaped pillows.

"Here comes Étienne," Nora looked out into the crowd of people.

"*Bonsoir,* Mister Meyollner," he stretched his hand.

Neil stood and shook his hand, "Always a pleasure Monsieur Deforest."

Étienne was the manager and knew Neil from when he'd moved to Monaco. Neil would come in and sit in the corner of the terrace staring out at the Mediterranean, order the dessert of the day, watch the water for an hour and leave. He never ate the dessert and always had it sent home for one of the waiter's kids or if they didn't have kids, for the server themselves.

Not because of his wealth or social position but Étienne, like everyone else, usually averted Neil's gaze after they'd shook hands and it was seeing another bow his head or avert his eyes that had still attracted Nora to Neil, sometimes Neil knew it, sometimes he chose to forget it.

Étienne sent a waiter over and everyone in turn ordered their lunches. Edwin ordered the 35€ burger to "Keep it chill"; Nora the marinated prawn with mango and fresh coriander, coconut milk panna cotta; Holly the veal medallion without the teriyaki sauce; and Neil ordered the pavlova and seasonal fruit sundae.

"You're not eating?" Nora looked at him across the table.

"I'm not hungry."

"Then wait and eat your dessert when we order ours."

"I'm not going to eat it."

"Then why'd you order it?"

Neil didn't answer and looked out towards the waves.

"Don't tell me you ordered it for the waiter Neil! They get paid you know. They can buy their own desserts!"

"What does it matter?" he heard the sound of a big one thrash against the rocks.

"You're impossible!" Nora laughed.

"Yeah! You're impossible!" Edwin choked on his water.

They all laughed. Neil nodded. Why, he wondered, did he always go to these idiotic luncheons with Holly and Edwin? When in fact he could order a magnificent meal with his love in the comfort of his home and eat it in bed with her. His home that was now being renovated… again, his *house* that he would have to get used to again and again at the beginning of every season when Nora bought new things and changed the décor. Why did he go to these lunches? Always armed with the foreknowledge that they would be boring and repetitive and the conversation would be without substance and pointless.

As the trio talked about the newest line of Versace furniture Neil looked out and listened to the sound of the water. That sound has been there since the birth of the Earth and will be the last thing to die when the world comes to an end.

"I'm going to the restroom," Nora stood up.

"Me too," Holly followed.

Neil stood as well and when they left turned towards the water again.

"… Think… investigation."

The word *investigation* piqued his ears, "Pardon?"

"Weren't you listening?"

"No. What were you saying about an investigation?"

"I got an email from Marco. He said they're looking into some accounts."

"Okay. That's fine. Protect confidentiality but we're aces," Neil knew they had nothing to worry about but then Edwin wiped his forehead with his *Mr. Porter* handkerchief even though he wasn't sweating.

"What do you think about Calvinho? We should hire him right? He made 32 million this year for one of the royal families. He has the connects and the influence."

"We'll see."

Étienne brought a pitcher of lemonades and filled the glasses. "Apologies for the delay."

"No problem, Étienne. Thanks," he looked at his blue cup and put it facing the water and looked through the glass at the waves trembling up and down.

The ladies sat back down and were talking about a new play that was coming out and expressing interest in wanting to see it.

The heat tore through the sky and made it almost impossible to breathe.

When the waiter came over with the food Neil's dessert wasn't on his tray and when he tried to walk away, "Excuse me. I ordered the sundae."

The waiter gave Neil a quizzical look and shot a glance at Nora, "The mademoiselle said you changed your mind."

"Did she?" he looked at her. "She's right. I apologize. I just forgot," he didn't want to instigate a fight over something so trivial. Edwin just laughed and made a bullwhip sound but stopped when Neil turned his neck towards him before their eyes even met.

Holly waved the waiter away but he only left when Neil smiled and nodded, "So are you coming to the play Neil?"

"Play? Yeah… sure," the water descended upon him and waved at him in the great distance that seemed not so great as his wife across the table from him. He lifted his glass and tilted it towards his new tie.

"NEIL! You're spilling on your tie!" Nora blurted out.

Holly was watching him as if she knew he did it on purpose.

The dance of the tiger, "I'll get it cleaned up."

"Ask for soda water and a cotton handkerchief. Oh honey! Your new Hermès! It's pure silk, Neil. Be more careful!"

"That was rather clumsy of me."

"Never seen that before," Edwin suddenly barked when he caught Holly staring at Neil, "You must be gettin' old!" to curtail and remind his wife who the young virile man between the two of them really was. Neil took the saltshaker and left the table.

In the bathroom he had a moment to himself and it had only cost him 200€ and the future nagging of his wife at having ruined a designer tie. "Not *just* designer hon, but *Hermès*," she'd say. As if the word Hermès or Prada or Chanel had any meaning past the price you'd paid for their objects.

"I came to help," Edwin came in, "Old man…" he clicked his tongue.

Neil thought about how women go to the restroom in groups and wondered why that is, he'd never asked them and turned to face Edwin, "That's what you're good at. Helping," he dabbed some salt and sprinkled some water on the stain.

"Why are there only waiters at these fancy places? Never any young, struggling waitresses who want to make it in the creative arts industry," he breathed through his teeth.

Neil watched him through the mirror and continued to dance with the tigers on his tie.

"Looks like you have everything under control," Edwin left.

Walking back towards their table, that old man with a cane across the street talking to someone caught his attention, and Neil stopped to watch him.

"Is everything all right, Mister Meyollner?" Étienne appeared beside him.

"Yes. Everything is perfect. … Do me a favour, Étienne…"

"Yes, sir."

He handed Étienne a 50€ bill, "Give this to our waiter when you have a chance."

"That is not necessary, sir."

"Please, Étienne."

"As you wish, sir," he took the cash.

Étienne walked over and handed the money discretely to the waiter and pointed to Neil in the distance. The waiter's wide smile and bowed head made Neil feel good about himself. There is not a single thing that is not for sale. How easy it is to buy things, even a smile.

The beep of his phone accompanied the water soaking through the tie and into his shirt where he felt a warming chill in his heart.

I guess it was too easy to simply send an email and find him. Where did you see that? Yes I am! I'll be speaking about some of the classics but the main focus will be on the Metamorphoses. Would you like to come?

Christina.

Neil sat on a chair nearby and wondered if it was possible to get into the penthouse and acquire his Ovid tape.

I figure I'll have to track him down some other way. I would love to come. Do I need an invitation?

The old man walked across the street but saw Neil and quickly retreated down an alley to his right.

Øde Ensomhed. Desolate Loneliness.

Poetry both seduces and repels loneliness. Knowing most of the romantic languages I find French rather cliché and Spanish too frequently butchered by others to use them in my writing. The rising and falling of Portuguese vowels are a different story.

This is subjective preference of course. Danish is the most poetical language I have come across. I have been watching people pander about in their futile attempts to mitigate their loneliness. In the Bazaar of Istanbul in Turkish; in the cafés of Helsinki chattering in Finnish; in Catalan and Spanish in Barcelona and Seville; in German skiing in Gstaad; and in French in Saint Tropez and Paris. I knew better. Loneliness is a necessity to existence; you're born alone and you die alone. Read and write between these two non-events so you're not ignorant of the existence of this eternal loneliness. Danish beguiled me because that curtailing of the loneliness, that tethered thread bordering propinquity was only perceivable in Copenhagen's *Ruby Bar*. Tied not to the language itself but the location and circumstance where its words fused and weaved the threads of my existence. Regardless, I had accepted my loneliness and was to some morbid extent proud of it because it meant I could pity the buffoons who actually thought they could curtail it. And then she came, Sophie, the Swede, the white feather that fell subtly and gradually on the still waters of my soul. She stripped me of my loneliness and I wasn't lonely anymore. I had a feeling she would abandon me to solitude eventually. It was a gut wrenching feeling in the pit of my stomach that we could not, no, *would not* be together. Suddenly confronted with my loneliness anew, this time I knew it would not be curtailed.

I have begun a paper on the differing conceptions of love and I have entertained the thought of writing down our interactions posterior to the experience in admittedly vain hope that the words will assist me in acquiring the necessary knowledge to pursue the necessity of propinquity.

Awareness of the fated loneliness guarantees its victory. Pursuing propinquity is inveigling loneliness. A writer is lonely. An artist is lonely. These are the necessities of their respective vocations. But lovers are the furthest from that loneliness even if they are writers or artists. So by seeking to be lonely no longer and failing, the representation of that newfound loneliness symbolized a deeper truth.

Flygtige ord translates to 'evasive words.' Evasive like happiness or love. Throughout my life I have been both master and slave of those sentences. I have thrown them left and right and hailed them above me or stomped on them under me. Sometimes they flee and don't come to me when I call. They run. They torture me. Why then does Sophie make me such a master of them? The mere mention of her name and the words, as if commanded by a God, flood into me and break the dams of my subconscious. Rhymes, cantos, verses, and delightful prose appear; prose I would not be able to write without thinking of her. Are we linked like two skies that meet and cannot differ any longer? Through the fields I saw a hawk circling above me. My mom bought me a book about birds of prey when I was young. Hawks fascinated me. They mate for life. Not even eagles mate for life. They are faithful but if a partner passes away they will find a younger mate. The hawk however, becomes a lone hunter. What a romantic bird. What a perfect idea.

III
The Flood

"He's talking to *me*. Me personally. He's talking to Neil."

"I think you're letting his words get to you," Christina shuffled her legs under the table.

"The words burrow into me. I can see him…"

"You don't even know what he looks like. It could be a woman for all you know."

"No. *You* don't understand. I can *see* him."

"Okay. What does he look like then?"

"Can I get you anything else?" the waiter came over.

"I'm okay. Would you like anything, Christina?"

"Yes. I'll have the dessert of the day."

"Excellent. And you, sir?"

"I'll have the sundae."

"Coming right up."

"You're letting him get to you, Neil. It's natural. You're reading someone's *journal*. It's their thoughts, their fantasies; it's their *mind*. It's normal for you to think you know the man personally. Normal to think he's talking directly with you. When we talk to others most of the time we're really talking to ourselves."

"You don't understand."

"How do you mean?"

"He's an *idealist*, Christina."

"We're all idealists when we're young, Neil."

Neil smiled, "Exactly. He's the idealist we all want to be but don't have the patience or guts to be. We jest and ostracize people like this."

"No, *we* don't."

"I don't mean *you* and *I*; maybe I do…" he drifted towards the sight of the waves pounding the sand in the distance, "… I mean society in general. He's a dreamer. Is it not nobler that he *knows* — despite having only read a few entries I understand him — that his dream will *never* happen. It's only a dream but he retains his existence because he has *dreamt* it. Listen to this..." Neil took the journal out.

"Should a muse choose to manifest through the soul, the question is never whether her attainment is possible but rather in the representation of the conquest within her independent existence. Can words transcend this conquest? If the question is not in attaining her or the ordained knowledge that she is unattainable, as all muses are, why then, after her manifestation, does my independent existence become dependent on hers?

Romances are thus illusions of potential conquests; their fulfillment is irrelevant and only present in order to unite that dependence. It is as if a flower was planted in a soul's garden but it was never allowed to bloom or it has bloomed but was picked too easily to have actualized its nature. Thus to rebel against this dependence, the muse's conquest must be timeless and eternal but unattainable at the same time."

Christina leaned in closer to listen and looked at Neil's mouth.

"Even 'blooming' or 'actualization' infer some timed essence and thus must be flawed and weakened in this description. This is why we assume romances have the potential for heartbreak when weakness seep in. This is erroneous. Hearts do not break, that is a sentimental notion thought up by foolhardy idealists and hopeful writers of the imagination. Hearts turn to dust when they're given to the muse — since she is unattainable — but they never shatter. They turn to grains and by the power of the wind find themselves by the water for redemption and purification. The Dead Sea, the Red Sea, the Aegean Sea; of stormy waves where each grain of sand on their shores is a dusted soul. That's why we never venture to count the grains of sand on a beach. The mere idea of partaking such a feat frightens us not because of its sheer volume, but because the increasing volume intensifies the truth that all our hearts are alone."

Neil looked up to see Christina in a reverie. "Do you see what I mean?" he whispered.

"He doesn't like idealists, Neil. You're interpreting it to fit your belief system."

"No. I understand him. He's trying to talk himself out of being an idealist. I'm a mercenary, Christina. Hired by society to be pragmatic. The most unsentimental; I can never allow myself to be sentimental about a company, about an investment, even about a person…" he looked into her eyes, which reflecting the sun off the water had turned greyish-blue. "… But face-to-face with him like this, despite the obvious pain behind each word, it seems like I'm the one who suffers by not dreaming. And to be honest, I can't afford it."

"I think if you feel that way, you can't afford not to," she tilted her head back and gripped her hand onto the chair.

"What do you think?" Neil looked over her shoulder, furrowing his brows when his fingertips touched the journal on the table.

"Me? I don't know much about idealism. Ideas are a dime a dozen, maybe pragmatism is a good thing… What do *you* think?" she shook her head.

"Me?" he mirrored her, "I think symbols take meaning to the idealist. A romanticism that hurls you into existence. He…" Neil lifted the journal off the table, "… Knows symbols are meaningless unless there has been an initial experience that has begun the creation of the motif. Then it evolves. Everything works that way doesn't it? You're hot one day," there was a cool breeze coming from Christina's direction with her back to the water, "And you drink a cold lemonade. You remember it. Lemonade now means something. Lemonade for Christina shall always represent fulfilling a desire. It's a compulsion that drives the idealist. A compulsion to immortalize the motif or symbol. I make you a bruschetta; you enjoy it and something happens between us. From then on the smell of bruschetta will remind of those moments won't it?"

The waiter came over and placed their desserts on the table, "May I get you anything else?"

"No, thank you," he nodded to the waiter and he disappeared into the distance.

"And? …" she continued the thread of the conversation, "The pragmatic can't be *compelled*," she watched him closely when she stressed "compelled."

"No."

"That's invalid logic, Neil!"

"I'm not talking about logic! Forget logic. I'm talking about intuition. The pragmatic has symbols too, of course. And motifs that give his or her life their designed meaning. But the pragmatic's symbol is born out of the tangible to the tangible," he took out his wallet, "My Bottega wallet and Amex Centurion symbolize wealth. All of these are objects. For the idealist the symbol might be abstract *or* tangible, but goes to the abstract or tangible."

"What? You've lost me."

"From the physical to the abstract or the abstract to the physical. It's in the elevation of a concept."

"Take a breath. You're not making any sense."

"Look," he took out a 50€ note, "Money. A tangible. Means success. Something intangible. And success means more money. From the tangible," he rubbed the cash together and then wiped his hand, "To the intangible," and pointed around him to Monaco.

"As opposed to what? Smell is tangible."

"The smell is an example. Think of love, that fleeting and idyllic love manifested somewhere in the recesses of the thousands of experiences we have. He mentioned a woman in one of the entries. I can't remember the..." quickly he leafed through the few entries he'd read and scanned each page with the precision he reads the account reports in the office, "Sophie. She becomes that symbol. It's a hierarchy, an existence upwards towards the soul. *Ours...* I mean the pragmatist is a horizontal existence, a circle with no beginning or end."

"You're making a symbol out of him by talking about him this way. When he comes to get his notebook, and he's *just* a man, and he coughs and drinks a latte and sneezes, the symbol will perish. What will you do then? ... What, you think this Sophie is something more than human?"

"That's what I mean. I know she's not. But the way he talks about her. The way he writes about her. He makes it seem that way. And I haven't even read that much.... I feel like I know him."

"My question stands, what will you do when you meet him and everything you're talking about now turns out to be a farce, and he's *just* a man who has good *ideas*?" she leaned back in her chair and watched him closely.

"Offer to buy him out. It's all I know."

"You think he has a price you can afford?"

"Everything has a price," he blurted out without thinking and in fear of offending her tried to backtrack, "Well, I guess you're right. Not *everything*. It's just... he writes things I think about. Things that have been in my mind for years."

"We all think about these things. Even if we don't admit it. Why don't you try to write something? See what comes out," she smirked.

"Me?"

* * *

The day's paper reported a murder had taken place the other night. There was a break-in at an apartment complex; when the woman had tried to fight back, the perpetrator, who was reported as saying *scusi*, had killed her during the attempted rape and robbery. Neil glanced at the article on his way to the financial pages and read that there also had to be more than one assailant since the family had a security system.

"How was your breakfast, sir, and thank you for sending breakfast to the car. It really is unnecessary," Alec looked at Neil in the rear view mirror.

Neil looked up from the paper in the back of the Bentley, "You're welcome, Alec. I hope you enjoyed it."

"You're the only one I've seen that still reads the paper, sir. ... You don't mind if I talk do you?"

"Not at all. What's on your mind?"

"I used to drive a cab in New York. People liked the conversation in those days. Not like now, always with their eyes reflecting that glass in their palm. Even newspapers are on them now."

"I know what you mean."

"Anything good in the paper today?"

"There was a murder," Neil flipped back to the local section, "A woman died in her loft," and scanned the page to read that the fight that led to her death was over the car keys to her Mercedes SLS, "Fighting over her car keys with an assailant who said *scusi*."

"So he's Italian?"

"They think there was more than one guy. She had a security system."

"All we have to do is find some Italian car thieves in Monaco," Alec shook his head.

"Are cars really that important to people?"

Alec ran his index finger over the leather of the steering wheel, "It's an SLS sir."

"It seems benign to die over car keys. The car was insured."

Alec pulled into the hotel, "Must've been animal instinct. To protect what you have."

"Like protecting your kids?"

"In a way. I don't think you make such decisions on the spot. These decisions are already made. When the moment comes you just act."

Neil got out of the car, "The decision's already made? I have to think about that. Thank you for the conversation, Alec."

"Thank *you,* sir."

"I'll see you later."

"See you."

In the lobby Neil's eye caught the lecture sign again and he slowed to read it for the fifth time, as if some information had changed in the interim of his breakfast with her.

"Have you seen this?" Nora pointed her uPad to his face.

"Morning, love," he looked at the screen: *Woman murdered in her home.* "Yes, I read it in the paper."

"I called the electrician and went down there. I want a better security system, Neil."

"You mean for the penthouse?"

"Of course. Are you listening?"

He pressed her to his chest and smelled her hair, "Yes. I'm listening. Whatever you want. Get a state of the art system. The best there is." She smelled of cinnamon with a hint of lilacs and carnations.

"Thank you," then she pushed him away. "I also wanted to order some new curtains."

"I thought we already ordered the new curtains."

"I want to change them. I don't know. I went in and saw the place and it didn't ... *feel* right."

"Sure. Get whichever one you want."

"You don't want to choose them with me?" she raised an eyebrow.

"I *trust* you," the heat had settled into his hair and he felt like he was boiling.

The stress on *trust* made Nora withdraw. She nodded and walked over and stood over the kitchen counter.

"Is the A/C on? It's boiling," Neil tried to see her face but she kept it hidden. "Nora?"

She turned around, "Huh?"

He looked at her.

"Yes. The A/C is on. It's actually a little cold. Are you coming down with something? You've been running hot lately."

"You're cold. Turn it down then."

"But you're sweating!"

"Turn it down if you're cold, sweetie. I have a meeting anyway."

"Another one? Is Edwin going with you?"

"I hope so but that's up to him. His accounts are solid."

"Aren't yours?"

"You can never have too many..." he stopped himself and didn't finish the sentence. "I'll send up some lunch."

She followed him to the door, "Neil, are you all right?"

"Of course," he pecked her on the cheeks.

Divination af Kærlighed. The Divination of Love.

We were sitting outside at a small café after class where a frustrated Benson fumed over the lack of actual analysis and critical thinking regarding previously accepted theories or arguments. We just recycle ideas and cannot challenge preconceptions simply because of the person who said them *even* though this is a fallacy itself. Our lecture was on Sartre's concept of *Bad Faith*, which makes no sense and has no logical congruency but the so-called *professor* refused to give a little leeway for our critique: that you are *fundamentally* free, stressing *fundamental* like that proved his point. Sartre knows more than we do and understands more than we do. This is counterproductive, since we are now arguing the merit of the *man* and not his work. Do we accept these theories because of the men and women who purport them, acquiescing because someone deemed intelligent says something. That doesn't mean it must be accepted without thought. That is relinquishing too much power. Example: couldn't Da Vinci paint something that wasn't a masterpiece?

In a moment of crisis Benson blurted out "Philosophy is useless," in his perfect Cambridge accent. Sophie and Simonetta both watched him closely and waited for him to go on. When he continued he said *we* philosophers sit around and discuss things that have no economic or political value and consider ourselves intelligent. I half agreed with him and mentioned that most of those political and economic theories derive from misused philosophy, "Born out of pedantic sophistry," and lit a cigarillo. "To discount the value of philosophy is the exact goal of the political or economical leader."

Philosophy demands inquisition. We are taught to question things and to never accept the appearance of a thing or a preconception of an idea or even the first impressions of a person. This is what it means to be a philosopher; it's more a lifestyle choice. An education of philosophy means nothing if you accept all ideas and philosophies at face value simply because you are taught they are worthwhile. Thus if we begin by considering the true philosopher as one member of society filled with non-philosophers who question nothing and do nothing, we, the philosophers see at once that the freedom not to be influenced by society's preconceptions on how a person *ought* to behave is in fact a necessary condition for people to develop and improve themselves *for* themselves and become compassionate human beings. The philosopher immediately realizes that the appearance of affluence that consists primarily in obtaining excess and objects does not assist in improving himself. And in fact, an *intelligent* philosopher—as with all things, there are subpar imitations of such categories—recognizes that leisure and objects filled with fleeting pleasures is not the blessing it's made to be. The great philosopher takes things even further, seeing that the privilege to live in a metropolis such as New York or Toronto or Chicago comes at a high mental and physical price. An *elite* education that demands you sell your values is itself thus valueless; social organizations that result in individuals being forced to alter their values for the profit of the organization must be wrong. Ad infinitum. Now, governments, religion, and the economic system at the behest of the banks, force the non-philosopher to forego their inquiries regarding how governments, religions, and banks are run and regulated. Governments thus demand that the non-philosophers sell their values for the social organization, stability, and *progress*. This is a critical word, for all three sectors use it; the non-philosopher, at the behest of the government, religion, and/or bank who lives in a metropolis thus must have *only* the freedom to go to the films, post whatever they want on surveilled social media, and the greatest freedom of them all: to be free to purchase things they do not require and in fact counter the necessity of self-improvement. The cogs of the capitalist machine must turn and they only turn when the non-philosopher is kept busy with movies riddled with propaganda about the greatness of the nation and its economic policies; newspapers shuffled with meaningless words that omit and obtrude facts to increase readership and legitimize the government and its economic policies. If the non-philosopher is not kept busy, he might convert to philosophy and think for himself and eventually trouble the leaders who profit from the turning cogs.

Question: How to utilize the vast knowledge gained from philosophy and its doctrines to better the economic and political sector without resorting to sophistry, coercion, or omitting rhetoric? Possible answer: By acting on the knowledge gained rather than boasting about the knowledge gained for the good of the non-philosopher and not the government or the bank. However, acting on the knowledge gained assumes a unity between the non-philosopher and the philosopher. Answer doomed since by nature we are all disunited, even non-philosophers among themselves and philosophers by themselves. We are all disunited in an inevitably lonely existence and a lonely death. Propinquity is an attempt to unity. Unity of two: love, of three: family, of four: camaraderie, so forth until we arrive at national or global unity. Love is a profound attempt to unify the loneliness of death. This is why humanity has created the metaphor of immortality through childbearing. To be remembered forever and through the generations is just as good if not better than actually living forever. But because there are many different kinds of love it is rare for two people, even the most passionate lovers for example, to feel the same love and unite. Against all odds if a love is located and approaches unification, the love takes unfamiliar forms, forms not sanctioned by social morality or governments, and thus forces one or both lovers to flee in apprehension. The moment that approaches unification is the same moment that renders the fleeing lover a social liability. There is no greater fear for society than the unity of two or more people. The paradox of unity: to say "I love you" is an attempt at unification for two people. It is necessary before societal or global unity. But love manifests in different ways, an expression among an infinitude of possibilities with no objective bearing. A writer writes for his beloved; an artist paints; a banker buys things. Thus affection and love are demarcated pertaining to the corresponding vocation at an attempt to propinquity. However, this is not enough for Love either. What love manifest demands is a caricature of unifying vocations. Demanding that the writer buy things, the painter to write, and the banker to forego greed and paint. This is both a realistic and conceptual impossibility. I must simultaneously be as crooked as a banker, as deceptive as a lawyer, as sensitive as a painter, and as well read as a writer all *to love*. And because these ideas contradict, to forego greed but be crooked for example, it is impossible to love someone in the way you mean when we say "I love you." An art that is never actualized with no masters to apprentice us, we are forsaken to social or institutional love, never real Love.

"We're here, sir," Alec opened the door.

"Did we have the A/C on in the car?"

"Of course, sir."

"I'm so warm. It's too hot!" Neil got out of the Bentley.

"It was set to max, sir."

"Yeah… don't worry about it. Thank you for the ride. You want to come hang out in the lobby and wait or do you want to get back?"

"It's up to you, sir. If you're going to call me back I can wait in the lobby if you like."

"Sure. Come in then."

They walked into Neil's offices. The front-desk receptionist worked on a rolling-basis from a temp-agency and changed every week and a half to ensure maximum detachment with the team. Receptionists know everything and information is power.

She nodded to Neil and greeted him.

"This is Alec. Please get him something cold to drink or any food he wants."

"That's not necessary sir."

"Don't be ridiculous."

"Of course, sir. Right this way please," the receptionist guided Alec to a waiting room and came back out, "They haven't arrived yet."

"Thanks. I'll head in now. When they come in. Don't send them right in. Make them wait three minutes. Call me. Then send them up in another two."

"Three. Call. Two. Got it."

Neil went in and splashed cold water on his face but it didn't allay his increasing temperature. *Love as unity. How to unite. What is to unite?* He thought about Nora and how they met, about how he started CAM and how much she supported him. He would've never done it without her, she pushed him, told him he could do it. He thought about her hair dancing in the wind and her body swerving on a cool summer night after some music festival they'd attended; a cool night he hadn't felt for years.

He ran a search for "Raphael Adler" on his laptop.

No results.

Love as unity.

11, 621, 000 results. Multiple articles and blogs on eastern philosophy and unity and love appeared.

"Love unity Raphael Adler."

One result. A non-fiction travel magazine piece from Istanbul appeared. He clicked on it.

His phone rang. "They're here."

He scrolled through the article; he didn't have enough time to read it now. Bookmarking the page he closed his laptop and walked over to the thermostat and turned the COLD to maximum. "Jesus it's hot."

Watching the clock in the corner, "Three… two… one…. Come in," he heard someone pause outside the door and watched the shadows of their footsteps through the opening.

"Mister Meyollner!" two men walked through the hand-carved wooden doors.

"How do you do?" Neil looked at both their tailored suits.

"I'm fine," it was clear one of them was the boss and the other was the assistant.

Neil wondered why Wilbert Schermer had set up this meeting. He and his firm had ties to the World Bank of Commerce and Trade. The WBCT had controlled governments and was responsible for its fair share of coups d'état and revolutions. CAM was a frog compared to the crocodile that was the WBCT.

"I don't like to beat around the bush," Neil needed an edge to assess the situation, "Why do you guys want to give your accounts to CAM? You have the WBCT at your disposal. You're more connected than we are."

"I like you *Neil,*" he called him by his first name and stressed the last syllable. Letting the L linger like the hiss of a reptile. "You get things done. We've heard a lot about you. Besides you've been doing business for us without even realizing it."

Neil smiled but didn't say anything. The silence did its job. The man nodded to the assistant who took over. A tall young man who spoke in short, glib sentences.

"One of your clients is really one of our clients. You already have some of our accounts. Call them, run tests."

Neil went through every account in his mind trying to discern which ones they were talking about. There were quite a few in Africa and even some in Asia and South America. He had okayed and followed up with each one personally and then wondered if they were one of Edwin's accounts. On that note he considered Edwin's recommendation to hire Calvin. They would need at least another person to assist if they took Schermer's accounts.

The personal flattery wasn't enough for him, "I have to ask, and pardon me for being frank, why not open your own firm? You know people."

"Everyone knows everyone in degrees."

His assistant looked at Wilbert and looked up to count in his head, "Boss, how many? … Six?" he whispered.

Neil chuckled and stood up. "I'll look at your portfolio and give you my decision." He extended his hand for the Tod's leather document holder in the assistant's hand.

Wilbert nodded and the assistant handed it to Neil.

"I look forward to hearing from you. I don't like dealing with assistants," he handed Neil a business card. "That's my personal mobile and home number. Please get in touch with me directly and permit me the courtesy to do the same."

Neil jotted his number on the back of a business card on the table, "Of course. I'll stay in touch."

"Good bye," Wilbert and his assistant left.

The chair creaked when Neil leaned back and looked at the sky. Dabbing the sweat off his face with a napkin he called his receptionist, "Morning. Can you get a hold of Edwin please? He was supposed to be in today." Fury built inside him. The weather, the journal, his life, had all conspired to strip the carefully cultivated meaning he'd built for himself.

An email chimed.

Dinner at Caina. We have our table!!!!! :)

WINN3R4EVA

He looked outside through the window blinds, causing black slits of darkness across his face and watched people walking. Like ants desperately searching for an anthill, each person was so sure that their existence was more than the summation of their chemical composition. 'I am more than my biology,' their subconscious buzzed. Each person moved with a confidence and certainty that the world stood for something more than actually perpetuating an existence that is without any purpose other than its perpetuation. He tossed the document holder in the desk drawer over the journal and sat back down. The clock ticked in the background.

He took the portfolio and went downstairs, leaving the journal in the drawer, "Let's go Alec."

"Yes sir," Alec drank the rest of his orange juice.

"The meeting go okay sir?" Alec started the car and turned onto *Avenue du Trois Septembre*.

"Yes it went well. Thank you for asking." He took off his coat and rolled up his sleeve in an attempt to cool down. He untied his tie and tapped on the window, watching a cloud in the distance slowly move towards the sun. "Wait, Alec!"

"Sir?"

"Go back. I forgot something."

"Yes, sir."

Lyden af Paradis. The Sound of Paradise.

Belief is not necessary when dealing with truth. What truth has imprisoned me with such a force that I am unable to liberate myself?

Sophie read to me in Swedish. First Tranströmer's *Open and Closed Spaces*; she pronounced it in Swedish: *Öppna och slutna rum*, with her voice rising on the N and falling on the CH which sounds like dwindling K, they are foreign sounds to an English speaker.

A metaphor about the constant renewal of the self. The allegories become literal with each subsequent verse. A mortal immortality that has blossomed since the first happy couple became unhappy in the Garden.

She reached into her bag at one point and began reading Goethe's poems to Charlotte Von Stein. It was a Swedish translation with the German worked in.

I found her swimming in the waves of my thoughts, devouring those dark lines that form the boundaries of my sanity. Beyond them there is only darkness, but with the passing of her agile wave a glimmer of light appears and I dwell on the idea of us being together. I have no intention of pursuing her, not since she mentioned in passing to a mutual friend that her boyfriend lives in a different country. Intention negates action but action is just as necessary as belief and truth. Still, the way the words connected and the way her lips and throat moved when she pronounced Goethe's name. *Go-teh.* She corrected me *every time.* It was a fiction we'd begun. I would pronounce the short *th* sound and she'd correct it immediately and smile. I found myself saying his name every third sentence just to see that smile form on her lips and the words to appear from beneath her slender neck to her throat and finally wave through the air as sounds. She *never* lingered over the monosyllable as a native Swede usually does. Purposefully and without restraint she hid her accent for a fear unknown to me; as if it meant something particular not to be taken for a Swede, but instead for a Dane or Norwegian. I found it odd, but if I listened closely, like the lingering smell of flowers after you leave a florist, sometimes there was the faint trailing of the Swedish umlauts above the vowels, "Us" and "Os" especially. Her voice, I decided, was among the most melodious voice I'd ever heard, like the sound of dancing trees in a summer night when they're covered by fog and dew. The lifting tones of her voice were enriched by an already beautiful vocal landscape and made it even more divine. I listened more and more and tried to focus on the intricacies of the way she formed sentences and rhymes and committed them to memory so I could analyze and appreciate their beauty at my earliest convenience. The rising and falling of Danish's glottal vowels were beginning to form the pattering raindrops that would purify my soul from within, but the only possible purification could come from a deep-seeded and treacherous corruption that simultaneously sounded like the soft and aggressive Swedish monosyllables.

We'd walked through the woods around my place after dinner and we came to a clearing where a small lake reflected the serenity of the trees. Two swans sat still on the water. It was so eerily quiet that I heard the sky heave for air. The absence of ripples on the water was a statue of breath and Sophie was… floating. She watched the swans gliding on the lake. With subtlety the sun lowered and the wind brought a storm cloud that stripped us of the silence.

"We should head back through here," she looked back at me when the sun pushed through the trees and lit up her face in golden stripes.

At home it was the candlelight that engulfed the blue of her eyes like a trapped ocean set ablaze from below.

"What do you think about children? Do you intend to have any? … No. You're too…" she muttered something in Swedish as she searched for the English sentence, "I don't know the word in English."

"What do you mean?" I watched the reflection of the flame in the deep of her pupils.

"You don't want to perpetuate existence. So you don't intend on having children."

"I think about the hubris required, the arrogance that approaches eternity, to nab a being from nothing and force it into this perishable meat…" I interrupted myself, "I mean… they're nice."

"Well, I think it's our goal to perpetuate our lives and benefit others. Maybe our children will change the world. Without us, the world would never change."

It wasn't her optimism that sucked the despair from the marrow of my bones, it was hearing her say *our children*. Even though I knew she was not talking about *us* as in her and I, but her and her boyfriend and my future-girlfriend and I. The anguish would return when I'd consider her bearing his children… but in that moment, and for every moment that followed with her in it, I wanted children. Question: How do we rid ourselves of romantic sentiments we know to be illusory without invoking apathy or becoming cold from the rest of this lost race? Answer unknown.

"So your ambition is what then?" she continued, "What's the meaning of life?"

"My dear Sophie, if I knew that, do you think I'd be here…" I froze, because I would've liked to have been with her, in that moment, for eternity. Perhaps *she* would be *my* meaning for life. "I don't know. I have to think about it. Perhaps money plays a role."

"I don't think so. People who pursue money are always discontent. The pursuit is eternal. The want for more prevails. People who pursue money will never be happy."

"As opposed to? Pursuing what?"

"Love," her eyes glinted in the dark. "That's just an example. Love can be anything."

"I don't believe in it anyway."

"You don't?"

"No. … But what else could it be? What pursuit other than love is worthy?"

The silence resembled the lake. After a few moments she whispered, "I don't know," and narrowed the gap between us.

That night I laid on the couch and gave her the bed. Unable to sleep I thought about ambition. Intention to be ambitious is just as bad as intending to do evil because it permits anything for the sake of the perceived end. The end? Perfection in all respects.

Intention negates action but truth negates belief. What then, is the use of intending to believe? Or believing that your intentions are good ones? Ambition and perfection go hand-in-hand and are both fated to failure and sorrow.

There's a story about Cézanne that had always fascinated me. In Paul Rosenberg's gallery there was a client who'd frozen in front of a painting drifting through the colours of the landscape. "It is a magnificent and captivating landscape," he'd said to himself loud enough for some of the patrons to hear.

Paul Rosenberg had laughed, "No, monsieur. It is a cathedral."

How easy it had been for that client to see eternity in art. What had been his intention and how had he acted upon that belief? Maybe he saw a landscape with a beach and a sky and sand and empty walls because he intended to drift through existence like sea waves. Maybe he wanted to believe and go somewhere and experience solitary bliss. And that painting permitted him the momentary rapture of that escape. So he saw what he *wanted* to see: a landscape, rather than what had been the objective reality Cézanne had portrayed: a symbolic cathedral.

Intending for more is a lack and a bottomless pit. More money. More understanding. More art. More beliefs. The thought hovered over me like mists in the night and its refreshing drizzle was only refreshing until it shook awake the fact that money, like love, is interchangeable with anything. Could it be that ambition is what leads to discontentment? Was this not the tragedy of Macbeth? If you want for the perfect poem, the perfect blossom, the perfect narrative, painting, or even the perfect person, are these not in their infinite futility bound to discontentment even more so than pursuing money? Is that pursuit not more rational? The pursuit of money is an easy desire to fulfill because there is a formula: lie, cheat, beg, and steal. The other pursuits, not a wasted life even if felt unfulfilled take on meaning and beauty as the pursuit intensifies. But is that not too fated for discontentment because humans in their mortality are fated for avarice? Where is the meaning in that? Renoir had wondered how Cézanne acquired such immediate meaning. "How does he do it," he'd asked, "He puts two lines of colour on a canvas and it is already *something*." Can there be an unconscious recognition that money, unlike a Renoir or a Cézanne, is tangible and thus can be attained and grasped but those other things are intangible and thus unattainable? Do such people see money as *something* and not as *nothing*? Question: do we so desperately yearn to feel something in our hands like money than to feel something in our hearts and souls like love? Answer unattainable. Question abandoned.

I drafted a letter dealing with these ideas and gave it to her in the morning when she emerged wearing my white t-shirt like an angel through dawning mist.

"Do you want me to read it now or later?"

"It's up to you. Would you like some coffee?"

"Yes." her pupils swept across the words, furrowing and wrinkling her eyebrows and forehead. She touched my hair when I set the coffee cup down, "Thank you. I'll respond soon."

The thought of that still lake with the swans lingered in me. A winter that hopes for light snow during the purple dawn; the coming of spring that lets us touch the frost on our windows without feeling frigid. The arrival of a summer where tree branches cut across the clear blue sky of her eyes; the autumn wind that whispers her name. That lake… that water that hankers for freedom. How does lake water ever attain that freedom? Water wants to be free but it never succeeds because the fires burning through its waves permit the night to depart and the sun to rise. Is this why all rivers flow towards the ocean? That is where their freedom lies like words rising with smoke shadowing the feelings of ambitious souls not pursuing money but something else.

"Where are we?" Neil looked and instantly felt the sun on his chest.

"Sir?"

"Where are we, Alec?"

"We are at *Caina* sir. As you requested. We arrived some moments ago but I didn't want to disturb you while you were working."

"Thank you, Alec. I'll see you later."

"Would you like me to wait, sir?"

"No."

"Very well."

"See you later, Alec."

"Yes sir. Have a good dinner."

IV
The Envy of Aglauros

Caina was one of the most exclusive restaurants on the Riviera. Booked months in advance and requiring a minimum purchase of 600€ which looks harrowing but with entrées exceeding 295€, every customer expects to go well over a grand for a nice dinner. Everyone loved going to Caina, everyone except Neil; the service was never top-notch and the food was far from what Southern Italian brothers Guido and Rinieri promised when they opened the place in the late 90s. Still, owning to its exclusivity it could afford to be whatever it wanted. The design was sterile; there were no personal objects of any kind on the walls. Everything was white except the menu that was white on black laid inside a Bvlgari document holder. The lighting was so bright Neil always felt like Guido was interrogating him inside a hospital's hidden dungeon. Despite having ate there every Thursday since he moved to Monaco he only just realized this. The emptiness of both the place and the people so hell-bent on getting the seats deserved for Neil and Edwin crowded him. It descended upon him like vultures over a man dying of thirst in a desert with only a mirage of heat flashes glimpsing water that does not exist.

Peculiar and ruined, he thought. Had Raphael ruined his life? Why had he been enraptured by a sullenness, now perceptive of things that had previously made him such a rational man? The minimalism of Caina, the designer decorations, CAM's accounts; they'd all reflected the harsh afternoon light of Monaco's blazing sky. His movements, ambitions; they *meant* something more than money even if money had now become an end in itself. Now he was about to get the Schermer account, the account that would make CAM an even better firm than it already was. He felt cheated out of his glee by being the type of person he wouldn't even meet with if there'd been a request. With tormenting futility he told himself that he loved Nora, that his life was great, that he was threading the wire to the secret truth of the world, and that he was in fact, more than the sum of his biological existence and his physical wealth.

Approaching the table everyone watched him with envy. An envy he used to relish and in fact love. Now he was exposed under those seeing spotlights.

"Neil?" Edwin slurred as though he didn't recognize him until his gaze fell to the unique design of Neil's old Hermès tie. "Welcome! We ordered drinks without you!"

"I can tell," Neil looked around at the people staring at them through the glass terraces. He didn't *feel* sick, but came to realize that he'd been ensnared by a fever all this time and had only just begun to sense it.

"Hello, Neil," Holly glanced over.

Neil nodded back as the waiter came over with an espresso. Nora followed behind him with an ear-to-ear grin.

"I just saw Melanie..." then she giggled, "She's gained 5 pounds at least. *And* they were in the main room!"

The three of them laughed while Neil looked through the glass towards the softness of the waves in the distance. "I can't see them..." his voice lamented, "...Why is everyone staring? Are we on display?" like apes watching the gorillas at the zoo, Neil could not escape their eyes. The eyes... they see everything if you look close enough.

"Because they all want to sit where you're sitting, big *dog*!" Edwin shoved him in the shoulder.

"I missed you at the meeting," he thought how intense and stoic Schermer had been, "Perhaps it was a good thing."

"I was shopping at *Missoni*, then I had to pick up some cologne. *Creed*. Les Royales Exclusive Collection. Jardin D'Amalfi, the Garden of Amalfi," he smiled as if swiping a credit card was a noteworthy accomplishment. "It's a fruity and wooden blend..." but Neil hadn't heard a single word past *shopping*, drifting into thought about reviewing those accounts when he remembered the bookmarked page on his laptop.

"Nora! Smell it. It's amazing!" Holly took Edwin's hand and shoved it in Nora's face but Nora was reluctant, not because she didn't appreciate the aroma.... Neil synced his phone to his laptop via uCloud. There were links on Florence, Amsterdam,

LA, Chicago, Hamburg, Helsinki, and some others. Neil clicked on Istanbul.

Guds ord som profit (vor civilizations kampråb). The word of God as profit (the battle cry of our civilization).

Istanbul. I've had trouble with the taxi drivers and the merchants. Most of them have been haggard thieves in fancy clothes. They all sell snake oil and none of them see past their own long noses. Today, I had the map booted up on my phone as to not be swindled by these con artists. When I informed him that I wanted to travel a particular route he told me he knows his great city better than a filthy Canadian. He refused my request to turn the radio down and said he loved the tunes, that "You of all people, being a westerner, should appreciate his freedom to listen to music."

Mid-way through the drive the city quieted with a mystical and eerie spirituality for *Ezan;* from the Arabic *Azan*, which means *to listen* and serves as the Islamic call to prayer. My driver turned the radio off and rolled his window down all the way. He whispered something to himself and finished with *Allah Akbar*.

I burst out laughing and could not stop no matter how hard I tried. He thought I was being purposefully offensive and began speeding and weaving through traffic in an attempt to scare me, whispering what I assume were curses upon my soul which periodically ended with a tsk and then "Canada" and "West." They are a proud people. Too proud. And pride, even a bit of it, comes at the price of ignorance. Turkey is no exception.

I found that one experience would exemplify Istanbul with fatal precision. A cab driver, who himself is a member of the bottom-half strata of society, would have no scruples swindling everyone and anyone who comes his way, but would turn the radio off and roll his window down all the way for the grace of God while forgetting his fellow-man, the very sin God would not forgive even his angels. Maybe that defines humanity. We have so much love and reverence for something we've been taught to love rather than choose something to love because it makes us a better people and then love *each other* because of it.

When he drifted back onto the second terrace Edwin was preening his new *Boglioli Stone* linen suit jacket with uncomfortable glee presumably at himself. Immediately, Neil felt a disdain crawl through him like a talking snake.

"I'll handle the Schermer account myself."

Finally Neil had wiped off that ignorant and buffoonish smirk off his friend's face.

"I thought we were going to handle that together!"

Neil knew a direct approach would only push Edwin into trying to prove his masculinity and ruin CAM in the process, "You have a lot on your plate. I only have two accounts right now. I'll pass those off to Calvin and deal only with Schermer." Paying a compliment to Edwin's choice regarding Calvin, Neil rued how easy it was to manipulate his oldest friend. He was like a monkey and you can trust monkeys.

I would like to come to your lecture.

Without rereading or second-guessing himself he tapped *send*. In the interim between her reply and the lecture, he would send her a designer charm portraying a Roman goddess. Juno, Minerva, or Venus. Hearing her speak in a field dominated by males meant he would have to sign it. But he wondered, what would it be like if he didn't? If he, in fervid haste would act like Raphael and follow the romantic yearnings of his heart? Would her mind drift through the titanic of suitors she would certainly have? And would he hint to his identity in an accompanying card, make his feelings known, and begin the unraveling thread of the crisis of his existence?

She would have a condign certainty that the admirer would be male, and touching the frigid gold would imagine him doing the same as he polished it. It might be one of her students. She would try to picture his face; it would be a normal face, perhaps handsome but a face people would be prone to trust. She would know this instinctively because she was naturally trusting herself. But the visage she imagined was no better than the thousands of sculptures trying to depict some God or literary character from a classic myth. She knew this wasn't her strength as a scholar of ancient literature. She was a collector of cold facts. Immediate in her organization and ability to connect and shuffle and fuse those relative ancient values into modern categories. Imprecision for Christina only invited sexist criticism that she wasn't smart enough, that she was malleable to others' ideas and thus not up to her male colleagues, that she'd only gotten this far because of her appearance.

Neil could sense that she was more professional than necessary, in a way like Neil himself but different. For Neil, unprofessionalism invited disarray, disarray meant imprecision and imprecision invited weakness. Christina's distance was a proximity reflecting her fatal curse. Letting the glimmering reflection of the gold course through her, she'd push a wayward strand of her light ash brown hair behind her ear and would worry her admirer already knew what she could only guess about herself. She would examine the charm for its opaque symbolism. What do such trinkets mean in classic literature?

To be thought of as *only* a beautiful woman was limiting and unfathomable. But Christina *was* beautiful. Possessively. Elegantly. Mortally preconceived. Yet the unbalancing equilibrium of respect she demanded from her male colleagues only deepened the pining of her heart: to let it open and let another person in.

Neil saw Guido approaching in the light and as if taken out of autopilot noticed that they had in fact, all eaten and were waiting for their post-meal drinks. Ironically enough, Holly had only ordered a double espresso rather than her regular long island iced-tea. When the breeze came in for a moment her profile glowed.

"How was everything?" and then like an old cop asking leading questions for the answer he wanted in the first place, "Nick of time, Neil! Nick of time. Barely got the table booked for you. If you and Mrs. Meyollner hadn't called…"

Neil never called and looked at Nora who averted his eyes.

"…When she did. Couldn't have done it. So busy. We're so busy. Ya know?"

The lingering disdain and the food that had left a bitter taste in Neil's mouth forced him to stay quiet until Edwin rescued him by putting Guido in his place for divulging too much information.

"Say… Guidinho, my small-business owner friend, you hear about that home invasion? They say the guys were *Eyetalian.* You don't have any cousins Paulie and Vinnie I oughta worry about do you? … We're friends, right?" he shoved Guido in the shoulder.

Guido tapped his circular belly, "Be careful, Mr. Voclain, you never know," he laughed and with cat-like agility he bid *arrivederci.*

* * *

"*Where* can I find love?" Simonetta sobbed after a recent break-up. Her tears came in steady easy streams like the shushing rain outside her window.

Sophie said something I didn't understand. I let my eyes fall on the world map Simonetta had framed on her kitchen wall breaking everyone down to the country that best represented them. The thought imprisoned me. Where *is* love located? To narrow the gap, and perhaps owing to my demanding vocation I ventured into high literature. Take arguably the most romantic character who had found love: Romeo.

Romeo thinks he's living in a romance. Upon first meeting Juliet he believes so fiercely that he is fated to be with his love that he works tirelessly and relentlessly to turn the pages and reach the end of the story; to skip the courtships, the games, the tribulations of young desire and circumstance, only to arrive to the fated elation he presumes lies at the end of their story. Only Mercutio had the awareness to realize that *fated* loves can *only* end in tragedy. The narrative demands the death of Romeo not because of his intelligence but in fact because of his comedic stupidity. He is such a wandering buffoon that he allows Shakespeare to use him as a narrative symbol only to prove that *star-crossed lovers* are fated to die by each other's side pursuant to the rules of tragic drama. What an insolent fool. Even if he had the capacity for self-awareness, the fool would think he's in a cheesy romance. Mercutio on the other hand, dies because he understands the world is filthy. He is the only character who socializes with both the Capulets and the Montagues because he *knows* that feuds are bloody, childish, and benign. He dies because the *world* demands his blood as it demands the blood of the intelligent and the aware, not due to Shakespeare's use of storybook motifs.

Now despite Romeo's lack of self-awareness, the spatial continuum of his love would've demanded his death regardless of Shakespeare's motives. He was, having been born a Montague in Verona, and having fallen in love with a Capulet, *simultaneously* fated to perish *simply because* of his existence. But it wasn't love that forced his death, it was his insolence coupled with his lack of awareness regarding his existence as a character in a tragedy.

Unawareness of both weaknesses and strengths, people are bound for tragedy regardless of the narrative structure set for them or their status as a literary character. In fact, *Romeo and Juliet* is a comedy until Mercutio's death. The real tragedy was that the only character privy to the incoming tragedy was the one that made the audience aware we were reading one.

Romeo lacked awareness of his strength. That he could at any time, being the sole heir to the Montague family, defy the feud and unite with the Capulets *using his love inadvertently* in the process. Instead, he was manipulated by Shakespeare and accepted his metamorphosis into the poster boy of tragedy and with it, also *lost* the love that gave his life new meaning.

The perfect foil to Romeo is Werther. Werther lacks complete awareness of his weaknesses. His weakness? His idealism and drive to turn unrealistic dreams into surreal realities. The ideation of his beloved coupled with his ignorant pride that he is smarter and more sensitive than those around him. Werther would not accept that Lotte wanted to be with Albert regardless of her being in love with Werther. He ignored Lotte's apparent and albeit illusory satisfaction with Albert, since she too, possessed an ideation of her relationship with Albert. In fact, Werther is selfish and uncouth. He only thinks about how sensitive *he* is and how deserving *he* is of Lotte. He he he! And the boorish imp considers himself the greatest gentleman, the greatest dancer, and the best read! All emblematic of Romantic rationality. *It just makes sense for us to love each other and be together*, is the mantra of the entire book. What a paradox! Even his suicide is more a metaphor of pride than of love. For if he truly loved her in the romantic way he would have us believe, he would do nothing that causes Lotte pain and accept his suffering in silence. And surely, since he believes she loves him as much as he loves her and is trapped by circumstance, he committed suicide with the knowledge that his suicide would cause her pain. As the reader we know this is not true but the truth is irrelevant. What matters is Werther's psychology. Ergo, his suicide is the final confirmation of his arrogance. True love is the persistence of suffering even when the person you love remains unattainable. You sit next to them but miss them. You dine with them but feel lonely. You talk to them but yearn for their eyes above the candlelight. You hug them not wanting to let go but *know* that you must. Love shatters you and many become jagged at the corners of their souls. Those it does not shatter it murders, though not as quickly as lovers. If you're not a lover don't woe, you too will be shattered but lovers take priority because Love loathes lovers.

A week later the boats in front of me swayed and their sails created long, triangular shadows over the green and blue of the Ligurian Sea on the Costa Azzurra. They moved as if they were lovers waiting to drown. The sun burned my fingers and my chest tightened every time the black of my pen and soul touched the paper. I waited to be shattered, at once both Romeo and Werther. As strong but stupid as Romeo and as idealistic but arrogant as Werther. I found that I must refuse my genre. To refuse to bend to the will of the writer narrating my story since I am both smarter than Romeo and more selfless than Werther. The writer will not choose my fate, he will not decide whether I am with her or not. *I* will, and in choosing I would leave the choice to her. Would she trade my real romance for her image of their illusory romance, which in reality is a vile relationship built solely in the sky with no foundation? That decision would be hers and not the writer's. I'll suffer because lovers suffer for being romantic, sentimental, and dumb enough to allow something so mundane to control their lives. I refuse to be a character in a novel, defined by my thoughts and actions on a page and moulded through a genre that makes those actions predictable.

Neil heaved hysterically over Raphael's vain attempts to transcend an existence that to him, *was purely* defined by words on a page and predicated upon a genre that defined modern love. A love, he then predicted, that would see Raphael suffer only to give his love a meaning that would otherwise simply be not getting what you want: the very definition of life.

"What's gotten into you lately?" Nora handed him the Illy espresso cup. It was from the artist collection when she went through her "creative artist phase."

"What do you mean?" he looked at her up and down in search of that location.

"If I didn't know better I'd think you were carrying on behind my back."

Neil laughed louder, roaring and crying with each fracture enlarging on the fault lines of his heart. "With who? … My gracious Nora? … Holly, I presume."

"Why not? She's attractive and seems to like you."

"That's not because of me."

"Why is it then, my *dear* Neil?"

"Two reasons. On the one hand she shows you *and* Edwin up with one move, and on the other hand, I wager no man has said *no* to her before."

"You still overthink things."

"It'd be like if you were having an affair with Edwin," he watched her body closely.

"PFFFT!" she chuckled with nerves, "You're crazy! … Crazy!"

"Maybe that's the best part about me. The insanity…."

"You don't sound normal. Are you sure you're okay?"

"Never better," he raised his espresso cup, "Did you know that a client once visited one of Cézanne's paintings?"

"Huh? … No…. He was an impressionist right?"

"Yeah. The guy stood in front of the painting, awestruck by the landscape. In its colours and brushstrokes When Rosenberg, it was Rosenberg's gallery, came up to him the client turned—"

Neil saw his wife's eyes through the glare of the uPad. "I'm listening. Go on," she swiped up and down.

"I'm going to hop in the shower."

"Neil, tell me the story! Don't be upset. I *was* listening! … Such a drama queen!" she whispered the last part; he didn't hear it.

Society has indeed killed even the most basic of human interactions. Rarely do we say what we mean with sentences into another's eyes or mean what we say with actions that illuminate our intentions. We exchange our most intimate moments with glorified hieroglyphics through a glass that others will carry around in their pockets or purses, never in their hearts. Our words are a miscellany of lonely letters that abbreviate and conceal their true meaning. We do not smile, we colon right parenthesis; we do not love, we less than three. That is how we have bested time; we cannot die because we are already dead. What better way to communicate with the dead than say what we will never mean because we haven't actually said it and thus can never mean it? What better way to live than to die willingly and refuse to accept such an affront and pillage of what was once something more than symbols on a screen or words on a page?

The Biotherm facial soap in the shower cooled his face only until "… Nora?" he waited for a response then listened for her Hermès slippers.

"NEIL? Are you okay?" she ran and stopped at the doorway when she saw him steaming in front of the mirror with the towel wrapped around his waist.

"Do you smell cedar? And…" he sniffed, "… A hint of tangerine and apples? Why do I smell neroli oil?"

She stuck her head in and inhaled, "I don't smell anything."

"Hmmmm. No one's been in here?"

"Maybe the maid."

He watched her shoulders; that had always been her tell. They would jerk up and outwards as if to shrug *I don't know* but only halfway. She knew. She *always* knew what she was doing.

"You're right," and when his phone chimed, a wave of relief washed over Nora and sent her shoulders back in.

It would be swell to have you. Just tell them you're a friend of mine. They'll let you in.

Fantastic. See you there.

With a simple 21 words, Neil forgot the fruity and wooden aroma in his bathroom. He forgot the motifs highlighting Raphael as a fictional character despite his attempts to escape himself. He forgot the shady business practices of the WBCT. In fact it was *he* that was forgetting everything that had made Neil the Neil Meyollner he had become. Worst of all, this meant he would conveniently forget to love his love, whom he'd promised to love until death by contract, and forevermore by soul.

* * *

That night Neil had difficulty sleeping. The old antique clock Nora had bought at an auction tried to tick-tock away the silence. The ticking lingered in the air between seconds like a phantom walking through their apartment and its vibrations moved the varying floors; the marble vibrated, the wood creaked. The silence asked the clock to let it reign but the latter would not abide its despair, and eternity ticked on with the assurance that Neil would approach it.

A loud noise interjected the conversation a few floors down. Someone had ordered room service and the tray fell and spun in the corridor. Spinning, he imagined the tray, like a disc in the air or a Frisbee. The ticking resumed and it sounded like an old pistol being cocked. An old pistol, like the ones Werther demands from Charlotte and Albert. How long had it been since Neil had read Goethe? Just prior to proposing to Nora he guessed. She used to read Goethe and Rilke and they used to talk about their books and their letters. He heard people cooing and aww-ing like pigeons in the university hall. He'd never forgotten that sound, of the people wandering by and pointing them out, just as he'd never forgotten the picture one of them took on his phone and later sent to him: of them sitting across each other reading *Faust* and *Paradise Regained*. Where an orchid he'd found laid next to her and his eyes wrinkled with amorous perplexity. And her, with her eyes fixated on one of Rilke's letters to young poets. He kept that picture in the jacket pocket of his old navy *Hugo Boss* suit, his favourite one, the one he never wore. Shuffling on the bed, he tried to silence the creaking when he rose and walked towards the closet to search for it. Sleep paralysis had set in; his body refused to move for him. The clock wheezed the seconds by and when he noticed the time he yawned. Nora turned towards the bed and her arm stretched towards the empty part, carefully moving her fingers up and down looking for his shoulder. She liked stroking the circular arc at the top of the shoulder blade. When she couldn't find him she shuffled again and rose for a cup of water on the nightstand.

"Neil?" she whispered.

"Yeah," he answered above the bed. There was an elegance in Nora's movements when she was asleep and when she had just woken. When she wasn't bound by the social obligations of class and prestige and could be herself. We are most ourselves when we sleep. That is when we dream.

"Where are you?" her legs shuffled under the sheet.

He walked around the bed and cuddled next to her, "I'm right here, love."

"You can't sleep?" she put her head on his shoulder.

"I'm asleep right now."

"HA!" she yawned, "It's nice to see you still have the same sense of…," her breathing slowed and she frolicked down the rabbit hole.

"Good night," he kissed her hair but she had already fallen asleep.

It was a dreadful sleep. He hopped from dream to dream. They were confusing dreams; he woke from them mentally exhausted and famished but dared not to move for fear of waking Nora on his shoulder. He tried to remember them but could never quite reconstruct the scenarios that could lead to anything symbolic or analyzable. The only thing he could remember, which he feared was due to an affinity to romantic sentiment, was a wiry and thin yet heavy figure behind a closed window that refused to open. Before falling asleep he tried to keep his thoughts on Nora; her face, her movements, the particular curves of her body, the slowly appearing wrinkles under her eyes that he loved and hoped the expensive Biotherm cream would not take away. It was Nora that could open the window for the figure outside. No. It was futile. Every time he closed his eyes Nora would find a place to hide and plant thoughts in his dreams that he would only seek her away from the enigma of misty dreams when he woke restless at dawn. But finding her only meant losing her throughout the day until the fiction would repeat that night. Seeing her in a dream was tantamount to not seeing her at all in reality. He loved to make money and she loved to spend it. Matches made in paradise are almost always against the categories we think would perpetuate the perfect relationship.

'Perfection is impossible,' he'd heard over and over again. That had never made any sense. Nothing is perfect only because we are terrified of what we would do if we were confronted with it. We treat perfection as if it were in an untimed vacuum. The perfection *now* that will never last. That is a future predication; we live in the present. When we worry about perfection not lasting into the future, we must confront the thought that when the future becomes the present, it will retain the same imperfections we felt in the past. Can the reverse be true? He turned and tossed. If the present dictates the future, our relationships may be as perfect or imperfect as we demand from ourselves and confront it without fear.

His lashes dropped under the horizon of his pupils next to the darkness and the silence. Both the darkness and the silence would accompany the symphony of dreams. Nora would appear and disappear and reappear along with the figure with the window between them. Always the window. His clouded mind misted through his eyes through the darkness, travelling through mountain terrains and spelunking through blue caverns echoing his feelings. The night howled with tragedy where the howls were weeping tears across cement floors.

V
THE SUN IN LOVE

SAINT PAUL'S CHURCH WHEEZED AND exhaled before chiming once, twice, thrice… six times past the window. It was quiet, so quiet that Neil felt like a hovering phantom. The smell of new wood and old leather lingered in the air until the vibrations of the chimes faded above the beeping slot machines of the Monte Carlo Casino in the distance. Neil gazed and analyzed the distance between himself and the podium. He lost count of the number of times he switched seats to get a better vantage of where he imagined Tina would stand. He'd started calling her Tina in his head and thought of her as Tina; it gave their relationship an intimacy without any risk to his marriage. It was an intimacy he craved with her despite the knowledge that he would never act on it. Some of the seats filled up but the room was far from capacity. A boring voice introduced her and listed her many accomplishments and degrees while Christina herself seemed to look on in disdain.

It was boiling in the conference room but Neil felt comfortable in his new linen suit. He'd spent three hours at Brooks Brothers trying to find the right colour to match her eyes. Now that she was staring out into the crowd under the light he noticed his suit was darker. Tina's melodic voice sung about Roman mythology. He decided to sit among the middle row in the last seat near the window to catch her eye more frequently than the others. To this day he would not admit it but it was of course not *what* was being said but *who* was doing the saying.

What does it mean to be unfaithful? Is there ever a justifiable reason to betray someone you're supposed to love? Does it consist in experiencing something physical? In kissing or hugging passionately or having sex? Or, Neil began to worry, did it consist in the emotional detachment of the person you're supposed to love and beginning to picture a future with another? Had he been cheating on Nora if he did nothing but think of Christina? What would life be like with her, what *would* it have been like if he married someone *like* her instead of Nora? No. What would it be like if he had married *her*? As Raphael would say: "Question: Does infidelity occur the moment desire is born in the mind, the moment you fall in love, or the moment the desire is actualized? Answer: Hopefully the last one. Thus to not act on a desire means you are as noble as others see you."

Neil thought, foolishly and with a stupid stubbornness, that if nothing physical ever happened between them, his relationship with Nora would be as safe as a GIC investment in Canada or Switzerland. Little did he know, machinations would ensure that all three of his criteria would be met before the new year. The more hidden a fire, the hotter it burns.

"Formally, *Metamorphoses* is an epic poem. It's a long poem written in hexameter verse. It deals with heroes and myths; I will speak more about the use and creations of myth as a tool for tragedy in a moment. However, it *doesn't* have an overarching plot like the *Odyssey* or *Aeneid.* The overarching story of the Metamorphoses, if you read it that way, is actually the entire history of the world. We begin with the creation of the universe in the first section of Book One called *The Creation.* 'Ere land and sea and the all-covering sky, Were made, in the whole world the countenance, Of nature was the same, all one, well named…' And it even goes further than Ovid's own death. He predicts he will live forever. It is either that Ovid has written the greatest epic ever written or that it's not really an epic. But if we define epic as a grand idea and the broadest terms, what could be more epic than the entire history of humanity? We cannot ignore the themes of love. The overarching theme of love creates a large tension in the work. Though Books and Chapters are unrelated, the theme of love binds the whole book together. The story of Apollo and Daphne for example. Apollo seeks to kill a large snake, which again is a nice epic activity. It's noble and heroic. However, Cupid appears and an argument ensues over who has the greater right to use a bow and arrow. This seems rather mundane, but it is in fact a thematic tool on which Ovid rests the arching plot of *Metamorphoses*. He shoots Apollo with an arrow; Apollo falls in love in Daphne. Then he shoots

Daphne to make sure she doesn't feel the same way," she seemed to look at everyone and everything except Neil.

"This is the creation of the myth, in what we know about Cupid and arrows, and tragedy, in what we know little about. The myth and tragedy that in a way carries on throughout the whole poem. Now...."

Neil had begun daydreaming; his hands fell motionless on his thigh. He was thinking about the other figures at the antique shop where he'd bought her charm. There was a coin of Hercules that he now wished he'd bought for himself. Hercules wasn't a God per say, which meant perfection wasn't an issue for him. Cacus, who had been terrorizing the countryside of Rome, had defeated him in battle but he retained his religious veneration as a deity of children and childbirth due to his many children. Many children... he thought. Hercules, who subdued and defeated monsters, bandits, criminals... was famous and renowned for his courage. He was renowned for his courage and wisdom but the ancients honoured him by building temples and altars for his wisdom and soul that earned those honours; nobility, strength, political influence, fame, these weren't and still aren't good enough. As a role model his foes were moral obstacles to further his wisdom and allegories to improve his soul. In one of the legends he's asked to sacrifice his demigod status for one of his wives. Threatened with this loss he immediately chose his wife and embraced his humanity. Why? Neil could never wrap his head around that; he had so many wives and children. Children... an impossible dream, a surreal sentiment that would make Raphael scorn.

"... Stories and myths create a sense of tragedy when one or both lovers are unable to live *happily* ever after not by bad luck but either circumstance or the ignorance of one of the lovers at the other's love. The last of the most tragic. Take Pyramus in Book Four. He is so passionate that he refuses to analyze the situation at hand and mull over his feelings. This causes him to make a hasty decision that eventually leads to the death of both lovers. Thisbe's suicide is tragic *because* of that overwhelming passion. Listen to the passage: 'She fixed the sword's sharp point below her breast, Then fell upon the blade still warm with blood. The parents and the gods received her prayer: The mulberry retains its purple hue; One urn the ashes holds of lovers true.'" The sun crept through the window and two strands of light striped across her mid-length afternoon dress. The applause shook the room.

Neil entered the reception and walked by two people discussing the recent home invasion.

"They have checkpoints at every train station and bus stop out of the.... It's absurd," one of them was saying.

"I know! I have to hire a car out and it takes twice as long as the train," the other sipped his sparkling wine.

"Did you hear that they were Italian?" another joined the duo.

"Yeah," the first one replied and snapped his fingers at a waiter for a drink.

"I tell you, we're being overrun," the third one looked around and whispered in a heavy German accent.

Walking away from them, he realized he'd become a body in two places. Rather, a man with two faces: Janus. Tasting sweet despair with one face gazing at the empty life he was unaware of not last week, and bitter elation in the awareness of Tina's rising and falling voice in the room with the other. Hope, he thought, was the seducer of futility.

Neil sought Tina. Tina. What a name. He felt a momentary flash and rebuked himself for the adolescent indulgence. Then immediately he felt partial for her and even, daring to think it, cared for her, and made a beeline down the spiral staircase towards the exit. But characters are unaware of their genres, and tragedy would not permit him to leave quite so easily; he heard the gliding sound of those little rubber balls exclusive to Tod's loafers.

"Neil!" she stood above him with her hand resting on the rail above him.

He was almost too afraid to face her at that point.

"You were going to leave without saying hi or bye?"

"I didn't want to disturb you," what a dreadful thing to say, a sell-out answer.

"It was only a chat about Hemingway's representations," she leaned towards him as if she were about to take off and fly. She stood there and he could see her in natural light coming in through the window behind him. It was liberating.

She smiled, like Michelangelo had *only* revealed the angel that was *already* within the block of marble.

"Of course," she stepped down and the rustling of her dress enchanted him with elation and languor. She put an earring in his hand. There was a tattoo on her forearm but the light slanted across her face towards her opposite arm so Neil couldn't make it out.

"What's this?" he whispered.

"It's one of my earrings. I lost the other one. I don't have pockets. Can you hold onto it for me?"

He put it in his jacket pocket.

Now face-to-face with her, the light of the lobby reflected by the white of the staircase and the blue on the wall had altered the colour of her grey irises. Looking into them he leaned back, but she negated his retreat by leaning and falling into him. Her lips electrified him and when he drew back, she kissed him again.

"I dreamt about you last night. And before you ask, no, I did not sleep longer than two hours."

A smile curved her lips towards the sky, "Even I was awake longer than two hours. I didn't expect you to sleep very well," in the seconds of silence that followed she felt pressed to ask, "Are you going to tell me what your dream was about? Don't say no."

Goosebumps crawled through my forearm, "You were awake last night? Were you just lying in bed? What time was it? If those aren't weird personal questions," I hastened to ask but forgot to answer, "Yes I'll tell you."

"It was between 2:30 and 5:00 I think."

I froze in place, "That's harrowing."

"Why? … Is that the time you slept?"

"Yes. It was 1:45 to 3:00. At 3:46 I walked to the kitchen for a glass of milk. And I thought I heard you calling my name."

"Uhhh," she paused, "I thought about texting you actually but I was afraid that you would be magically asleep. That would've been around 3:45."

"I hope you're joking," I tried playing it off, "I heard you in the kitchen," laughing and making it seem it was just entertaining to keep this conversational thread going.

"Did I just say your name? I don't remember the exact time but it *was* around that time… that's funny. Time…."

"No. You called my name and said something but I was dozing in and out of consciousness so I don't know what you said."

She leaned back thinking about the scenario in her head and what she'd said the night before. It *had* happened and neither of us would've realized the connection had a single temporal iota been out of place.

"Turn the light out," Nora shuffled towards him on the bed, "You're keeping me up. Let me sleep. I have clients tomorrow."

"Sorry, love. A couple more minutes."

She yawned and turned away from him.

The rain pattered behind the sound of the wind knocking on the glass. The candlelight illuminated the deep fire of her cavernous pupils and played the strings of her dampened heart.

The long silence was broken, "You can't deny we're drawn to each other," she leaned closer.

"I wouldn't dream of it," I smiled, thinking of how many dreams I'd had of her since we last talked. She had, with a mere touch of those magical fingertips, cured both my insomnia and migraines. But they return with full force when I am not in her proximity. Is it selfishness then, to want to be with her? Because she's good for me? Because she diminishes my ailing heart and twinging mind? In fact there was a newspaper article regarding parents who are unable to care for their children that day. The elite opinion at the university was either to not have kids or put them up for adoption if you can't care for them. Otherwise "You're being selfish," Benson had quipped. Yet no one would argue that pain exists regardless.

Ever since he'd read the words, his imagination had begun to plague his soul; impersonally and subtly at first, so subtly that he hadn't noticed until he'd seen Tina. When he saw her, he knew definitively that those words associated themselves with her, and he loved the words. He knew there'd be no forgetting, and thinking of Nora he was filled with profound regret as if he'd embezzled his clients' money.

VI
Daedalus and Icarus

A canal cloud opened up over the meridian the following morning. The water had yet to freeze but for some reason the temperature in the clouds was below freezing. Ice crystals formed and set off a domino effect, causing the water droplets around the crystals to evaporate and leave a large circular hole in the cloud. As if the universe was speaking directly to him through the patch of visible blue sky, Neil had made another 890,000€. The list of available choppers for sale was only an inevitable weave into how the recent purpose of his existence had been actualized. His wife's happiness meant his own and he wanted to actualize that happiness as best he could. He knew of course that any happiness that is tied to externalities means, by its very nature, that such elation is improbable. Tina's lecture echoed in his thoughts when he laid in bed and when he woke; ecstasy linked to external objects means unhappiness. Are people also external objects? If Nora is unhappy then Neil is unhappy. But Nora's happiness *was* tied to external objects, and though Neil could make her temporarily happy an infinitude of times before her death, was he too, not fated to unhappiness?

He was rolling the Lancôme *Rénergy 3D Yeux* anti-wrinkle ice ball under his eye and remembering those lonely nights; when he was on business or Nora was away visiting her parents, when he was younger and circumstance wouldn't permit them to have a moment alone together, *when when when*. He was working to give Nora whatever she wanted. To give her the very things that gave her existence purpose and thereby gave *him* purpose. *Give give give* his uncle had said every summer when he visited the farm. "Give and you will receive" he used to say. He certainly gave to his three ex-wives and they certainly received. The ice closed the wrinkled gap above his left cheekbone. To be in love depressed him; he wanted to love no longer. Edwin for example, would have no scruples about deceiving the barrage of gullible and naïve women he'd "bedded." He knew women too well to love any of them longer than the time he spent on their mattresses. Neil envied that ignorance, that happiness nature had gifted to Edwin, a man who could never love anything but surfaces. How many times can a man love the internal before he breaks? Neil got the emotional security because he deserved it; he paid for it every time with his money *and* his soul. The pattern that had repeated throughout his existence was the emergence of heavenly love brought down to the caverns of despair and suicidal pain. It was always: woman, love, heartbreak. There was always the potential of a different woman or a different kind of love, but the heartbreak resiliently came last, never contracting or lessening his pain. On the marble counter, to the side and next to his *Czech & Speake* zebrano wood shave-set, laid Raphael's journal. He turned the pages with his pinkie and read the section on the location of love again. Closing the book he fixed his eyes on his reflection in the mirror where the forlorn look of unhappiness and pang stared back. Neil reviewed his life thoroughly; youth and wrinkles, comedy and tragedy, heartbreak and love. He was slow to dress and even slower to the office.

The exhaustion overwhelmed him when he ordered the Eurocopter EC120. He was too tired to read and research other models and trusted Edwin's judgment in such things. The office went through an abrupt peace when he sent the email confirming his intention in purchasing the chopper. The skypunch had followed him when he looked through the golden-striped blinds of his windows. Immediately he received an automatic reply from the dealership highlighting the appurtenances of owning a private aircraft and the chime of his laptop disturbed the emanating silence of the hall and the soft pattering of rain. Still the sun shone heavy. Still it was hot. It would be the last of those marvellous moments of tranquility before his assistant came along with his agglomeration of clients wanting to get rich quick because they read about some investment strategy sponsored by some conniving capitalist in Forbes. The office caged the inanimate objects and made them seem real and alive. But Neil found no peace in the momentary serenity that could've enraptured his soul. The collar of his Tom Ford shirt tightened and he felt feverish; the air decided to oppress him. He tried to enjoy the moment: his wife's absence, Edwin's withdrawal from the Schermer account, Holly's diminishing interest in him. What weighed on him was the inevitability of its fleeing; once the calm departs and the clatter and chatter of society enters, he would again have to confront that nothing had been resolved. He muted his laptop and walked over to the window. Watching the people walk on the street through the blinds and counting the raindrops landing in a puddle near an intersection to his right. Fiddling with the Davidoff cigarette between his fingers he heard someone approach the door from outside.

"Neil?" a voice called through the door. He crushed the unlit cigarette in the ashtray by the windowsill.

"Yes," he opened the door.

Holly walked through and stood in front of him, "Can I talk to you?" she closed her Burberry umbrella and left it outside the door.

"Sure," on the opposite side of the room near a coffee table sat a pitcher of iced lime water, placed there every morning and never used. "Lime water?"

"Please," she sat down across from his desk.

"I'd offer you a Long Island Iced Tea but you didn't drink at Caina the other day," he watched her. Holly's tell was different than his wife's, she was more submissive and thus to compensate would put one foot slightly in front of the other as if to give the impression of an incoming attack.

"That's what I came to talk to you about."

Neil made sure the room was silent when he poured the water and set the glass down in front of her.

"Can you sit next to me?" she pointed to the seat next to her, "Otherwise I feel like a client and not a friend."

Neil didn't listen and sat in his chair, "Would we be friends if we bumped into each other Holly? Would we become friends, have coffee or dinner if I hadn't met Nora and you hadn't married Edwin?"

She took a sip and grimaced with pain and he noticed how weak and fragile she was. She was delicate and vulnerable and he couldn't remember the last time he saw her like this.

What had she done to deserve this existence, he thought. Better yet, what had *we* done to deserve this existence? She looked around with the glass in her hand, her eyes were fixed on one of the blinds near the top of the window, it was jagged and crooked and she stared at it until the silence of dust falling was broken by the rain speeding up and tapping the window.

"Thanks," she set the glass down on the coaster and looked at Neil with a smile. Neil leaned back and looked at her aglow, then he realized this was *Holly*, a person he never really liked; he opened his mouth to ask again what she wanted but something stopped him. It was a thought. Why had they never felt at ease with each other? It couldn't *just* be that Holly was interested in Neil, for the sexual tension and attraction was posterior to the feeling of unease. Her attempts to seduce him were only to ease that tension. What was it that had kept them apart mentally? He opened his desk drawer for another Davidoff cigarette but her glow made him put it away again.

"What is it, Holly?"

She leaned in and crossed her legs on the chair, "My emotions are wreaking havoc on me right now. I have two things to say and I want you to forget them both the instant I say them."

"All right," he answered but what other answer could he give? How could he promise to forget something? If only he knew *all* things he would already know what she was going to say and take a position on it being worthwhile to forget. For the third time his fingers reached for his cigarettes but his hand fell asleep and then onto his chair. It wasn't only his hands that refused to instil order in him, the expression in his eyes and his roaming thoughts were coming to him in indecipherable languages. Welcome to the desert, his body said. There were no signs to point him in the direction he wished to go. "Is the A/C on?"

She paused and twitched like she'd contemplated leaving. Nonetheless she felt compelled to speak and no longer cared if he understood her or not. She wouldn't choose her words carefully, she would speak until she said everything she wanted to say, "Would you forget it? Of course you would. I'm certain of that. You don't think about me. You don't care about me. You never ask me how I am or what I'm doing and the only time we talk is when I have to tell you something Nora wants so you can retain the romantic ideal she has of you; an ideal that is not far from the truth. An ideal that you would retain without me. But I relish that opportunity. I wait for it. Sometimes I try to manipulate her into wanting something and wait a couple of weeks for her to bring it up so I can mention it to you. So I can corner you on the way to the restroom or in the hotel bar and have a moment with you. If I left right now you would forget me the instant I walked out. Even if you didn't, how long would it take for you to forget me? The things I've said or done, the clothes I've worn or the places I've been. I remember all of yours Neil, everything you've said; everything you've done for Edwin, for Nora; the patterns of your ties! Even their damn patterns! *La Danse des Tigres* with the facing tigers clawing each other, *Ara-besques* highlighting the long feather of flying birds. My favourite is *Maki Love,* the two kittens with their tails tangled into each other. How long until you forgot about me? A year certainly or even less than that. After a year my face would be a thing of the past, and even *if* Edwin kept a photo of me in his place, would you remember my face? Then even more time would pass…"

Neil leaned in then got up and walked to the window, wondering how and why he was so hot even though the air felt cool and seemed to want to welcome the rain.

"… And you wouldn't recognize me even if I walked into your office and sat in front of you. Nothing about me would reveal to you that I am your friend's wife. To you Neil, that's all I am. I'm just a woman you have to put up with, you didn't choose me. Edwin did. You had no choice; you said it yourself, we wouldn't have met or even spoke to each other if we'd met outside of the circumstance of my being Edwin's wife. You don't speak to me because of who I am, you speak to me only because of what I say and do; you judge my actions. If Edwin had married someone else… or if someone else had walked down the aisle even after he proposed to *me*, you wouldn't even notice and you'd treat her just as you treat me. And even if I came back one day and said to you, 'Neil, he proposed to me! That was an imposter who walked down the aisle!' It would still take you an indiscernible amount of time to get used to me. And what kills me is that even if I came back you might still prefer the other one," she talked on the verge of tears the whole time and hadn't looked at Neil, then being unable to resist the urge to face him any longer she looked him right in the eye and noted the scarring but noble wrinkles and the desolate but widened eyes staring back. "You don't know me; no one does," she felt and held her lower stomach, "We don't know each other. I could leave right now and what you, Edwin, and Nora would lose is only the company and gain only the extra seconds it always takes me to decide on a drink."

He walked over and sat in the chair next to her; he'd purposefully lowered the two chairs so his own was slightly higher.

"Neil, I'm in love with you. I can't stop thinking about you. …" she watched him and when he said nothing she continued, "…When I'm with Edwin all I can think about is how much you're not him. How are you two even friends? How do you get along so well? You're nothing alike! … Completely opposing forces!"

Finally he moved and lit the cigarette by the window; how did I get into this, he thought. He breathed in the smoke and sent the smoke into the rain in small bursts, "Holly…" he turned around and saw her staring at the smoke and the cigarette between his fingers. Flicking it outside he sat back down next to her and was gripped by the moment where she ordered the espresso instead of the alcohol. Now the avoidance of smoke, smoke and mist that had never bothered her before. "What's the second thing you want to say?" he looked at her stomach.

"You already know, don't you?"

He made sure she saw him looking at her hands holding her stomach. "Edwin's right. How do you know these things? Was it the espresso? I always drink right? Because all I really am is a rich alcoholic."

"No," Neil watched her legs, "You were, and still are *glowing*," he knew full well that this would destabilize her emotions further but he had to be honest with her.

She bit her lips and covered her face with her hands, "I think he's having an affair."

Neil wasn't surprised but feigned a reaction, "What do you mean you *think*?"

"It's just a feeling. I have no proof of course… only an absence of evidence. Something feels off."

Having to bear the bullet himself he tried vainly to hit two birds with one stone, "I think he's a fine man."

She saw his move immediately and scoffed, "What does he know about children Neil? He barely shows any interest in me. Why didn't you and Nora have children?"

The question left a bitter sting in his mouth, "We keep our relationship *intuitive* and *natural*." He believed nothing that came out of his mouth, "If it happened, it happened, if not we weren't going to force it. Edwin's a fine man and he'll make a wonderful father," in between his mistresses and the emotional torture of his wife.

"I'm unhappy, Neil. Now I have a child on the way with a man who understands neither me nor the child."

"What do any of us know about happiness or children, Holly? We're born wanting to be happy but no one explains to us what that really means. We only learn later that it's because they themselves don't know. We don't give a thought to it when we're young; that's why the young are happy. The moment we think about happiness and yearn to *be* happy it ceases. The stronger the desire to grasp happiness the unhappier we are when face to face with its impossibility. And because it's impossible to grasp it; we're unhappy until we die. Then we die unhappy. Happiness isn't something you can attain. People only say it is. Don't listen to them. Don't believe a word of it. Happiness is either *in you* and stays with you all your life or it ceases and you have to deal with unhappiness for the rest of your life."

"That's not true. I have been happy many times in my life."

"Was that *happiness* in the way we're talking about it? Or was that what *you* thought happiness *ought* to be?" That *poor* child, he thought. That poor child, the thought repeated over and over and over again, playing images of Young Versace and Burberry Junior.

She drew back and thought about what he was saying. The silence untightened around Neil's neck and Holly shifted on the chair, but the beeping of his office phone startled them both.

"Mister Meyollner," his assistant chirped over the line, "Your 11:30 is here."

"You have an appointment. I'll leave now," the vulnerability in her voice was as real as the sun and his belief in Edwin as a father as fake as Sophie's dedication to Raphael.

She got up and approached the door. Walking her out, he paused and put his hand on her shoulder, "Holly..." and he let her name trail in the air, "I wish..." he stopped himself, "I want... No. I don't have the words..." he wanted to apologize for being unable to reciprocate but he knew that would break her heart and he didn't want to do that to her. He couldn't. Then he became the Neil he knew he could be, the Neil that could unflinchingly support his friends and family without expecting anything in return. "Anything you need, Holly. You come straight to me. I'll set you up myself. Make your decisions *yourself*. Do what *you* think is best for *you* and that *child*. But you spoil that child. You love it with all the love you have. You love it until it kills you. You love it until it hurts you. Then you love it some more."

She smiled and it was the first time he'd seen her smile in all these years. It looked different. Not a momentary measure meant to convey a social persona but Holly was smiling. Holly herself, not Holly on the second terrace of Caina. "You can't give me what I really want, Neil. You *can't*; I accept that. Goodbye." When she walked out for a second, Neil thought he was never going to see her again but before he could say 'wait' his client squeezed by her and entered and she disappeared down the spiral staircase.

* * *

The air in the room thickened even after I'd opened the window. There is a tension between the desire of coveting someone for the sake of lust, and the love that enflames and burns for eternity. Tension and heat rise like gusts of winds through winter twilights. Sophie seemed to move on instinct. Turning out the living room light she misted through the darkness and lit a candle. Though her back was to me, I felt her staring into the flame and bathing herself in its orange light. She must've known I could see the silhouette of her body. Her shoulders glistened like milk, and only darkened when a gust of wind nearly blew out the candle, where the constellations on her back reflected the orange of the flame and absorbed its fire. She let her sweater slip off where her marble shoulders were now reflecting the candlelight and lighting the birthmarks on her shoulder blades. They were stars that orbited her body and tightly gravitated towards her eyes. I imagined them as constellations: Taurus, with its antenna like points that connected to a single dot near the arch of her back; and Delphinus, with its four starred dots curving an imaginary line towards the top of her neck.

She turned and faced me when the candle's reflection sparkled in its crystal cover and formed long triangles at the edge of the coffee table. I could not eject the thought of her submerged in a maple syrup bath, perpetuating and reaching the apex of the incredulous innuendo we'd been swimming around for weeks. Her glistening thoughts darkened and made even sweeter by Canada's best. The candlelight dimmed behind her, overcasting the night with slow, dense clouds floating across the purpling sky. Balls of yellow lights from the city in the distance tried to brighten it but the darkness prevailed, as it always does. It was warm and humid despite the sleet, despite the storm, despite the season, despite the climate; the farmhouses around us became dormant walls around the prison of my heart. The only glow was from that candle, and her eyes. The latter flooded out and spilled its aura into my soul and the garden below, where the desolate winter land was blackened from the darkness and the dead until that moment, which now looked like the first waking blinks of a monster.

"I'm unbelievably drawn to you," she pounced towards me.

"That's troubling."

"Why?"

"Because I'm taken with you as well. Fatally. Obscenely. Inexplicably. That never happens to me..." I looked through her and at the flame for a moment, "We're not going to act on it. We can't."

Gravitating closer to each other as each word left my mouth; an enigmatic conductor struck the strings of our hearts and bridged the gap between our bodies towards the lively fourth movement of a divine symphony. Our lips touched. Her tongue was a flame. It was a fire that burnt under her icy heart. It was a frozen lake that burned hotter than the sun. It singed my lips. It charred my heart. It scorched me to the depths of my soul. We both pulled back at the same time.

"Is Toronto safe?" she asked to lighten the air.

"It's like any other metropolis. *For the most part* yes, it's safer than Chicago or New York or LA," the air thickened and a section of the city in the distance lost electricity.

"I read there was a murder in the afternoon the other day. There was an article in the paper. I'll send it to you," she got up and opened her laptop. The glare of the screen lit up her in face in blurry black scribbles and reflected the words of the article across her chiselled cheekbones.

* * *

Pages 36 to 52 were missing proceeding this entry; tear marks edged the inner spine of the journal. Neil flipped back and forth a couple of times hoping that they would *appear* only because *he* wanted to read them. The next entry was "*Hvad er forskellen omsorg og kærlighed?* What is the difference between caring and loving?" a few pages later.

She had made things purposefully uncomfortable whenever we were together without recognizing the paradox of it. One time she extended the gap between us to gauge my reaction and I had to laugh.

"What?" she raised her eyebrow, and even made a joke of it later by quacking and pursing her lips. The tension threaded forward and back, swaying like boats over the Italian Riviera.

Neil looked left over the water and behind the yachts towards Genoa expecting to spot Raphael across the Ligurian.

The paradox was left unseen like the background of a portrait with fading and greying colours. Feigning discomfort was the most comfortable you could do. No one *wants* to be uncomfortable, so to create discomfort requires a profound level of comfort. "You are free to do as you wish," I had implied, "Even be uncomfortable." And like a sparrow that flutters its little wings from place to place, she had chosen, albeit oddly, to perch upon a thin branch that ran of risk of breaking rather than nest on a thousand year old tree. On the walk home from the train station the next night, the moon was full but my mind emptied its sentiment, switching between fury and despair and settling on suicidal anguish. I held back tears on the way to the farm wondering how to finish the novel I desperately wanted to have a happy ending, if only to prove to myself that happy endings and *hope* were possible and I wasn't a sentimental romantic fated to be consumed by the world. But now, under the sombre blue glow of that lune, there would only be one ending.

Neil shut the book.

VII
Jupiter and Europa

Reading a poem about Sophie's eyes as serene ocean waves and her hair as the dawning sunlight, Neil heard ambient chatter approaching his office.

He used to be a creature who could laugh and smile even if he didn't mean it. Now he had to only approach the threshold in his mind where Tina, Raphael, and Sophie laid dormant and he would feel like Atlas wanting to shrug. He compelled himself to be satisfied with what the world had gifted him. He was not only among the most successful of the circling vultures he called his friends and clients, but he was among the *most* successful people in the *world.* What's more, he was inconspicuous, no magazine knew his name, no one recognized him. He retained his privacy and his identity with no apprehension of ever being bombarded for a comment or a photographer trying to catch a glimpse of him and Nora. These thoughts brought him no peace.

"But he's the boss," one of the voices said.

"Trust me. Just come. He won't care," the second voice was Edwin.

"This is highly irregular."

Neil put his cigar on a stand he'd gotten from Marseille. The room was stuffed with smoke when Edwin and Calvin walked through the door.

Edwin pretended to cough and held his lungs. Neil smiled because he almost made a comment regarding his drug addiction but hailed himself for his self-control.

"Hello, sir," Calvin walked towards the desk and held out his hand.

"Afternoon," Neil shook his hand. He held Calvin's grip for a moment and stared at the solid colour of his tie. It was maroon. Tightening his grip, he attempted to size up his newest recruit.

"It's an honour sir; thank you for the opportunity," Calvin loosened his grip but Neil didn't let go.

Neil picked up and puffed on his cigar as he sat down, "Don't thank me yet. Let's see what you're made of," he slid some of the accounts across the table.

Calvin looked at Edwin and Edwin shrugged his shoulders but then smiled at Neil.

He flipped through the papers and handed them back to Neil. "This one's embezzling your money. 240 a year," he pointed to the account, "This one could have a higher return but your trader is lazy, he made six trades where eight would've been more optimal. Coup de grâce is *this* one," he removed a sheet and put it on top, "I'd rather the second guy than this guy sir. He's overzealous. Makes more trades than he or she needs to. Fourteen trades when four good ones would've yielded the same return without the risk."

Neil spun the sheet towards Edwin.

"Those are *my* accounts," Edwin craned his neck towards Calvin.

Calvin shrugged his shoulders, "Sorry, boss. I didn't know."

"An honest trader. What a world," Neil smiled. "Welcome, Calvin."

He got up, "Thank you, sir."

Edwin squeezed Neil's hand, "Later, gator! Where are we eating tonight?"

"I have nothing planned," he tapped the wood of his desk.

"I'll set something up with Nora."

Neil stared through his eyes and into the deep of his pupils, well, he tried, but they only went as deep as his green suit pants with his red tie.

"You and Calvin will handle the two Arab brothers."

"Sounds good," Edwin tapped Calvin on the back on the way out.

When Neil sat back down there was an email waiting for him from Schermer.

Hello Neil. I hope you've had a fantastic week. I need some of the accounts to be moved from bank to bank. Attached are the transit numbers and the required signatures.

Neil followed the transit numbers and the wires to a Dutch bank in Africa.

Afternoon Dr. Schermer, I have followed your instructions. Attached is the confirmation of the wires to the listed bank. Would you like me to execute trades and futures from this account from now on?

Spinning in his chair waiting for Schermer's response he leafed through Cervantes's *Don Quixote*. The belief of something out of nothing. The belief that knights and gentlemen and romance mustn't be allowed to die and an effort is made to perpetuate them. What does it mean to believe something like that? To exist like that. What does it even mean to be? Not exist per say, because you can't choose when or why to exist, but only *how* to exist. Again this is not an attempt to argue for existentialism and choice. Rather, how to exist within different settings. The way, for example, how people queue in line in a new country or wait for trains in an underground subway. Sometimes we perceive people breaking these boundaries and pretend not to notice. But the reverse is also true; some people recognize with immediate intuition and precision how to behave. Even further, two people who are seen as *compatible*, are they unified souls? But if we don't know what the soul is, how can we know what we've unified?

An older woman with a hunched back approached him on his walk home.

"Do you believe in the lord and saviour Jesus Christ our Lord?"

Almost as a secondary thought, Neil reached into his pocket for change. It was her raised and insulted eyebrow that made Neil answer, "Yes I do."

"How about angels?"

"What about them?"

She wrapped her hands around her neck and unhooked her necklace, "This is a medallion of an archangel."

Neil looked at it, "It's a woman."

"Angels are pure, aren't they?"

"That makes them women?" a car sped by and honked because he thought Neil was standing too close to the curb.

"Of course," she answered.

Oh no, he thought. When the woman had mentioned *angels* his first thought was not his wife sleeping peacefully next to him on those sunny mornings without makeup but it was Tina standing at the top of the stairs looking like she was going to take off and fly away.

"There are wicked angels, and pure angels," she continued.

"The wicked ones are male right?"

"Not all of them," she waved at no one in particular and walked away.

Wicked angels? That's a new one. But the more he thought about the biblical stories of angels the more he understood what the woman could've meant. He sat on a bench on his way to the hotel and mediated on the idea. Suddenly his thoughts raged and stormed at the boiling sky and the bubbling waves of the Riviera.

She was right. God's angels are indifferent and apathetic. They have no feelings. They know nothing of passion, of love, of beauty, or even of justice. They understand nothing. They are the indoctrinated employees in God's investment bank. They do nothing but praise themselves and each other and their boss and their company. Opportunistic cheaters and thieves of love and justice and beauty they are. Their CEO though, isn't God but Satan. Though without a doubt on the surface it seems as if angels work for the Lord, and they love our God and praise Him, but secretly and really, they answer to the major shareholder, Lucifer. They bow to him unconditionally and without thought. They themselves, like the weak-willed *who ought to have fallen*, the sheep and the scorpions, lacked the courage and bravery to stand up to God when he founded the bank of existence. They agreed to the company policy but work secretly to overthrow it in disdain at their creator's vision. The boldest and courageous of the angels is in fact Satan himself. He stood up proud and said to God,

"I will not serve them. I will serve you. I will never serve these dirty creatures that you created from the dust and mud and formless dirt of the earth. These weak and unfulfilled things that for a loaf of bread will forego You, father, and your kingdom, and their saviours, and justice, and love, and passion… forego everything and everyone…. These squalid beings that for a piece of lamb or some grape or some fine wine or money will bow to anything and anyone else but you, and will close their eyes towards the sky and You, God, because the loaf of bread demands it… I certainly will not serve them. How can you ask this of me? To serve these envious, filthy, greedy, money-loving, hoodwinking, hypocritical animals? Slimy beings that even when they want to show their loyalty to You will bring only a piece of dying grain or wilting flower that they themselves no longer need. Beings that for the sake of their wife's beauty or their mother's love will forget you. A putrid being that *actually* contemplates murdering his son, and in fact murders his brother to prove his so-called love to You. How can you be so blind to the wickedness of these beings? Look at what they've done to the earth you gave them, look at what they've done with the time you've given them; how filthy it's become since you created them. These sordid beings that without remorse or a second thought will murder Jesus, Malcolm X, Gandhi, Zachariah, and Saint Stephan only because they *can*. Not even because those beings, those that truly believe in you, have great personalities, old souls, strong bodies, firm beliefs, and only because they pursued truth their own way and wanted to fight for the freedom and beliefs and love and passion for the very people that would eventually murder them! These beings too afraid to change for the better but sprinting so quickly and hastily to change for the worse! How tortuous their existence is to our kingdom father! Why did you create them? They are driven only by the hatred of each other, and their snake-filled hearts build walls around their false-beliefs to sting anybody that gets in their way! And once they sting someone or are themselves stung because evidence of their cruelty manifests, they are grudging and feral in the face of even a little pain. How do they satiate this pain father? They alleviate their mild pain, barely noticeable to every other creature, this minute sting of a hair, by inflicting tortuous, murderous, flaying, burning, and agonizing pain on their fellow humans who tried to alleviate and understand this anger and grief. They are only calmed by the blood of their fellow man and not only that, they enjoy it! And only bathed in their enemies' blood are they cured, momentarily and fleetingly of this ire! They are violent father! So quickly they fall behind Nero, Commodus, Hitler, Stalin, Nixon, Trump…, every being created in the opposite of your image, with tongue-twisting words and manipulative tricks to fool their fellow animals into more blood and intestines and guts spilled further into your earth. Am I to use my own light? My own soul and my pure fire that burns without smoke and without scorching anyone but me.… Father, I am supposed to serve and pray for these statues of decaying and bloodthirsty and bloodhound pieces of corrupt flesh?"

And in the same anger Satan spoke of, the same ire and fury that builds and is only allayed by blood, the fury that parallels with the most wicked humans, God banished and punished his greatest son to a lake of ice that burns him for eternity. All for what? Pursuing and pointing out a great and universal truth? In His image we were created after all....

But the other angels, who watched this interaction in disbelief and widened eyes, and who on the surface sided with their so-called father and not their brother, nevertheless chuckle and laugh *with* their brother. They betray themselves and their mighty father every day. Are they not, in perpetuating the corruption of these beings by omitting their guiding auras, not contributing to Satan's version of humanity? Perhaps we'd think, "No, that's too pessimistic. Everyone is different. Don't be bitter. Don't make the earth seem evil and wicked." And perhaps we'd be right; I don't know. But if Satan and the rest of God's angels are not allies in corrupting us to be the worst we can be rather than the best, if they did not share Satan's beliefs in our filth and lack of spiritual ambition and disbelief in each other and a never-ending thirst for crushing each other, for blood, for our own gains, for money, for power, for influence, how do we then consider the end result of what humanity has become and will surely become before our deserved extinction?

Unable to sleep once again that night, Neil thought about moving closer to Nora and feeling her warm body, her creamy skin, and her soothing touch. Now that Holly had all but confirmed her infidelity, and though general infidelity might not have bothered him, it was the fact that it was with Edwin. Edwin! Now the proximity of her body bordered disgust and wrath. He listened for the slightest noise emanating through the building to justify his insomnia and to redirect his feeling to the origin of the sound that never came. It was as quiet as death. Even the clock had stopped ticking. The paling glow of distant stars floated through the window. In the darkness next to his wife he made out the darker outlines of the furniture in front of the new curtains. The vanity mirror reflected the probing lights of airplanes flying to distant lands where these complications simply ceased to exist. Every couple of minutes he would stare at the digital clock on his nightstand, which only reminded him of his insomnia. There was now nothing but mist in the deep valleys of his cavernous heart. The fire of desire had burned and dimmed without him having realized it, and that little dimming no longer bound material objects to his heart. Beside him Nora slept like an angel and her breathing galled him as if she were sleeping peacefully purposely to unsettle him.

"Nora?" he sought his wife, and when she shuffled closer to him, he wasted no time and whispered, "Have I given you everything you've wanted?"

She thought for a moment… "No," she yawned and squeezed his forearm.

This was a tacit agreement between them. They were to be honest with each other no matter the circumstance or mood when faced with a query. This agreement was not only the reason why they rarely asked either other questions, but also why they were both unhappy; their answers rocked the pendulum towards extremely hurtful or incredibly endearing. People always remember the pain and never the pleasure.

He got out of bed four times: to go to the kitchen for a glass of gin; to the window to look out at the wealth and squalor of Monaco's shady existence; to watch Nora lie still with the bed sheets rising and falling with her breath, and lie convincingly with each breath when she would wake; and finally, to his desk drawer. What cruel, invisible hand had guided his to select that book? He outlined the tear marks along page 35 and then prickled his fingertips past them on page 54. Are books meant to serve a moral purpose? Why then, had this ruinous turmoil of unhinged sensations erupted in his heart? Words. Arranged in a particular order meant to symbolize purpose. Random, meaningless, useless words that conveyed only the vague fading gestures of lost souls in search of something greater than the summation of their biological and material desires. Words that press the same piano keys of a heart and become benign with repetition. He drifted through the drawer, waiting for the insanity of the words to enrapture his heart, but the futile dancing of the sentences refused to cage him. Instead his soul reached for far away horizons with never-ending frontiers to cage it. And with each new thought in this frontier he became more aware.

Though she could, Sophie never relied on her body to attract or seduce men for her benefit. She was, rather pleasantly, refined and sensual, talking about nature or trees while the grooves of her fingertips would graze your shoulder at the mention of *serenity*. She could, on command like snow in Canada, traverse through the realm of desire and demand your soul in a way that would drive you insane with passion while *simultaneously* making you incapable of defending yourself from something you *knew* to be natural and spontaneous. Every man she encountered was unable to flee from her onslaught, plunging headfirst into those waving eyes against all reason with the belief that the love was as real as a snowflake when in fact it was as simulated as a fictional romance. The only thing that was real with her was the cold. The cold that made the Canadian winter the warmest place on Earth. Canada. Home. Question: If home is where the heart is, is Canada no longer home? Answer unknown. Expansive follow-up: Why do I anticipate not feeling at home in Canada anymore? Unanswerable. Question abandoned.

With no other alternative, I sought the bittersweet solace of my narrative. My novel refused to work with me. *Refused*, as if it didn't want to be written on principle. Normally I'd write until words disgusted me and then I'd write more out of disgust to be rid of them. This pursuit, whether it be for Beauty or Happiness or even the perfect novel; a novel with no extra words, no mislaid commas, no plot holes, or dull and contradictory characters; is it not fated to disappointment and misplaced ambition like any other pursuit? I've written and thought extensively about this. The answer remains elusive. *Flygtige ord.*

Question: What is an authentic ending and how do I write one? Answer: Is that not the magic of literature? Interpretation? The writer is in fact a prisoner of his own mind. And like a prisoner that lives inside a prison he knows is impossible to escape but lacks the reservation for suicide and simply exists, he remains at the beck and call of prison guards. Guards who take everything from him except his pen, periodically handing him a piece of paper and saying "Go." He sprints as fast as he can, to the lands of his mind, to the lands he imagines have beauty, those lands that have justice, that have happiness; those lands that have… love. Then just as he approaches those deserts he runs out of ink and they laugh.

Sometimes they let someone in. A woman, to keep him from floating to the sky and escaping, and she brings him down as hard as she can. He crashes back into his cell like an asteroid and leaves a crater where his heart used to be. Bound by limits he neither agreed nor set, every person is caged in flesh too small to contain their souls should they seek to pursue anything higher than those limits.

Nevertheless, these dances were necessary in an existence without meaning or purpose, which was every time Sophie and I said goodbye.

Does every writer tie his worth to the words that waltz or tango for him? And does he define the meaning of his greatness by whether the truth he wishes to expose is the last he is permitted to unveil? Death gave birth to Time, that's why time passes. With each passing moment we are closer to a reckoning we do not control. We are Death's prisoner, never free and always at her beck and call. Is not the most free thing we can do, the most liberating and meaningful, the denial of that existence that summons Death? Is that not how a being could take control of its *own* existence? Summoning the most dominant figure in the universe by mastering its own time and asking her to do her job? I'd like that, to one-up the master of the universe. On the off chance that these thoughts in fact do deem me insane, I will first attempt to master the sentences that must form before I can dominate the Master of Being. On this thread, what is the depth of the soul? And if it extends beyond the frivolity of what we can and can't perceive, what shape does it take? For if the depth of a person differs based on their soul like mountains of different heights and terrain and depths, how deep does someone else's soul extend? How do we gauge even our own? Is this why some people are incompatible? Because one soul is only skin-deep and the other is as undiscovered and deep as the ocean?

Love was everywhere; those who search for it can have it. You could love anyone at any time. The catch is you can't keep it. It flees. And you have to chase it and then die for it. I was ready to die for her. She wasn't ready to die for anything, let alone for me. My existence had become an amusing paradox. Most of the time I was okay just hanging out listening to my friends talk about useless tidbits of information. But the instant I would see her or talk to her or even think about her, harsh realities would set in and I would see no purpose in perpetuating my existence past the next month if I could not advance the novel to my liking. Whenever I felt my work wane, without hesitation I would plan to end it all the following day. By some mysterious force however, there always seemed to be some new plot point or dialogue in my mind as soon as the sun began to rise.

The words were appalling. Sentences formed as if I was writing a cheesy romantic best seller, *die for her?* Come on....

The adjectives and nouns were despicable. No organization! No passion! I crossed everything out and began anew.

All poems are about love except love poems. Love poems are about agony. It was a quiet, dull, dark, and misty morning in a surprisingly warm Danish winter. Nonetheless the warmth did nothing for my heart; the thick clouds hung lower and lower with each passing night. It was a new moon when I traversed alone through the dreary country road from the train station while the early darkness of the winter afternoon lingered on, until at last I was within view of the melancholic farmhouse I shared with a pleasant Portuguese man named Luís. The petrichor reminded me of Sophie's freshly washed hair and with no visible moon I ghosted in the shadows with only the spark from my cigarillo marking my glowing yet dimmed presence. Imagine a gazelle in the jaws of a leopard, being chewed and savoured ever so slightly. That's what being in love feels like: being eaten, and surviving.

* * *

We'd been introduced after a lecture about the interpretative power of language. "Wittgenstein's Meaning and Human Language." I'd noticed her before that; she spoke with a British accent because she'd studied there but our first real conversation would be at the Ny Carlsberg Glyptotek museum.

"Do you come here often?" like a purring jungle cat I was already well within range of her claws before I even knew she was there.

I turned away from Stephan Sinding's *Adoration I* and watched her eyes glint through the skylight that lit up the sculpture's knees. "Yes. I like this sculpture. He wasn't considered a romantic. We would be hard pressed to think this wasn't symbolic of a romantic time. It's called *Adoration One*, after the pursuit of the muse always left unfulfilled."

"Have you seen Adoration Two?"

"I have not."

"What if he attained her in Two?"

"I don't think there is a Two."

"There must be," she smiled.

"Do you know Goethe?" I watched her reaction carefully after mentioning his name, "*The Sorrows of Young Werther* was partly based on his own life. He was in fact madly in love with a woman named Charlotte. Lotte in the novel is actually Charlotte. He couldn't even bring himself to change her name.

… He could never have her. It nearly drove him insane. This," I pointed to the sculpture, "Is the threshold of that insanity."

"It's pronounced Goe*tt*e. Hard T sound at the end," the silence echoed until a boy's footsteps tapped then disappeared towards the French Art hall. "Simonetta said you might be here."

"I wondered whether we were ever going to bump into each other here."

"You wondered?" she looked at the man's lips on the sculpture.

"I noticed you in class."

"Simonetta mentioned you're an author."

"Hence the wondering," I smiled.

"I'm sorry?"

"It's part of the job. I wonder how people behave."

"Really?" a raised eyebrow of disbelief veiled her true intentions behind her eyes.

"Yes. That's how I know you're not British. Despite that perfect accent, you're hiding your real voice behind an unfavourable stereotype."

She gave me a perplexed look of acquiescence.

"I saw you at the lecture. You wear a light coat despite all the other students wearing their winter jackets. I would've thought you were Danish but you asked the one sitting beside you to translate something. You're not Scandinavian or Canadian— I'd recognize the accent, and unlike all the others, you weren't cold, well maybe not in that way. So you're either Danish or … Swedish. Your hands told me which…"

Her fingers twitched but she controlled them and hid them behind her back. "What?" she stretched the W sound to make herself sound as British as possible. I had my answer.

"Your hands are wonderful. I would paint them if I could."

"My hands mean I'm either Danish or Swedish?" She rolled her eyes incredulously.

"Of course. We wear our masks under our skin; Russians have coarse hands. And I *imagine* yours aren't."

"Imagining. Is that part of your job too?" … When she received no reply she filled the silence with, "You imagine a lot."

"It's all I have. I'm quite taken with you. I don't believe in illusions; such things are new to me," I glanced at the woman on the pedestal of the sculpture and feared she'd followed my gaze.

"What things?"

"Overwhelming thoughts."

"Doesn't explain how you'd guess I'd be here."

"Your hands. You must paint or sculpt yourself. And though there's a closer museum to your place than this one, anyone with a sense of romance and appreciation of architecture would naturally venture here."

"What if I just wanted to see *you* because I find *you* interesting?" her smile sparkled along the lips of the woman of the sculpture whose knees were being kissed.

"I wager those doe blue eyes of yours see more than they let on."

She ignored me and looked at the sculpture, "Her face and body language. … She's so cold."

I looked at her, "Yes she is."

VIII
The Raven and The Crow

Neil watched Nora during her morning ritual. Applying her anti-aging creams and masks, reserving various restaurants around the city, preparing their morning coffee. He watched her for any sign of her infidelity but saw nothing. We are the seedy underbelly of the universe. The blank slate for a failed civilization. The sun shines above the clouds but beneath them, down here in the gutter with us, is a darkness formed in space itself. Flickering neon lights that only perpetuate the unnecessary isolation and desperation created by the blurring urban sprawls of our major cities.

"You know what's funny?" he asked when her back was to him.

"What? Did you learn some jokes?"

"Even when the sky is clear, we can never see the stars. But they're still there, right? With their points like tips of flames and their glinting like the eyes of lovers. Why do they only shine in the darkness? It's a necessity, otherwise we would never see the eyes of our lovers," his left shoulder had started falling asleep. He had to massage it thoroughly to loosen the muscles and even then the tingling sensation would remain for a while thereafter.

She chuckled, "Yes. That's hilarious Neil.... Are you all right?"

"Why do you keep asking me that?" He rubbed the new curtains between his thumb and index finger.

"Neil, you hardly make sense anymore."

"Anymore... that's a funny word. You know what else is a funny word? Goe*th*e."

She smiled, "It's *Gottei* honey."

"Yes it is! Yes... it is. How exacting your words, my wonderful, exotic," he fumbled for another adjective, "*happy* Nora."

She walked up and put her hand on his forehead, "You're burning up."

He looked outside at the sizzling cement, "Aren't we all?"

"Your book is here," she ended the conversation, "It was forwarded from the penthouse. I signed for it."

"Thank you, my lllooov…" he couldn't finish the word. In his office the sun hid the stars. He had forgotten his order of an old reprint edition of Hesiod's *Theogony*; he flipped through the pages that looked like they were about to disintegrate into ash and float up towards that blue sky that mirrored only his soul. Cursed be the sky to shine upon the wicked where thorns and thistles grow over infertile lands, for words are taken out of nothing for the meaningless letters than they are, and to nothing they return once they're no longer read.

Dear Mr. Meyollner.

We have received and confirmed your payment. Your Eurocopter is now available for delivery to a helipad of your discretion. Please note that the Monaco Heliport is the only helipad within the municipality of Monaco. The Heliport is located on Avenue des Ligures. For delivery to another municipality please let us know 12 hours in advance. If you are sending someone to pick up the helicopter, please fill out and enclose the attached form in your reply with the person's full name as it appears on their ID. Enjoy your purchase. We hope to hear from you soon. Warren Franklin, President of Sales, Monaco Heli.

Neil wanted Edwin to supervise the drop off from Monaco to Nice. Filling out the form with Edwin's information Neil recalled a conversation he'd had with Nora when they'd first met. She'd said his sense of humour was odd and macabre. He didn't understand what she meant. Now, years later, and only *after* he'd sent the form to Warren with Edwin's information and he'd informed Edwin that he, and not Neil would be picking up and surprising Nora with the chopper he understood what she'd meant. Angst choked him until the asphyxiation turned him blue. Its knots tightening around his neck over each broken promise falling into the hallow cavern of his heart where there used to be only love. When had this pain started and when would it end? Was the allotted love for another person, like matter and time, in endless supply? Like a bacterium that turns into a virus and cannot be eradicated even from the most forlorn soul? Even if he had the answers, who would've guessed if he'd believed it when face to face with such a brutal truth that he would not have chanced into such a crisis? To learn that love in fact was like matter and not time; it could be transferred, stolen, or lost. Even worse, it could be taken from you and spilled everywhere, and like money and corpses surrounded by vultures, it would then be irreversibly picked apart.

"Something's been bothering me. I will be dropping in today *personally*." the voice at the other end of the line called.

"Is everything okay, Doctor Schermer?"

"Yes. Urgency demands immediacy," click.

"I'll see you later to…" Neil realized he was talking to an empty telephone.

At the office his assistant handed him the day's appointment, "Everyone's here."

Neil looked at the paper and remembered the scheduled staff meeting. Today of all days, he thought. A day he wanted to be alone; a day he wanted to see no one and talk to no one except Christina. He massaged his left shoulder. Now that he was across others, now that he was at work, his spiralling descent no longer weighed on him. Lifting and reshuffling the wooden chair to cease its wobbling, he peered into the status report spread in front of him, "Where's the Habich account? … McCarthy."

Simon McCarthy was responsible for the U.K. and North American portfolios. He'd studied in Tennessee and always made sure everyone knew it. Neil had hired him because he reminded Neil of home. From the long end of the conference table he tapped his class ring on the table.

"Yeah, boss. It was me. Lot of yeehaws on that horse," he snicked his cowboy boots together.

Neil flipped through the account, "You're not maximizing. Two or three more derivatives would've yielded a higher return."

"13.4% gross return, pardner. Highest in the office I imagine," he clicked his tongue.

"Your return is good but it could be great. I want greatness, not contentment," he turned to everyone for the last part and approval echoed back from everyone at the table.

Neil's leadership had never been called into question. No one likes staff meetings; both errors and innovations are amplified but human nature tends to focus on the former. Neil had thus reduced the number of staff meetings to once a month and made attendance optional. Usually everyone showed up except Edwin if only because Neil could make a mental note of who had attended and who hadn't, and those that hadn't appeared would have their mistakes further analyzed one-on-one with Neil.

"Karina," he looked around the room for Karina's long flowing blonde hair, "Nice work on the Sørenson account. He called me personally to extend his gratitude for the last private equity investments you'd requested."

She smiled. It had always been her smile that made the clients sign on the dotted line; it melted hearts and froze assets. Her beauty was second only to her brilliance.

"Thanks. It was more intuition than anything else. It could've gone either way."

"Where's Edwin?" Neil played the regular fiction, *hoping* that Edwin would walk in at that exact moment. Anna Leopoardenzähne, sitting at Neil's elbow and whose name no one could pronounce looked around and breathed a sigh of relief when Edwin didn't walk through the door. She was as exceptionally cold as she was seductive. She'd never known pressure and her youthful charm coupled with her pretty face meant she had always coasted through life.

"Should we wait?" her blue eyes asked out of politeness.

"Of course not. We wait for no one."

"I want to talk to you after the meeting," Anna went on in a whisper.

"Sure," Neil looked at her and then glanced at Tadeu Sousa, the reserved Portuguese head of the Trust and Fiduciary division who had made a name for himself as an intense and serious investor. He played no games, he made no jokes, clients would tell him what they wanted and he would get it done. Neil was hard pressed to remember when he had last seen Tadeu smile. It was the office Christmas Party when he'd met Mélanie. She asked him to say something in Portuguese and he quoted Camões's "*Since my eyes don't tire of weeping,*" the rising and falling of Portuguese vowels were like pattering raindrops in the wind. She'd countered with a Rochefoucauld maxim in French: "Love, like fire, is sustained only by constant motion; and it ceases to exist when it ceases to hope or fear." Sousa had taken off his thin rectangular glasses and smiled as an excuse to disengage and not seem *too* interested. Since then Neil had taken a liking to him. Responsible for the Italian, Spanish, and

Portuguese Rivieras, Neil had always taken extra care to recommend him to his best clients. Now watching him clean his glasses and hold them up to the light, he wondered why he hadn't recommended Sousa for the accounts he gave away to Edwin in lieu of the Schermer account.

Neil remembered what Calvin had said about Edwin's portfolio. "We work directly with the clients. Do not settle for short-term gains when it might be detrimental for the portfolio long-term."

A bird landed on the windowsill and started singing. Distracted, Neil followed the lines of its feathers shining in the sunlight, "Simon, some of the investments are being routed through Switzerland and the Netherlands. Why? You can route through Toronto or New York or London. Go through Chicago if you have to."

"I tried sheriff. They told me there was some investigation and had me reroute through those banks you see on that sheet there."

He sifted through the papers, "Did anyone else have to reroute?"

Sousa raised his hand, "I had to go through VGT."

"You had to go through Vaduz?"

"Yeah…" he pinched his nose, "Some new law about all private banking assets coming through Lichtenstein having to go through the Vaduz Global Trust Bank."

"Hmmm," Neil looked at the various routing banks, "That's weird."

***

Anna was waiting in his office when the meeting ended. Neil wanted to be alone and went to the one place he knew he could find solace: Edwin's office. Dust flew across the lines of light seeping through the blinds. The perspiration tickled his triceps and gave him the sensation of lobsters being cooked and baked alive. Edwin was never in his office; he preferred to take his clients to Muse, Caina and other restaurant hotspots along the water. Neil's left shoulder tightened and he felt hot and faint. He stood over the air conditioning vent to cool himself but then his shoulder tingled and pained his neck.

He tapped on the window looking for the sparrow that had landed on the window of the conference room when his neck went numb. Massaging it and waiting for it to tingle out of numbness, Neil saw an envelope on the cherry wood table.

"Edwin," was etched across with a fancy fountain pen in Holly's writing. It was sealed. She knew that Edwin barely came into the office. Then why had she left it there? Did she want the head start? Did she want him to see it the next time he bent an assistant over that wooden finish and that sweaty aroma mixed with Holly's scented candles? Moral dilemma aside Neil put the letter in his inner jacket pocket. How could Edwin live like this? Whenever he felt himself feeling or experiencing something outside the realm of the material, he would simply quip, almost predictably, like the ticking of a clock, "Two reds don't make a green," which was practically the opposite of what he really believed. Everyone laughed whenever he said it, not because it was funny, but because he said it too often. Even Neil laughed and he suspected that's why Edwin said it so often. But Neil laughed because it was so quintessentially Edwin: benign, predictable, drab. Green was what he also called money and red what he called emotion. Neil only laughed because Edwin was saying money over emotion, which *also* happened to be great advice for market hedge funds. A happy and stupid idealist is a loyal idealist. So what if that ideal is money? What would Raphael think of Edwin?

Neil sighed and stepped into the hallway where the assistant, probably having heard Edwin's office door open, was waiting right by the door. Startled at the sight of Neil, she pretended to need his signature on a schedule update moving Edwin's meeting with the Arabs from Friday night to the following Thursday afternoon. Behind her Sousa and McCarthy were talking about the home invasion arrests.

"They *actually* got them?" Sousa almost didn't believe they could be caught.

"Yeah! String 'em up I say. HA! I don't know how you guys live without the death penalty."

"That's what we do because we don't have it. Live..." Sousa delivered this line with such a cool air that Neil thought he was sure to smile after that. He didn't.

"This isn't the Wild West Simon," Neil walked by them but then asked out of curiosity, "Were they actually Italian?"

"It didn't say," Sousa looked outside the window.

Neil pressed on towards his office, returning Karina's smile in the main hall while the assistant tried to get his attention again.

"Yes?"

"Don't forget, sir, you have another appointment on his way."

"The Schermer account. Forward all relevant files to my laptop please."

Finally back in his office he sat down across Anna on his own chair. He wobbled it to make sure it was sturdy and was almost disappointed when the chair reacted the way he wanted it to.

"Are you all right, Anna?"

"Yes," she searched and translated the words from her native German to English or French, "May I be frank with you?"

"Always," Neil wondered if there was a Swedish idiom for 'May I be frank.'

"Edwin is still married correct?"

"Yes."

"He's been messaging me and saying… rather colourfully unprofessional things. And I like this firm. I really do. And I like you Neil. You're a great leader. But I wanted to speak up and let you know if there's anything you can do."

"Anna, I'm so sorry."

"You didn't do anything. Maybe I said something and I…"

"No. I'll handle it. Please think nothing more of it."

She looked distressed when she stood up, "Dankesc… *thank you,* Neil. I really do love working here. Everyone's so nice."

"Don't thank me, Anna. I'll take care of it. Please give me 3 days. You can go on vacation. Go down to Nice or Portofino," Neil's eyes burned into Edwin, wherever he was.

She smiled and nodded. Neil tracked backwards through his memory to remember when the last time he'd actually seen *Anna* smile. He was certain she had mentioned in her initial interview that she had a fiancée living in a third-world country somewhere. But which one? Had he even followed-up and asked? The corners of her eyes looked so desperately lonely and Neil, despite being incessantly told how good of a leader he was, felt guilt ruminate through his heart because he had never taken a *personal* interest in the members of his firm past their credentials. They could all be interchanged with others on the street, even each other and nothing would change, Neil knew nothing about their identities past what he'd seen at Christmas parties; the words they used or the expressions they let slip through their masks. Holly had said the people in his life could be exchanged and he wouldn't even notice. He was beginning to wonder whether she had been right.

"I'll see you later, boss."

"How many times, Anna? … Call me Neil. And I'll see you later," Neil shook her hand and felt her skin warm his palm.

The assistant knocked on the door as Anna made her way out.

"Sir, your appointment is here."

"Goodbye, Anna," Neil said in German. "Show him in please," he only wanted another moment alone, just one moment, to email Nora and ask her if Holly was all right.

"Neil," Schermer walked in. It was a carnival of first names. And though Neil always preferred to be called by his first name, there was something about the way Schermer said it: *Kneel….*

"Afternoon," Neil opened his cigar humidor, "Cuban?"

"Yes," Schermer reached for a Siglo VI and sniffed it, "You're a man of good taste."

"I can afford to be."

Schermer laughed as he sat down, "I didn't know taste could be bought."

"Anything can be bought with enough *will* Wilbert," Neil smiled.

"Alliteration. That's very clever," he lit his cigar with a Dunhill lighter and puffed smoke in the air. "It's too cool in here."

"It's not too hot?" Neil flapped his tie hoping for some cool air to sneak in through the holes between the buttons of his dress shirt.

"No. It's frigid actually. But I didn't come to discuss your internal climate."

"Surely not. Is everything copacetic?"

Schermer took a drag of his cigar, where the red embers of its tip reflected through Neil's irises, "Do you know your Hesiod?"

"Enough to get by but not enough to say yes."

"The nine muses have always fascinated me. Even the word *museum*, though Latin, takes its origin from the Greek. *A place holy to the muses.*"

"I did not know that," Neil asked himself why he didn't read the *Theogony* in his study at the very moment Wilbert was asking about it and berated himself for not having this information.

"It overwhelms my thoughts Neil. Back in the day artists and creative types, whoever what have you… they had to ask *permission* from the muses to tell their story. Homer had to ask Calliope, the superior muse, whether he could be inspired to write *the Iliad* and *the Odyssey*."

"You don't like to ask permission?"

"No no no. It's not that— well no I don't care to, but what I mean is this. There are *nine* muses. I'm interested in only three of them. Thalia, the protector of comedy, you know with the comedy mask? The famous no face smiling mask?"

Neil thought of Edwin, "Yes of course."

"And Melpomene, she's the *opposite* of Thalia, she's the protector of tragedy, inventor of rhetoric speech, and Melos. She holds the frowning no face mask. "

Neil thought of himself, "Melos?"

"The succession of tones in a melody."

"What about the third? Calliope?"

"No. … Come on, I'm no Homer! … *Erato*. The protector of love and love poems, sometimes weddings. Erato comes from the word *eros*, which describes the feeling of falling in love."

"How can you tell which is which?"

Schermer let the smoke of his cigar linger in the air for a second and loosened his tie, "You're smarter than those Hermès ties make you look Neil. That's exactly my point. Exactly my point! What if you ask Calliope for permission but get Erato instead? You're asking to invoke justice and serenity and instead you get the pain and calamity of love. What if…" he sucked some smoke through his teeth, "You ask for Erato but get Melpomene?"

"Often I think Erato and Melpomene come hand in hand."

Schermer puffed the Cohiba in quick succession and coughed, "I knew I made the right choice. We're going to be great business partners. I'll ask you to liquidate and invest in some equities in a little while," he doused the cigar and coughed again, this time his lung hacked and knocked on his ribs from the inside. Neil handed him a napkin and Wilbert wiped his mouth. "Thank you."

"No problem."

When Wilbert approached the door Neil asked, "That's why you came to see me, Doctor Schermer? To talk about Hesiod? That's what was so urgent?"

"Of course," he shook his head as if the answer was obvious. "Muses always demand urgency," the last part he muttered to himself as the door closed behind him.

Neil followed the tigers' claws on his tie with his finger and tightened the knot around his neck before shoving it off and tossing it towards the window. He sat in the silence and watched the sparrow flap from windowsill to branch to windowsill to car to rock. The air conditioner circulated the smoke and the harsh taste of the cigar lingered in his mouth long after he'd finished smoking. When he looked up, agony swallowed the stars where only darkness reigned over the sky.

BOOK TWO

THE VILE

I
La Donna Velata

The Riviera's chilling breeze did nothing to cool my ailing heart. Instead the sun only singed the corners of my soul. My thoughts were a carnival and she was every attraction imaginable: her hands, her fingertips, her face where dimples had left immutable wrinkles. "I have wrinkles!" she'd whispered and smiled to show them to me. "You're crazy…," "No you don't…," "Don't be absurd…," were my stock responses whenever I denied their existence. I only pretended I couldn't see them to keep her smiling whenever she attempted to prove her point. Down the windy benches of Cap Ferrat parallel to the shore I saw people sitting and reading newspapers and magazines. Another dead. Another robbed. Another war. Another rich banker. Another new uPhone announced. Another another another!

"Why are some lovers cruel to each other?" I asked a random bystander who only chuckled and walked through me. Behind the rain the sun touches the meridian in the horizon and Lady Night will soon set her foot on Monaco's sands.

Neil read the sentence and fidgeted across the bench. He looked left and right and at a man walking by him expecting to see Raphael writing in the very notebook he was reading. The baby in the man's arms began wailing as soon as his eyes crossed Neil's.

'I don't even know what he looks like,' he thought to himself. And then he looked up at the man with the cane walking towards the shore below.

To get my mind off her I emailed a friend of mine who is seeking to become a police officer. I inquired about the murder Sophie was interested in only to find out that the detectives on the case are stumped. My friend Martin was elated when I contacted him; he thinks it would impress the captain if he solved the case and make a name for himself on the force. Now he has asked for my assistance because I have a large body of work in true crime and noir detective stories and he thinks me familiar and intelligent when it comes to the ooze of human nature. He does not understand the simplicity of mankind. We are not complicated. Greed drives us, vanity sustains us, lust perpetuates us.

I await him to send me the necessary files not classified as evidence. I will know only a little more than the media. The police often withhold facts to confirm or deny a confession or to trap a suspect. The information I will receive ought to be more than enough. It's people who commit crime, and like them it's not complicated.

When the email arrived my instincts told me something wasn't quite right. The victim had gone unidentified for two days and already this was suspicious. Most murders are solved within the first 24 hours and once past the 36-hour mark the odds of *solving* the murder drop significantly. Martin also mentioned that the detectives have a huge casework and this one was simply chalked up to a carjacking gone wrong. The questions to solve a murder are always the same. Who was the deceased and who benefits most from their death? The benefit can be material *and/or* emotional. The latter is often ignored; this is why spilled blood and goes unavenged.

Giltbert Maurus was found shot in his Land Rover in Midtown Toronto well past midnight. The coroner put the time of death sometime between midnight and 2:30 A.M. and the cause of death was multiple gunshots to the head through the passenger side window. One of the crime scene photos I saw had that window open and not shattered by the bullet. Thus either the window was already down or Maurus lowered it because the killer was someone he knew or was expecting. Who *was* Giltbert Maurus? Search engines turned up nothing on him personally but the Maurus family runs various trusts in a Dutch South African bank and has another investment package in Lichtenstein. The vile conspirator in me warned against blaming everything on the bankers like every other quasi-intellectual hipster looking forward to landing a Wall Street job once their music or wood design careers don't work out, but the romantic in me hoped I wouldn't listen.

I requested Martin discreetly follow up on why Maurus was in Toronto and whether he was in fact connected to that same family. What if it was just a carjacking and I was seeing patterns that do not exist? And if it wasn't, what did he know that would merit death?

"One thing, I prefer to say this over the phone instead of email," Martin called me.

"What's up?"

"The car. The car he was in. It was a black Land Rover registered to a company called GeoTex Corporation. I've tried investigating them but nothing popped up. They're a security firm he'd hired. No specific ties to Maurus."

"Thanks."

As I meditated on the idea waiting for happiness to find me Sophie surprised me with homemade chocolate cake.

"I don't eat cake." When the blue of her eyes orbited and sucked me through reality, "... Screw it."

"You are weird," she tapped me on the shoulder.

"Aren't we all?"

"Fair enough."

I sliced a thin piece of cake and it was as succulent as her lips whenever she pronounced the umlauts. "I looked into that murder case in Toronto for you."

"Uhh... why?"

"You seemed interested."

"Only because it was Toronto. It's probably someone wanting to get richer."

"Yeah but that doesn't happen too often there."

"So who did it?"

"I don't know yet."

"Are you going to find out?"

"Certainly."

"How can you be so certain?"

"Crime is not complicated."

"Nothing is complicated."

I looked at her, "That... is not true."

"No. Things are simple. You just complicate them."

"That's not true," I repeated. "Blatantly and unequivocally untrue."

She walked over to the terrace and opened the doors where the sun bathed her in its light. Her hair sparkled like lines of sun-rays. There was not a cloud in the sky other than the one brewing the storm that was sure to happen in me.

"I'm not materialistic," she touched my designer uPad sleeve. "We'd never get along."

"You assume I am?"

"I don't know. You're hard to read," she traced a line from my cheekbone to my lips.

What is the most drastic and charismatic thing I could do for her, the self-proclaimed not-materialistic? What is materialism? Possession. How do we possess things? Money. Where does money come from? Banks. How convenient.

Challenging the banks is no easy task. They have a hand in *everything*. Only a few searches proved them to be behind every major war of the last three decades and either directly or indirectly involved in the global arms trade. Certain regions are kept destabilized to retain or if possible increase their profits. The small percentage of banks who steer clear of the obviously illegal trade acquire profits from other means. I found that the WBCT charges an extra 12% on cash deposits over a million dollars and transfers from unverified or suspicious sources. This tells me two things. One: that they make a minimum of $120,000 from every "suspicious" transaction; and two: that they must *know* "unverified" or "suspicious" sources really means "proceeds from illegal transactions or business practices." It is legal racketeering and money laundering. If by a divine miracle a bank is exposed in their participation in this global fraud, such as the Global Commerce Bank of Derivatives and Trades (GCBDT), the board of directors can simply plead ignorance and deny any culpability and involvement in any misdeeds that *may or may not* have occurred. When no one can be held accountable, ignorance of the law becomes a defence against its violations. Now smoking a joint is a punishable federal offence in the great United States of America, carrying a sentence of up to one year in prison and hefty fines. Yet taking 12% of proceeds from the sale of that marijuana is completely legal.

Necessary steps must be taken to curtain this corruption.

"He's insane," Neil shook his head at Christina, whose eyes were focused on his nail-bitten hands caressing the cover of the journal. "Seriously. Crazy…" he slammed the book shut as the sound of his voice melted away like the mist that had been settling over the now cloudy sky. This sudden turn in Raphael's mood, the sudden realization of a lonely manifestation that mirrored his own muted the reality of Nora's affair, of Edwin's betrayal, of his increasing desperation that Tina desire him. These silent thoughts gathered like storm clouds around ridged textures of disharmony, like whirlpools and twisters blending the internal expanse of his soul spinning into a frontier of lost space.

The air was thin and cool and accommodated Tina's laughter. He committed which of the words that instigated a reaction so he might try to make her laugh at his command.

"It's not funny." Searching for that lost frontier, he moved through the constellations breathing in moments that might best represent happiness like implosions that end in stillness.

"You have to realize Neil, that people don't want change. They don't need nor want heroes. How easy is it to flee from an oppressive relationship that's both loveless and dead? How simple to move to a city that has more of what you want? But we don't do it; we envy birds because they can fly but we root ourselves to our problems. Why?"

Neil looked up at the sky now covered by a blanket of grey, "I don't know."

"Look at classic antiquity, literature. When has change ever come willingly? Both internally and societally? Never. Because of fear. We fear change but we also fear success. We fear that we just might be happy. That fear overpowers everything else. We're never happy and if we're unhappy, we're never satisfied with our successes."

"That doesn't make sense!"

"People prefer suffering to happiness I find. No that's not *how* I want to say it. ... They fear suffering less than they fear happiness."

"Why?"

"For some it's probably easier to suffer than be happy. You can always find something to despair over. But you have to *try*, actively and infuriatingly try, to simplify things and acquire a measure of happiness. Maybe by nature it's just easier to suffer," she sipped her macchiato and watched a waiter clean up a table near them.

"And the others?" Neil tapped on the journal with his fingertips and having bitten his hangnails earlier that morning each sent a shivering pain through his hand.

"Hmmm?" she focused on a strand of hair that curled near his forehead.

"You said for some. Means there are others."

"Suffering makes them feel alive," her eyes scanned the water and settled on a small wave that hopped its white foams towards a rock and bounced back.

"As opposed to?"

"The sublimation of happiness… maybe, I don't know maybe it's too much to bear."

"That's too many maybes to me *Tina*— I mean, *Christina*…"

She smiled, "The future is a maybe. A large part of the unknown is a maybe itself," her eyes now reflected the grey of the clouds closing access to its blue hue, "Tell me about her," she raised her eyebrows and pointed to the journal.

"Sophie?"

"That's the same one we were talking about at breakfast that day right?"

"He calls her that. Who knows how much of it is true? Haven't you been listening? He's crazy! … *Insane*," he repeated more to himself because it was a convenient answer. Now he was too tired, turning too frail, too old to entertain the idea that maybe Raphael had actually made some sense.

"Do they love each other?"

"No. … I mean yes. I mean I don't know. Maybe," he tapped his fist on the table.

"There's that magic word again."

Neil guffawed, "She has someone else."

Tina mumbled something to herself.

"Pardon?"

"Beautiful women always do."

Neil watched her neckline tighten and loosen around her where her shoulder bone met the upper part of her chest.

"Tell me about her *true* beloved then," Tina would replay this conversation in her mind over and over again and sharpen this sentence. She would add all the things she *could've* said, and with the intricacies of the English language; where a noun can become a verb, where the meaning of a sentence changed based on the stressed word or syllable, she stressed or distressed one or more of the words she'd used. 'Her *true* beloved then.' 'Her true *beloved* then.' '*Her* true beloved then.' 'Her true beloved *then*.' Her real beloved as opposed to the one she didn't love. The one she didn't love. The one she loved because everything was about her. Her beloved at that exact moment in time. She had of course, actually stressed the word *true*. She wanted to know which man Sophie loved and yet she couldn't decide whether she was being sardonic or not, whether all her classical education had warped her image of modern society and in fact turned *her* into a cynic. She would decide she wasn't being comical and that the matter was in fact grave and deserved the highest analytical attention.

Neil glared through her eyes and analyzed the distance between two waves by the silent gap between the rock being slapped.

"I don't know," she shrugged her shoulders and the bone spun under her skin, "What's his name?"

"There are only allusions. Raph never mentions him by name. If he's melancholic it's 'true beloved,' if he's angry it's 'oppressor,' but if he's depressed and dejected, it's 'the vile romantic.' I told you… he's insane. Obsessive."

"Raph?"

"Give me a break…"

"All right. What else? Read me a passage."

She said it as if she'd issued a command that Neil couldn't refuse. He flipped through the pages of the journal, running his fingers over the fading words: "'Having slept on the couch I could only imagine what her quixotic Don Juan thought of her in the mornings. Where the swaying aromas of a delicious breakfast would fill the room like lines of light escaping through veiling curtains. I envisioned him sleeping with the serenity of Siddhartha under the tree before he sees Govinda for the final time. He would undoubtedly crack his joints and stretch when he woke, as one does after having slept so peacefully. He would feel the ripples of his muscles traverse his body. His muscles would be sturdy and strong due to the nature of his status as an army man. But that's not why he would stretch them. He would stretch them because his muscles were all he had. His muscles and his beard. That ridiculous beard that was as part of him as those shallow set eyes and those small lips that saw nothing of value, said nothing of importance, but had kissed the most valuable thing on this Earth. He would keep that beard whether or not Sophie liked it. It had taken so long to grow and maintain that shaving it would be tantamount to stripping him a part of his identity. He would be someone else without that beard and he feared that Sophie would never love someone without that beard. That was what made him a telling romantic, his ability to manipulate. For one must be at once both as strong as a lion and as sly and duplicitous as a fox to trap a leopardess.

It was however…' this part is good," Neil looked up and tapped the page, "… 'Their interactions that interest me, since my words border vituperation and my thoughts and emotions may be chalked up to bias.' He admits it!"

"Yes he does," Tina had closed her eyes to listen but had now opened them and the reflection from the black of her macchiato turned them sandy brown.

"'They had not a common language between them. I'd wager my love for her she thought their interactions, from the moment they'd met to their latest conversation about … *whatever*, had been *intuitive*. Now for someone as intelligent as her it is certainly short-sighted to think that the inability to communicate in a common language can be curtailed in lieu for *intuition*. While it is true that she could potentially *learn* his language—this would amuse me more than it would shatter me—it would still take *years* to attain the sort of linguistic mastery required for passionate and ferocious communication. The latter point stands if by some miracle *he* learns her language. Ergo, either she is not as intelligent as I believe, or he is an avid manipulator of ideas and future-projections, with Oscar worthy performances portraying himself as the victim in a drama all to retain an emotional dominance over her.'"

"That is a lot of spite."

"I like it. He doesn't joke around. I can't stand people who wrap the truth in jokes because they fear being serious when telling the truth."

"I think you were right when you read the banking piece. He's obsessed. Crazy. You're reading what you want because you're buying the image of this Sophie he's selling." She tapped her nails on the tablecloth waiting for Neil's answer.

"He doesn't hide behind a mask. I value that."

"Maybe he does. You're reading his journal. We have no idea what he's *actually* like in real life."

The *we* had sent Neil drifting over the primary colours of the Riviera during summer and a breeze washed through him.

"You don't even know what he looks like!" she went on, "He could be *that* guy!" she pointed to a waiter, "Or *that* guy," she pointed to a guy in a hat across the street, "Or even *that* guy!" she nodded to the man with the cane sitting on a bench in the distance who had been staring in their direction.

"There's some pages missing!" he turned the book around to show her the tear marks, "From page 36 to 50-something."

"And you can't rest until you find those pages right?"

Neil breathed in the cool breeze just before the rainstorm that wouldn't come.

II
La Belle Jardinière

There was a newspaper article regarding parents who are unable to care for their children. The elite opinion was either to *not* have kids or put them for adoption if you cannot afford them. No one would argue that pain exists; we blame parents for bearing children but never God for creating an existence He has never provided for. Either He created us deliberately or He didn't or He doesn't even exist. If we take accidental creation, we may operate on the same basis as the atheist, which is more of a religion about screaming louder and patronizing interlocutors. The atheist understands nothing and knows nothing outside of the process previously available to him. Amusing that they think themselves the freethinkers of our time.

On the other hand, we think the politician maintains political stability whatever the cost. We believe the politician we have voted for is honourable and the subjects have therefore consented to some extent to what it takes to seize that honour. Both slave and master are talking about stability. But to really be a politician is to perpetuate your nation and prolong your power and seek glory. The entire modern liberal tradition pretends that the way to perpetuate that glory is through honour. That is an illusion. The great measure of modernity is to suppose that glory is the deserved reward of honour. The argument is that it is thus rational and in the best interest of *everyone* to be moral and honourable, but experience *has* effectively demonstrated that it is more often than not both dangerous and irrational to be honourable. This sort of argument transcends humanity above animals, and we are only animals living in an ecosystem looking to exert control over our territory, roar at any new animal that attempts to ingress, and to keep power localized to our own cabal.

"You know what my uncle used to say?" Neil sipped his water.

"Yes, Neil," Nora scoffed, "A thousand times."

Neil shut the journal, "You're probably right."

"The happiness index is out for the year," Nora flipped the pages of her magazine.

"Luxembourg, Switzerland, or Canada?"

"Denmark."

"Danes are the happiest people? That doesn't track."

"I know…," she flipped back and forth again, "It's always dark there!"

"We should look into it."

"I have too much to do," she laughed, "I don't have time to look up why Denmark is a happy country."

She moved down the list with her finger, "Luxembourg… Luxembourg…" she whispered to herself, "Luxembourg is twenty! Canada is…" her eyes flicked up, "Six."

"The Swiss?"

"Two."

"Maybe we should move there."

"Switzerland?"

"No. *The happiest place on Earth*."

"Why? Are you unhap—" just before she increased the pitch in her voice to formulate a question she corrected herself, "But we're not unhappy," she shrugged her shoulders halfway.

"How would you define happiness, Nora?"

"Nora?" she closed the magazine and looked up at him, "*Just* Nora? … Since when do you *just* call me Nora?" her shoulders tightened and stood as high and still as a mountain.

"Hmmm?" Neil crossed his arm and fiddled with his cufflink. "What do you mean?"

She mumbled something in German, "Neil, is there someone else?" this time the increasing pitch denoting a question and demanding an answer was not open to interpretation.

"Don't insult me," even though he had been consistently insulted by her every word since he knew about her and Edwin. Even then, he dared not ask her the same question. "How would you define happiness?" he repeated, "My gorgeous, gracious, loyal, magnificent, Helen of Troy; my absolutely excellent indelible paramour, my Hera of Olympia."

"*That*," she smiled and crossed her legs.

"What?"

"It's not a *thing,* Neil. It's the *kind of* life you lead that makes you happy."

"So what makes a life a happy life? … Don't say virtue."

"I wasn't going to; that's archaic. You're happy when you set rules for yourself and follow them."

Neil glanced at the journal under his hand then back at his glowing wife, "How do you mean?"

"You're asking a lot of questions."

"I'm curious."

"Following your own rules then, that's what makes you happy."

"Leading the kind of life I imagine myself to live?"

"No. Because you can be an athlete and imagine being a chemist, and you'll always be unhappy. You have to find cohesion between the rules that dictate your identity and the nature of your identity. Example, as a private banker you can set a rule for yourself that *there's a sucker born every minute* and that it's your job to… to… *liberate* them of their excess assets."

"So it's vocational?"

"Not necessarily. At least I don't think. Take me for instance; I'm materialistic. So I'd be unhappy if I attempted to live the kind of life that banished possession."

"I think you're dumbing it down for me. It can't be this simple."

"It's not. If you're feeling alienated from the *real* you, a real you crafted from an image and over years of memories and interactions, it's because there's a friction between the rules you had set for yourself and the ever-changing nature of your identity."

"You mean the rules I had set for myself are changing?"

"Maybe."

"Without me realizing it?"

"Of course. You can be happy and not be aware of it."

"So happiness is also a concept, mutually exclusive."

"You mean *of*-predication? Like Beauty, Happy, Large, Tall?"

"No?"

"Predications belonging to their corresponding metaphysical realms? … That's not what you mean?"

"I don't even know what you're talking about."

Nora scoffed, "The form *of* say, beauty is prior in its beauty to Helen, *of* love is prior to Dante's love. Helen can't be beautiful without the form of beauty. … Don't you read all those fancy books you buy?"

"Not as much as I like," recently Neil had forgotten how educated and refined Nora had always been. There is an infinite gap between what someone knows and what they want to show they know.

"Everything has its ontological priority. Remember that."

"So there's an ontological priority to my happiness?"

"Of course."

"And it isn't virtue?"

"What is it with you and virtue? It's so dated! What does that even mean nowadays? Virtue! Like what could that entail? You thin down your personal profits so your investors make more money? You pay your taxes instead of opening accounts in Monaco and Belize?"

"I mean following that rule you're talking about. If I set a rule for myself to lie and cheat to get to the top and follow it I'm virtuous because *I'm honest with myself.* Then I can be in a state of happiness."

"But happiness can't be a state, because then you can be happy if you're being tortured or if you're homeless," she looked up at him, "And I didn't mean *you*, I meant you as in people. I know you pay all your taxes."

"Ideally… yes… and I know."

"I think virtue would help because the alternative is vice and vices are negatives. Virtue is a positive trait. Of course it's better to never encounter a drowning child. A 'virtuous' person would save the drowning child but that doesn't mean saving drowning children is the path to happiness."

"So we can't pursue virtue because it's a state, but that doesn't work because that means I can be happy while being tortured and or homeless. But because I'm removed from pain and pleasure in following my rules I attain happiness?" Neil then remembered that today would be the day the chopper would be ready for pickup. He had already emailed Edwin about it so he had the day free.

Neil walked up and kissed his wife, caressing her body from her nape to the small of her back and the insides of her thigh but he could go no further than that. An intimate relationship like a marriage exists independently of social categories and time. It is a realization and acceptance that time structures are benign. Giving and sharing are simultaneous expressions of happiness rather than responses to socially programmed rites. There are no games in intimacy since there are ulterior motives, but that intimacy is only possible in a relationship where the absence of fear permits complete awareness. It is a region where beauty is no longer seen as valuable or useful, possessiveness is no longer seen as an envious goal to obtain an object but to exist alongside that object. When affection grows in a relationship, it allows both partners to be creative, spontaneous, curious, free from fear, and aware of each other. The logical phenomenon of intimacy transcends social norms, thus a surprise bouquet of roses picked from a garden is more of a spontaneous and authentic expression of love and intimacy than a set of Cartier earrings gifted on the socially programmed anniversary. A forgotten anniversary or birthday is not a tragedy for the truly intimate; such moments fabricated through time are only tragedies for those whose relationships exist only by virtue of social rituals.

A happy marriage is a marriage where intimacy reigns. But because intimacy is hard to fathom and attain, we borrow the image of a happy marriage from romanticized fiction. The husband has moved up the corporate chain and is now partner or has started a highly successful company from his mother's basement; he comes home with flowers, 'Honey, I'm home,' to a radiant, slender wife who's gotten home from her job just before him. Their home, just short of a mansion in an elegant suburban neighbourhood with marble counters and floors and big booming windows, where the lit candles stand tall on the dinner table and Barry White plays by the fireplace. Troubled marriages and relationships are those where such illusions shatter, where the husband has to work longer hours to maintain his partner status and pay for the Mercedes and mansion and the wife is alone and dines and drinks alone. When the husband no longer buys bouquets and the wife no longer leaves love poems in his lunch, where they stop calling each other just to say they love each other.

"I had the weirdest dream last night," he sat down next to her.

"Was I in it?"

"In a way. You hovered at the edge of the dream," he closed his eyes to remember.

"Who else was there?"

"Thalia."

"Who?"

"She's a muse. The protector of comedy."

"That is peculiar."

"I was reading Hesiod and then a client came in and started talking about the Muses."

"How'd you know it was *her*?"

"I didn't. I don't know what they look like. I've never seen a painting or anything of the sort. It was just one of those things you *know* in a dream. Like I knew the mist at the edge of the dream was you. The woman I was talking to was Thalia."

"What was she saying?" the corner of her lips quirked up.

Neil suddenly felt the air thicken, "It was gibberish," he blew into his shirt.

"Are you hot?"

"You have no idea."

She walked over to the thermostat, "It's on sweetie. In fact it's a little chilly."

"You can turn it down if you like. It's just the air."

"Maybe we *should* move there."

"Where?"

"Denmark."

"It's cold there right?"

"Yes but it's cold *outside*. Right now even here it's not that hot. Maybe it's something inside you," she filled the kettle with water. "I'm going to take a shower before I head out."

"Okay. I'll see you later today," he tapped the leather chair with the tips of his fingers which hurt because now he had no nails.

"Sure."

Once she disappeared into one of the bedrooms Neil got up to leave and noticed that the Hermès chess set had been opened and placed on the side-table closest to the window, where the Riviera's winds blew across the changing tides of nihilistic solitude.

The king's pawn had advanced two squares. Had Nora begun a game or was this part of the new décor?

Neil imagined Nora's elegant hands gripping the pawn and sliding it across the board; his first instinct was to move the pawn back to its original position but he had already noticed the piece and couldn't retreat without berating himself for it.

"Nora?" he said into the bedroom. "Nora?" when he heard no response he walked into the bedroom. … "Nora?"

"Just Nora again?" she called out from inside the bathroom.

"Did you move a piece for its Feng Shui?"

"Hmmm?" she stuck her head and part of her body out from between the door, revealing her *Agent Provocateur* Terri bra in navy. The orbing softness of her breast, hidden in expensive silk behind the delicate weaving of laces left just enough to the imagination to invoke mad passion.

"A pawn was moved to E4," he blurted out mechanically because she'd unbalanced his thoughts, and he remembered how easy it'd been for her to seduce him when they were young. Unhappy circumstances demand recollection.

She smiled and the last thing he saw before she closed the door behind her was her bra slipping off her body.

He overthought his move and eventually decided on advancing the queen's pawn one square to D6. Feeling proud because of the sophisticated and multifaceted symbolism of each of their first moves, Neil made his way out.

* * *

On the way to the office Neil steamed up his window with his breath and doodled spherical and cubic shapes with his index finger. Ordering Alec to stop at the *Yacht Club de Monaco Gallery*, he ventured into Brooks Brothers looking for a new summer suit to keep him cool. Suits rainbowed across the back walls and smiling shirt collars populated the centre tables of the stores. Beside the *Summer Accessories* section was a set of blue case-wrapped hardcovers where the floral aroma of wood lingered around him. Neil's eyes glanced over *Classic Wisdom for the Good Life* and *How to be a Gentleman* but stopped at *How to Raise a Gentleman.*

"Are you expecting?" a man in a summer Regent Fit 1818 suit approached.

"No," Neil looked at him, "But my friend is."

"Is it a boy?"

"I don't know yet."

"This one is for gentlemen."

"Do you have one for ladies as well? … I'll get them both."

"Unfortunately not. These are special editions."

"I'll take it anyway," he handed the book to the employee. A 50/50 investment was for Neil the worst kind of investment because it made people lean towards the positive where they should be leaning towards the negative. Children are no different. God decides, almost on a whim and at the toss of a coin whether an extra man or woman ought to walk the planet.

Are children a necessary step in the ladder of existence which apexes at the moment of death? Are children also a step in the ladder of love? Now, in the ladder of love *and* existence, must you have children with someone you're in love with? What if you fall in love with someone who wouldn't be a good parent? Isn't it unfair to snatch a soul from the abyss with someone who wouldn't be able to provide the best type of existence? Being responsible for an existence that only perpetuates despair is itself deserving an agonizing existence.

The yacht club was only a five-minute drive away from his penthouse and he walked in with renewed joy as he wondered what Nora would think about all the recent changes she'd outlined coming to fruition. *Home* sweet home, he sat down on the sheet-covered floor between newly painted walls but his arrival carried at most an expatriate's joy. He failed to recognize the parts of the penthouse that made it their home. He felt as if he'd been gone for years and not only a few weeks. The hotel, despite Nora's efforts and expertise in interior design, was far from their home, but neither was the perpetually renovating penthouse. *Home*, the senseless idea of *home*, failed to attain any meaning.

He found his *Metamorphoses* tape in a box in one of the bedrooms labeled *Neil Tapes* in Nora's bold yet curly handwriting.

The bone-biting winter replaced the autumn deluge with winds dwindling through blasts of cold fronts across the flat Danish plains. It was the perfect moment to show her some of the poems I'd written for her but such moments flee just as often as they arrive. She played her favourite piece: Uchida's interpretation of Schubert's Piano Sonata No. 20 in A in Andantino against the backdrop of thundering rain. The notes pressed through poignant melancholy because all elation is melancholic. My poem would do neither of us any good but it was like every meaningful moment; a passing reminder of a singing bird at dawn or a breath from the lips of Beauty. It was the voice of silence and crowding loneliness.

Something stopped me. Her mention of the word *lover*, as in 'I've had many.' Clarification: it was not that she'd had X amount of lovers in the past, wherein some threshold of numbers makes her a coquette. It was the fact that I had no way of knowing whether or not I would be relegated sometime in the future to 'I had a lover who....'

The following day Benson and I were having drinks at my place and he noticed Sophie's sock under my couch. She'd taken it off the day before while napping under my blanket on the couch while I worked on the hero's call to action and subsequently ended up with a romantic subplot that dominated the narrative.

His eyes drifted to the black stripe that ran through the centre and gauged the amount of GlenDronach left in his glass.

"I'm reading *the Sorrows of Young Werther* again," he rinsed his mouth with the scotch.

"Don't," I warned, "Dreamers and idealists ought beware venturing into that novel."

"I've read it twice already!"

"But the circumstances which you read it before and the circumstances you'll read it now have changed."

"The source of my joy is also the source of my sadness," he poured himself another drink.

"We lose everything when we've lost ourselves."

"I thought about calling my ex-girlfriend."

"I have to recommend against that."

"What's the point..." he looked out the window into the pitch-black darkness of the fields, "...If we can't be ourselves?"

"Why can't you be yourself?"

"I don't know. I feel like if you're not there, or if Simonetta isn't there, or if Sophie isn't there, or if Josephine isn't there; I've gone on two dates with her. She's cool. But still it's strained. It's straining. Being alone I mean."

"Alone...," I drifted into the dark space knowing full-well what he was talking about.

There were always narratives in her voice, in the way she said good morning or good night; fluctuations in intensity and tone that always left me wanting more. Her memory lingered in my soul, heart, and mind. Even when she wrote and showed me what she wrote, looking either for validation or praise, I was left in awe at each page. Sometimes she would rip the page up to prove a point, 'Kill your darlings Raphael, but I don't have to tell *you* that!' she'd said on countless occasions. I imagined myself in airports around the world waiting to board somewhere far away from her: to Nice, Toronto, New York. Imagination is not reality. I stayed. Everything has its price, even red roses.

Question: Which is worse; falling face first from the top of the CN tower, or falling in love? Answer: They are the same. Equal in their end and purpose.

"OY!" he snapped his fingers in front of me, "Where are you?"

"Apologies. Sometimes I drift," a lingering bitter taste, to accept that the most profound and major emotions of a human: love, fury, agony, and elation are as separate and distinct as the falling sands in an hourglass.

"I know."

Before he left to catch the last train at midnight we bid each other good night and shook hands. He was in love with Josephine, though that word was too saintly and sacred to be uttered by either of us. This didn't take me long to figure out; it was both cruel and fascinating that he loved and hated the same thing and how quickly she would destroy him from the inside despite never having done anything. It's impossible to bluff at the cosmic poker table. You play the hand you're dealt. Some of us are dealt pairs while others are dealt straights.

III
The Entombment

A picture of him and Nora before they'd moved to the coast was lodged between a tape of Gogol's *Dead Souls* and Nabokov's *Speak, Memory*. They were both smiling, with Neil squeezing the rainwater out of Nora's dampened hay-coloured hair even though it was cut just above the shoulder. Enviable young love. Enviable experiences long past. That was the first time Neil had felt he was truly in love with her, and someone, either Edwin or Holly, had captured the moment. Walking to the bar it'd started raining and Nora had reached for Neil's closed umbrella. He'd pulled it away and she reached for it again; every time she reached for it he pulled it away, until he finally left it there and when she abruptly grabbed it, he reeled her in for a hug. Afterward they held hands and even now he remembered the thought he had whenever the breeze pushed the rain towards them and he felt the drizzle on his face: A great woman is like the wind. She comes and goes as she pleases. It's nice when she comes but now he was beginning to realize that when she leaves she leaves a chill across your every bone. Now that their words floated through an impenetrable surface of despairing silence, where both sat speechless even during heated conversations and alone despite lying next to each other every night. Can a marriage survive beyond the turbulence of separation and division through a love that exists beyond rapture and hate? Regardless, the potential of separation always persists; hate and happiness and agony remain as essential conditions for marriage and being. A person entrenched in such concepts can never be at ease, never relaxed, even here on the meridian, the consummation of happiness is immeasurably impossible.

Neil had to wonder, whether due to his love or due to his deeply romanticized, borrowed and misplaced account of marriage, his unhappiness had begun at the precise moment Nora's had begun. The paint fumes were making him dizzy and he opened the windows and listened to the sound of the coast. The rocky and distant shore hiding behind veils lit by up sunlight but retaining their gloom. He breathed in the dust and took off his jacket when he felt feverish. Was marriage not mutual happiness? He'd taken her hand and there was a delicate transfer of felicity when he'd felt her slender fingertips. It was more intimate in some ways, than some of their sexual encounters, mechanically performed because it was either convenient or part of a necessary social ritual.

She bit her lip to keep from crying just before they went into the bar. "It's impossible not to wonder," he'd said, "Whether there is a sense or meaning to life. … As opposed to it being a tragic aberration of cosmic fate." He realized that he was traversing through memories and images of their fading joy. Memories are not factual; they change because we do. The person who *had* that experience is not the same person remembering it. The world was suddenly significant, unlocking all its mysteries and dissipating all its mists through the love nested in his heart. The love that was at risk of flying away in search of another heart. His greed yearned to hold onto that elation alone. A breeze came in through the window and hovered around the photograph. It circled around above the rain clouds forming along the horizon and sneaking between blossoming carnations. But that same waving feeling, that tiding and blissful breeze was inside the both of them as they'd walked hand-in-hand across cement roads that felt like incandescent fields of fertile pasture. "Plant a seed and it will grow," she'd said later that night when they were walking back along a lake. The manifest joy that at that moment had belonged not only to him but to the sunshine, to that lake, to the sky, to the clouds, to her; and even to the drunk buffoons who slurred their words when they hit on her and could not retain their balance. His elation was implicit and had manifested in Nora. She was herself, in her youthful gaiety, sparkling with grandeur; he could *feel* her exhilaration. How to make that feeling last? She was natural in every movement, every word, and every stare. It was a universally significant happiness that begun in the palms of their hands through infinite lands that he thought would last for eternity. What do these things matter if we are all happy or unhappy together? Are such feelings not singular? Was holding onto the fading moment of that bliss more important than the bliss itself? The intensity of that reality which had only been possible in Nora's presence meant—his phone chirped.

Think of the devil…

Where are you? We have lunch reservations! ;)

A.

I will try to make it. You guys begin without me.

Love,

Neil M.

I can't get hold of Holly. See you there if you can make it. <3

O.

Mirroring the tacit precision of her chess move, what Nora was *really* saying that she would be lunching with Edwin unless he joined. Great winds always choose the direction they blow.

I saw a video of her singing and I *knew* I wanted to be with her. Her voice pierced through souls. I knew I would be happy with her. But I dared to hope, and once you dare to hope you court disappointment.

"To be happy is to fulfill desires isn't it?" I asked when the video ended.

"It's intuitive to agree," even her speaking voice lifted me into the air.

"… Doesn't seem right. … What if our intuitions are wrong?"

"That would be… upsetting," she moved closer to me and slipped her leg across my thigh on the couch.

"What are you doing?"

"It feels natural."

"Are we trusting what feels natural now?"

"Yes?"

"Is that a question or a statement?"

"Both."

She put her legs against my chest and pressed. I caressed it and kissed her toes. We are all islands, but if you believe in souls we each have within us a planet and even a universe. Why else would we see the sky in a person's eyes or shining constellations on a person's back? Take the Earth's perspective. Aren't some souls worth more? I sought to detach her from herself. To me she was something more. She wasn't *just* an elegant person or a beautiful woman meant to instil desire in my heart. She was—

"Raphaello! … Come back to me!" she tapped my shoulder and left her leg hanging there.

I lost myself in the sea of sentences that were drifting out of me onto the shores of my mind. Stroking her leg with my fingers I whispered, "Let me take your celestial leg, the perfect metaphor for this planet. Here…" I slid my hand across her inner thigh and she moaned, "We have Copenhagen, the start of everything. But traverse south along the two branches of the Old Rhine," the words flew out of me as if I were a bird migrating north for winter, "To find the birthplace of the mighty Rembrandt," I kissed her thigh. "Where you were born. Across that river to the south," with my other hand I traced a line down the centre of her breasts, "We have the bureaucratic Hague," I kissed each of her thighs. "Now once you go east," I switched to the right thigh again, "You arrive at Amersfoort and its medieval centre," I sucked that tiny part of her leg. "This tiny mound," I traced the bottom circular part of her left knee, "Is Bronkhorst," I traced the circle with my tongue. "On the other side of the North Atlantic, Canada is your gleaning calf, your shining ankle, your divine heel," I sucked her heel. "Now if by some cosmic miracle you love me, your soul, Toronto, is your delicious toe," I bit and licked her toes. "Lying here, Canada seems unimportant, but try to stand by your heart and soul, and you'll find that balance comes from here," I traced her calf with my fingertips and breathed slowly on it, "Just as *my* balance now lies in the Netherlands…" I looked into her eyes, "Now… where are we right now?"

"Copenhagen," she put her fingers on my mouth and traced my lips.

* * *

In the horizon the sun was setting and the clouds closed the purpling colour of the sky. In a last ditch effort sunlight snuck through the deep frost covering the windowpane.

Her finger cleared the ice by drawing a heart. "Look," she giggled, "It's your heart."

"Melting?" I was writing in my dream journal.

"No. Icy."

"*I'm* the frigid one? Now you're deliberately being funny," a comedy bound for… tragedy.

"Not deliberately."

"Accidental comedy is the best form of hum…" a thought grabbed hold of me and I had to jot it down before it was lost in the ocean of consciousness. I found myself *hoping* that we would be together. I never hope. In my attempt to seize the moment I fumbled out of it and completely detached from what she was doing and saying.

"… So it makes sense really, for me not to get along with her."

"I'm sorry, my dear. Who?"

"You weren't listening?"

"No."

"It doesn't matter. It was gossip anyway."

"You don't get along with people because you're intimidating."

"I am not!"

"Don't pretend like you don't know what I'm talking about. Do people *approach* you or are they friendly to you a posteriori?"

Her silence begged me to go on.

"You're pretty and smart. That is a fatal combination. So you won't get along with anyone unless *you* actively make an effort."

"That's faithful. Shouldn't you always make an effort in hope that something wonderful can blossom?"

"I'm not one for charity."

"Charity?" she was kneading dough to bake bread.

"To give myself completely to another per—" I interrupted myself, "Unless other abstracts are involved."

She latched onto my thought almost at the same time I had it, "What other abstracts?"

"Hmm? I wasn't listening."

"No you weren't. You were focused. … Whatever."

"Giving yourself fully to another is being charitable. In healthy relationships both parties have a *choice* to be charitable to each other. They hope that their faith in each other will be rewarded in actualizing the idea they've created."

"I have difficulty understanding you."

"You and me both," I put down my pen.

She scoffed, "I can never tell where the intense line begins and the glib line ends."

"You and me both," I smiled. "By the way, I followed up with that murder in Toronto again."

"Hmm?"

"The murder you brought up."

"I was just making conversation; don't actually try to solve it! You're insane!"

"Yes, I am."

As far as the Internet will take me, I found that Maurus's family had close-to-controlling interest in a French bank based in Belize. With offices in both places, I found that every time a threat of civil war popped up in the news, their bank grew consistently at 4%. That means one of two things: either their revenues are off the books and unreported, or their revenue is illegal. Why was he killed? Who knows? Motive is irrelevant at this point. It could be as simple as human nature, greed and power and someone consolidating influence; or as complicated as a long disputed feud that culminated when he looked at his foe's wife the wrong way.

Nora tapped Neil on the shoulder, "Neil, wake up!"

"Huh?" Neil's eyes flickered before coming into their own. "What is it?"

"Edwin called. Thrice."

"What'd he want?" still waking; he put his hand on her shoulder to feel its movements.

"Something to do with the SEC. Some guy named Marco wants to see you and him or something. I don't know, honey."

"I have the Monday morning blues," Neil groaned.

"It's 1:30 on Wednesday sweetie."

"I have the hump day afternoon blues then."

"Then take the day off. We can go out. Just like old times," she giggled and squeezed his forearm.

His eyes lit up, "Just like old times?" he repeated, while imagining coming across an elk near a lake despite there being no elks where they lived.

"Yeah! We can go to Hermès and check out their window display. They finally removed that horrible jellyfish thing, then to Cartier and check out their stationery. You love their stationery!"

Neil's eyes blinked open, "I love their stationery," and he shoved the blanket aside, "But I have to go into the office. Call downstairs and have them bring Alec around."

"Okay."

On the way out Neil noticed that the white queen's pawn had been advanced two places to cut off his advance. Her two pawns stood shoulder-to-shoulder ready to attack and defend at the same time.

Neil sat on the couch and looked at the board. It was only the second move, why was he overthinking it? He began to wonder whether Nora had *ever* beaten him and couldn't remember. Nora *had* beaten him, with consistent and unhesitant precision. She had *improved* his tactical foresight. This was what actually made him excel in his job even though Neil was himself unaware of it. She never took any mercy on him and this was something he appreciated whether he was aware of it or not.

"Queen side knight to F6," he whispered to himself and smiled.

The elevator jerked up and down and stopped, "I'm sorry, sir," the attendant shuffled nervously, "We'll be up and about in a moment."

"It's not a problem." Neil sent an email to Edwin asking to have Marco meet him at his office and to forward him Marco's information and supervisor. Knowledge is power. Neil hated having to take on faith the fact that no one did anything wrong. He couldn't trust Edwin, not really. Edwin was predictable in his rampant unpredictability. If he thought he could get away with murder and gain something Neil wouldn't bet one way or another what he'd do.

"It happens when it rains."

Ding. The elevator doors opened to everyone from the doorman to the Russian oligarch renting out an entire floor fanning themselves from the heat. Nature is the great equalizer.

"I thought you said it only jerks when it rains," Neil handed the attendant the copy of the *International Times* he was given.

"Uhh…" the attendant blushed, "Sorry, sir. It happens sometimes."

"Very well," he took a step and then paused. "I was only kidding."

"Yes, sir. Very funny."

Neil stepped back towards the attendant, "Can I ask you something?"

"Of course, sir."

"Why don't you engage in normal conversation? I don't want to be rude. Have you been taught and trained that way?"

"Sir?"

"Never mind," Neil shook his hand and tipped him 200€. "I didn't mean to make you nervous."

His status had isolated him. Everyone refused to communicate sincerely with him, even to befriend him because they were afraid of upsetting him. But why? Because of his money and affluence?

Alec held the car door open breathing heavily and wiping the perspiration off his face with his driver's gloves.

"I have the A/C on max sir but I don't know if that will help."

"It's the humidity."

"I don't understand. The water should cool everything down."

"Maybe the water's boiling too. From the bottom."

"Are you okay, sir? You want me to stop somewhere and get something cold?"

"I'm fine. You may stop if you'd like something."

"No, sir. I don't want you to get heatstroke."

"Call me...," he looked outside and followed Rue Bel Respiro towards Avenue de Roqueville where he saw two kids sitting under a tree colouring a page with crayons, "Never mind."

The interaction with the attendant had jolted through him like a lightning strike. He had nothing. Nothing except his Eurocopter and his Monaco Penthouse and his Swiss investment firm. And how much is that to have?

The sun decided to set early today. The streaking rain clouds along the horizon rotated between pouring and drizzling depending on how they felt. It was drizzling when I sat on a bench across the Frederiksholms Kanal and tried to follow that last sun ray with my eye across the water. Its purpling orange bathed the canal and long string of rush-hour cars in pale, darkening yellow. I walked alongside a wall where old murals had been painted in brick-red. The colourful buildings of the city, edging along the distance were all reflected in the still canal and the cars' brake lights had all but turned the water red. When it started to pour I ventured into the Thorvaldsens Museum. Someone buzzed me in; the air was calm and the glass lockers in the cloakroom were delicately arranged by number. I took number 15.

There was a *Venus with an Apple* sculpture that I couldn't get over. Every male artist treats the nude female body as he sees a woman. Thorvaldsen's *Venus* wasn't any more beautiful or feminine or sensual than the Medici Venus, yet she lingered on my imagination. She stood as a fusion of nature: undisguised and barren. Canova's *Pauline Bonaparte as Venus* in Rome for example, is clothed below the stomach and sits seductively as if she were a femme fatale. We never see what Venus had no shame in showing. The apple she holds is meant to symbolize Aphrodite's victory in the Judgment of Paris by offering him the most beautiful woman with her charms and flowers. The most beautiful woman being Helen of Sparta, Paris of course accepted— who could resist beauty? And gave Venus the apple that signified her victory. Thus began the Trojan War. But that's Canova. The apple is power; she holds it firm because she won. Thorvaldsen's Venus was something else; she was naked and her arms were in the same plane as her body. Her fingers didn't reach out and her arms weren't outstretched to create more space in vanity or power. Her face was sullen and introverted, purging all prior preconceptions about what Venus represented. Her melancholy disposition was a future predication on what the apple will cause: the Trojan War. The apple is a lament; she wants to let go of it and let it drop hoping that would stop the bloodshed that she would cause. Across the Venus, Sophie was venturing room to room looking for a sculpture to sketch. She settled on a *Cupid and Psyche*, an allegory of the soul that searches for eternal happiness. It was a myth not because of its figures and subjects, but the fact that Cupid finds eternal happiness. He's struck by love when he meets the divine Psyche and eventually they end up together. A happy ending. A myth. No one ever asks who'd shot him with his own arrow. All happy endings are unrealistic because they're born through plot holes.

After the museum she frolicked past me down the steps outside and looked back. Her eyes refracted the moonlight across the canal and onto my chest. Gradually her gaze fell into my pupils and paralyzed me. Does a moment disappear when it's gone? Every person perceives moments differently. And when we hold on to moments, what is it we're holding on to? When moments and relationships change, for the better or for the worse, what happens to the moments before those changes had occurred? What happens to the experiences one has had when lives change completely because of them? Are we, as beings who experience one moment after another, forced to *hope* that these experiences will be eternal or infinite contingent upon their elation or despair? Answer… undeniable.

IV
Transfiguration

"Sir, the investigator is waiting in your office."

"Thank you… wait. What's your name?" Neil had seen this assistant two weeks ago.

"Sir? I'm just a temp."

"You were here two weeks ago."

"The other girl was sick."

"A temp for a temp?" Neil chuckled and extended his hand, "My name's Neil."

"Nice to meet you, Neil. My name's Sophie."

"Sophie… what a fantastic name," Neil couldn't see that this wasn't the same Sophie he'd read about nor that the reason why he liked her was simply because of the notebook.

"He's still waiting in your office." Sophie answered the phone, "Please hold."

"Oh… right. Thanks, Sophie," Neil took a step towards the staircase, "Sophie?"

"Yes, sir."

"Are there any performances of *Romeo and Juliet* or *Faust*?"

"I don't know, sir. Would you like me to check?"

"Yes."

"Two tickets right? For you and the missus?"

Neil was thinking about Christina but the words that came out of his mouth were refracted by the sunlight through the window and into Sophie's eyes, "Yes, of course, of course."

"Very well, sir."

"Of course of course," and Neil found himself mumbling before bumping into Sousa in the hall.

"That's horrible," Sousa looked straight at Neil.

"What?"

He pointed to the folded newspaper tucked in Neil's hands. TERRORISTS TAKE FIVE MORE IN FRANCE. "Oh yes."

Neil opened the paper but forgot that he'd hidden the notebook in the fold and it dropped.

"You keep a journal?" Sousa picked it up and handed it back to Neil.

"Me? No. I mean it's not mine. It's someone else's." Neil jerked and snatched the book from Sousa.

"You're reading someone else's journal?" Sousa smiled.

"No. They're just notes."

Sousa laughed, "That's why you're the boss," he walked into reception, said goodbye to Sophie and walked out.

Edwin was waiting for Neil at the top of the stairs.

"Neil!" he whispered and waved him into his office.

"I'm meeting Marco. What do you want?" Neil's hand twitched.

"Get in here!" Edwin looked outside through the blinds and the sun flashed across his face in thin lines which cut across his empty eyes.

"I don't think we should keep the SEC investigator waiting."

"*We*?" Edwin opened his collar to let air into his chest. "It's hot."

Neil took a step towards him, "What did you do?"

Edwin paced around the office.

"What did you do?"

Edwin ignored him again.

Neil leaped across to force Edwin to change the pattern of his pacing, "Eddy!" His southern accent lingered through the air, "Where's Holly?"

Little did he know, Edwin's pacing had nothing to do with Holly or her pregnancy. "Holly? What are you talking about? She's in Cannes. No wait, she's in Saint-Tropez. Or did she say she was going to Missoni?" a shark smile curved from ear-to-ear.

"Is that the same suit you were wearing yesterday?" Neil walked around and sat in Edwin's chair.

Edwin stared at himself on the window's reflection and wiped a bead of sweat on his forehead. "This?" he looked at his suit, "This is Gucci."

"I don't care. Is it the same one you were wearing *yesterday*?" and before waiting for Edwin to answer, Neil opened the drawer where he imagined putting Holly's letter and slammed it closed, "*Where*… is Holly?"

"HOLLY?" Edwin yelled and looked in the direction of Neil's office, "Holly?" he whispered. "Why do you keep asking about Holly? … You know if I didn't know better I'd think there was something going on between you two."

Neil got up. The silence suffocated the room. A bird flapped its wings outside the window and the sunlight lit up half of Neil's face, "Get yourself cleaned up. Meet Nora at Missoni. I'll join you guys later." He approached Edwin and knocked some lint off his *Gucci* jacket.

The door squeaked closed.

"You're the only person that has ever kept me waiting," Marco stood up in Neil's office.

"It's because most of the people you investigate are guilty. You're looking for more evidence to use against them. So they want to meet you as quickly as possible and then get rid of you," his fist twitched.

"But knowing that, wouldn't keep me waiting mean you want me to think you're innocent?" he extended his hand.

Neil gripped Marco's hand and pointed to the drink table, "Our thoughts are our own. I'm not worried because I did nothing wrong. So I don't care whether you've ever been kept waiting or not eh."

Marco nodded to the sparkling water and sat back down, "Very clever." Neil put the drink in front of Marco.

"So how can I help you?" He put the journal into the left drawer.

"Maybe you can start by giving me that ledger."

"Which ledger?"

"The one you keep close to your chest. The one you just hid away."

Neil laughed, "That's a journal. Not a ledger."

"You keep a journal?"

"No. It's someone else's."

"You carry around someone else's journal?"

"If I had an apt return on every time I've been asked that. I'd owe you guys quite a bit of money."

Marco smiled and opened his laptop, "I need to see what trades your clients are demanding and what trades your employees are executing as a result of those demands."

"Do you have a subpoena? All of our trades are confidential, as is our client list."

"May I be direct with you?" Marco closed his laptop.

"I can only hope," Neil tapped the left drawer.

"I'm only interested in one set of trades executed on behalf of one client. I don't even know if it was your firm that executed the trades. It's set off a series of events that culminated in the destabilization of a major geopolitical location."

"For the record. You're saying you're not investigating my firm but a specific person or organization. And you *suspect* them to be our client."

"Exactly," Marco exhaled.

Neil leaned back in his chair and lit a cigar. Watching the smoke dissipate above him he dozed off into thought. We choose our pursuits, whether consciously or unconsciously. If they are unconscious pursuits, pursuits that begin and gain momentum before we realize we are in a chase, our intelligence is taken by surprise and then detests us for acting on emotion. If we choose our pursuits consciously, we are sentimental. Sentimentality is loathsome and equated with indolence. Either inexperienced emotions that we weren't born for, or indolence for which no one prefers. Neither option is ideal yet on every occasion we either act consciously or unconsciously; thus we must fuse the two together to achieve equilibrium.

"Okay. Tell me whom you're looking for," Neil leaned in and opened his laptop that had been sitting on the corner of his desk.

"Do I have your word?"

"That's all I have isn't it?" he tapped the drawer again.

Marco chuckled, "Somehow I doubt that." He took out a piece of paper with suspected trades and handed it to Neil.

The sheet slid across the table and stopped just short of the edge. The A/C feathered it back towards Marco. "I'll give it a look later. How can I get in touch with you?"

"My personal number is at the top," he got up. "Thanks for the drink. And I appreciate the help."

They both stood, "No problem," and shook hands. "I'll stay in touch."

Neil walked Marco to the door where he heard footsteps retreating towards the other end of the hall. "Good day, Mister Meyollner."

"To you as well."

Marco took a step towards the staircase but doubled back, "Say, you think we'll beat the Swedes?"

"Pardon me?"

"It's a stereotype but you said *'eh'*; I thought you were Canadian. My mom's Canadian and we're playing the Swedes in the World Juniors next month."

"Oh," Neil retraced the conversation in his head to pinpoint when this had exactly occurred. "No, I'm not. But good luck!"

"Thank you."

"Sophie. Find me the best private investigator in Europe." He would deal with Marco later. He knew he couldn't trust anyone, let alone an investigator who works on a commission contingent to how much illegal assets or gains they uncover.

"You want me to find a P.I., sir?"

"Yes. I want the best. Forward me their details when you find one."

"Right away, sir."

He heard the same footsteps now approaching.

"I'm meeting Nora at Missoni later. When did you say you were going to join us?" Edwin tried to hide that slick pride under his slithery smile but couldn't.

Neil clenched his teeth at the mention of Missoni. The fact that Edwin didn't know or care where Holly was mirrored the fact that his understanding of Raphael was slipping from him. He opened the drawer and took the notebook out. When Edwin approached the table Neil took the paper Marco had given him and folded it into the back of the journal.

He looked at Edwin up and down. Those thinning little hairs desperately clinging on to an empty head. That rounded head whitened with anti-wrinkle cream in a futile attempt to stagnate the cracking wrinkles on his face. That porky belly hidden behind a loose shirt and a tight belt over his stomach; he was a poster for youthful imprisonment.

"We'll see. What do you want?"

"What did he want?" Edwin poured himself a drink and sat down across Neil.

"What do you think he wanted?" Neil stood in the shadows where the sunlight came through the blinds.

"They're investigators, Eddy. What do *you* think they wanted? They wanted our entire client list and trades executed."

"You told them to scram right?"

Neil emerged through the blinds where the light hit him directly in the face, "Something of the sort."

"Good," Edwin got up and backed away. "I'll see you later, man. … Oh. I almost forgot." He took the glass and gulped the tequila.

"Sophie, is the air conditioner on?" Neil took his jacket off and unbuttoned his shirt where some of his chest hairs escaped through his grey undershirt.

"Yes, sir. It's on maximum."

"It's so damn hot," he got up and fully closed the blinds where without lights the office was submerged in the darkness.

My heart's roundabouts, that's what she called them. "I never want to see you again but I wish you were next to me right now."

I should've hung up on her and said "Fine" and moved away. Instead I showed up to her place with maple syrup and made her eggs. Sunny-side *down*. Happiness is an avalanche without snow. She let her cardigan fall like Egyptian silk. It glided to the floor and her warm, sweaty body slipped into my arms. Her hair smelled like lemon sage; her body, like paradise. What you feel and what you know you shouldn't feel are almost always at odds.

Canadians fall in love twice in their life and always love the second. Swedes fall in love twice in their life and always love the first. We were each other's second love.

"Mister Meyollner?" his phone beeped.

"Yeah!" he shook off the sentences, "Excuse me. What is it, Sophie?"

"Karina was trying to get a hold of you."

"I've been in the office the whole time."

"You weren't answering," there was chatter in the background.

"I must've drifted off. Is she still in?"

"Let me check. Please hold, sir."

"Okay. Take your time."

Sophie, he said her name over and over in his mind.

"Mister Meyollner? Are you there, boss?"

"Yes, yes! What is it, Sophie?"

"Miss Holst is available. She's about to step out but she'll wait."

"Thank you, Sophie."

"Is that everything, sir?"

"Yes…" Neil paused and looked in between the blinds at a cloud in the distance, "Sophie?"

"Yes, sir. I'll have the P.I. information for you later today. You wanted it sent to your inbox correct?"

"No, it's not that. Take your time with that. I wanted to know what your name means."

"Are you okay, sir?"

"Of course. What does Sophie mean?"

"It was my great-grandmother's name. It comes from the Greek *Sophia*. It means wisdom. After a mythical saint who died of grief when her daughters were martyred."

"Oh. Sophia. Like philosophy in Greek translating to lover of wisdom."

"Exactly!" she giggled.

"Thank you, Sophie," Neil exhaled.

"You're welcome, sir. I'll send the information your way later today. Please do not forget about your meeting with Miss Holst."

"I won't."

"Also, sir, there are no showings of *Romeo and Juliet* or of *Faust* at the Opera house. The closest ones in the coming months are in Paris and Berlin and Copenhagen."

"Okay. Thank you for checking."

"My pleasure, sir."

Neil lit another cigar and stepped towards the door. He stopped in the middle of the hallway in front of Karina's office and emailed the temp agency that had hired Sophie. He demanded that the rotation stop and to keep Sophie on permanently.

Karina's door creaked open, "Whoa, Mister Meyollner," she flinched, "You startled me."

"My apologies, Karina. You were trying to get a hold of me. Is everything all right?" he refreshed his outbox to make sure the email to the temp agency had gone through.

"Yes, everything is fine. I wanted to show you this," she turned her uPhone towards Neil. "There's an email. One of my clients wants to meet you. I consulted on a merger with a Dutch bank and it paid off. They said they wanted to meet the head of the firm."

It would be a great honour if we could invite you and your boss to our city and show you around. Neil read on the screen near the bottom.

"I thanked them but told them it's impossible. That you never meet with clients directly."

Neil nodded, "You're right," and then retraced the conversation with Marco in his head, "Where are they?"

"Malmø. I mean, it's just over the Øresund..." her pronunciation slipped into Danish and he watched the dimples around her lips vibrate with life.

"The what?"

"The Øresund Bridge. It's a bridge. *The* bridge. Connects Denmark and Sweden," she smiled, and Neil suddenly remembered why she had the most clients. Recalling her interview, even before she'd told him she was fluent in 5 languages, Neil knew he was going to hire her. Beauty and intelligence are a dangerous combination. Any beautiful person can beguile and coax but it takes intelligence to recognize the varying angles posterior to having beguiled for a cause.

"Ah yes. And you're from Copenhagen, right?" *Here we have Copenhagen, the start of everything*, the words echoed in his ears; the start... the start... the start of *every*thing.

"Yes. And Malmø is just over the bridge."

"Your pronunciation of Malmo is different than my other friend."

"I'm saying it the Danish way. We don't have the umlaut. It's M-A-L-M, but the O in Danish is pronounced *eu*; you know the O with the line through it?"

"Of course. Oresund has one too right?"

"Yep! But in Swedish they have the umlaut so the O has the two dots above it. It changes the pronunciation."

"Interesting. ... I'd love to go."

"Sir?"

"Call me Neil. I haven't decided whether to meet with the clients but I want to see Copenhagen. And Malm... eu."

"That's great! I'll write you a list of places you have to see!"

"That would be perfect," Neil felt a breeze wash through him, where the carrying Ligurian winds of the sea's drizzle cooled his face.

Why was I here? It was a futile attempt to get away from her. It is a fallacy that fresh air and natural water clear the heart and mind. Thoughts and hearts know no geography. Now that I was here, I tried to work, *tried*, and failed miserably. It rained the whole week, and finally I searched, and found some board members of the WBCT. A simple Internet search revealed their names but this was of course no help because locating them was another task altogether. Their senior trustee, Mackenzie Agnew, stood out only because he was also the CEO of *GeoTex*. GeoTex, where have I heard this name before? I navigated to their website and clicked on their promotional video.

A shot of a crowded metropolis cut into a shot of plains and wheat fields and then cliffs and rocks. A determined voiceover enunciated every word with guided precision. *With over 40 billion dollars of funds*, a shot of a CCTV camera panned across the screen, *GeoTex unites a web of staunch elite companies devoted to security and defence.* A shot of ballistic missiles and a tank flashed across the screen and then one of an F-35 fighter jet. *With unsurpassed expertise in Africa, including the services of four former prime ministers, six former presidents, a director of the MI5, and the former director of the RCMP*, there was a close-up of a fighter jet maneuvering past an anti-aircraft gun, *GeoTex is proud to lead the charge in the battle against tyranny.* There was a shot of an African child playing football with what looked to be a soldier and/or GeoTex employee followed by a shot of a peaceful Johannesburg, where a couple sat on a bench holding hands with a Yamaha Raider sitting behind them. *GeoTex. … Refuge against Danger.* A shot of a tree dancing in the African sun faded out.

Imagine my surprise when their *Contact Us* page listed a station right here in Cap-Ferrat. I use *station* loosely, because the address for their office was above a *Saint-Tropez* boutique across the water. I did notice the shiny black Range Rover Sport parked in front, and I doubly noticed the burly and peculiarly scarred bald-man inside, rather than the regular dainty and charming French girls who work in such places to coax the old men with money who come in to *shop* for clothes… amongst other things. I knew I was in over my head the instant he inquired whether I wanted a new life jacket because many people have drowned in these waters. Someone shuffled behind him in the back. I was in too deep anyway, I had to press on for Sophie. Even if I don't find anything, or even worse, if I do and it kills me; it is the only way to exist.

The entrance bell chimed, "Are you looking for anything specific?" he immediately asked me.

"Yes. I'm looking for the GeoTex office listed on their website. Do I have the right place?"

The door behind him creaked again. I felt the Riviera air drain my lungs; "It's a billion dollar corporation, and their offices are above a boutique?"

"We have some people come in and look for their offices. I don't know what you're talking about. There is no upstairs."

"But the logo on the front of your boutique… the world with the red sash through it. That's the GeoTex logo," when I start doing stupid things, there is very little that will stop me.

That door behind him was as silent as death, and it suddenly opened where a petite woman with long blonde hair wearing black-rimmed designer prescription glasses stepped out, "I can help him Francis, *merci.*"

"Hi," she said to me and the ice in her veins cooled my bones.

"Do you work for GeoTex?"

"How can I help you?" she guided me to that back room where some scattered swimming items idled on the wooden shelves and two chairs were placed directly in the middle.

I took the seat *not* directly under the lamp; it had the interrogation vibe and I had to keep my eye on the exit.

"I wanted to ask you about one of your clients. Gilbert Maurus? Do you know or remember him?"

"Maurus, Maurus, Maurus," she repeated to herself, "No. Doesn't ring a bell. Should I?"

"He hired your security firm in Toronto. And you guys advertise yourself as the best firm in the world… but he was killed."

"That's unfortunate. I'm not at liberty to give you client information you see, but between you and me," she smiled and leaned back in her chair, "… I still don't remember him."

"How about the WBCT? Have you guys ever been hired by them?"

"Are you a reporter? I didn't catch your name."

"I'm not. I'm a writer doing research on security firms that work in Africa. I noticed that one of their trustees is your CEO…"

"…I don't mean to be rude. I just don't see how I can be of help. We are a satellite office you see. We're only here in case one of our clients finds their way here and requires assistance." she slid the chair away from under the light and her face sank into the darkness, "It's bewildering, no one has ever mentioned the WBCT connection before."

"Can I ask you something else?" I remembered my conversation with Martin.

"If you have to," she stroked her chin as if she already knew what I was going to say.

"The car Maurus was killed in was a black Land Rover. It was rented by your firm. Like the one parked out front."

I could tell she enjoyed the theatrics, shaking her head as if to play the role of the dumb blonde, *why I'm just an innocent little girl working in this little shop, I don't know anything*. I knew better, her eyes glanced towards where the car was parked and then back at me in the faint darkness.

"I wouldn't know anything about that. The company rents us these cars. We're just given the keys you see," her expression never faltered, which both impressed and frightened me. With a woman like this, you could take over a country.

"Hmm…" I realized it was *her* getting information rather than the other way around. "Can you tell me the names of any other offices in the area? Or the address for the one in Toronto perhaps? I didn't see one listed on your website."

"We don't have an office in Toronto," she rubbed and crossed her thighs.

"How about one of those… what'd you call it, *satellite* offices?" I had to get out, but how?

She chuckled, "No. None of those either."

"Hmm…, how would I hire you in Toronto? … *If* I were a client for example?" the door creaked and I sensed the man just behind it.

"We're a *global* firm you see. You can hire us from anywhere to anywhere, but the *physical* offices you're looking for… why they just simply don't exist."

"So the name Maurus doesn't ring a bell at all?"

"Nope, still nothing," she answered a little too quickly now, "Are you personally invested in this?" she pressed her glasses towards her eyes as if she were really thinking about the matter.

"In a way," the bell outside chimed and I heard what I assumed was a couple browsing the swimsuit section.

"Well… thanks for your time. I think this was a dead end," I got up towards the door.

"You're welcome," she overtook me but let the door linger for a moment before opening it, "May I ask *you,* how did he die?"

"He was shot. In the head."

"Interesting," she turned back and I noticed I was now standing under the light bulb, "Did he die right away?"

"I don't know," I tried moving towards the door but she blocked me.

"I never believed that getting shot in the head is painless. What do you think? It must be agonizing, especially if you see it coming."

"I wouldn't know."

"Let's hope not," she opened the door where the bald man turned towards me and watched me leave.

I could swear a different Land Rover followed me to the Fairmont. Its plate number was V 188. What am I into?

V
The Three Graces

Not only does everyone have their weaknesses, but everyone has weak moments. The longer you go without a *moment* of weakness increases the probability that the next moment will break you. The only thing that had made Neil weak was the fear that he wouldn't understand someone he sought to know. Right then he sought to know Raphael. What's left of those who live without knowing why they're living? Not knowing or being able to uncover what life and feeling really is, living an existence without faith or reason and refusing to react to the most rudimentary abstract manifestations like feeling connected to someone, loving someone, or helping someone; is that preferred to living with the foreknowledge that faith isn't reasonable and reason never sides with love? What then, are we left with other than the meditative introspection that reason is the soul and the soul feels everything? Apathetic and indifferent to the suffering of our fellow man and disconnected with the divine, we are guided by our misanthropic tattles as we prance and surrender ourselves to pointless sensations and driven logic, long cultivated along pastures of what is deemed *reasonable* hedonism and sentimental logic.

Reason and sentiment meet where happiness and love intersect. Are people not happiest when they're in love? A love like the waves over the Riviera.... *Neil looked up from the page and watched the waves in the distance*. Sometimes the tides pull the waves together and sometimes they drift. But the sea never stands still. Fate is never kind, how I should've taken her hand and made her mine. Never right or wrong. Now I don't belong in this city. I've been here too long and it was time for me to go.

I wanted to hurt. I felt nothing. Less than nothing. Yet I knew she meant something to me. I wanted her to hurt me like she'd promised. "Promises promises," I kept saying whenever she made a future predication. So when we drank too much I told her to hit me as hard as she could.

"Hit me. Hurt me. As hard as you can."

"Okay," she smiled and didn't move.

"Don't be afraid."

"I'm not."

"Okay…" I arched my eyebrows.

I tried to forget every moment with her. I couldn't get her out of my mind. I *wouldn't* forget her nor did some part of me want to. I could see her take my face into her hands and trace around my eyes. I could feel the singeing penetration of her gaze into my soul like a cold diamond, and how it shone when I'd handed her a poem I'd written her. I would see her again and again but none of them would be enough. How many times would her eyes shine at the reception of a poem? She wouldn't smile or hug me and tighten her arms around my neck. She wouldn't look at me from afar with a gaze that says *I love you.* How pure and uncontrolled words can be when idling in the dictionary but corrupting and meaningful they are in the mind of a being who knows how to combine them.

I would've liked to have been with her. Alone I mean, alone in the entire world. Love. Passion, and embrace is more than bedding a woman. She looked so at peace kneading that dough, and I looked forward to the aroma of fresh bread to fall over the house.

Nothing is eternal. Each moment can be undone by the next one if the next one fails to transcend mere words said, mere actions undone, and mere thoughts unfelt. Just as the seasonal changes of the Earth's fluxing weather takes us from breezy spring to hot summer to chilly autumn and finally: frigid winter; so can each moment that thus followed descend the hierarchy of words and feelings I'd said and she felt. *Love. Like. Friendship. Acquaintance. Disdain. Mistrust. Foe. Indifference. Apathy.*

* * *

On the Riviera I smelled lemon sage and thought about her every waking moment and dreamt about her when I passed out from drinking too much. I knew she wasn't worth a moment's thought but all I did was think about her. The daughter of a Swiss banker I met on his yacht said Sophie didn't deserve me and to forget about her. Sophie would've enjoyed that, that I was imprisoned at the thought of her. Her movements were never about getting from A to B; they were all about the theatre. She knew how to move from to A to C without ever hitting B. If B was in play, you were in trouble.

At a going away party for Katja, one of our mutual friends, I met her boyfriend for the second time. What an upstanding gentleman he was. He greeted no one and introduced himself only to the women in turn after everyone had liberally partaken of the available booze. She crossed her arm and rubbed her opposite shoulder anytime I felt her gazing towards me. After I saw her in class after a long break, she did the same thing. She had nothing to hide from me. The mark of a talented writer is in his ability to predict and understand behaviour and body language and what they symbolize based on a person's natural baseline. I was arrogant enough to think I had talent. What then, did she have to hide from me? I already knew everything there was to know. Or did I? Had she been with someone else? Someone I knew? Someone I didn't? Both? She crossed her arm again. That's twice now. The shoulder blade rub; that was her tell. How did I know that she hadn't sought intimacy with anyone else other than me? Even her boyfriend, who didn't want to move to this gloomy city, whenever she talked about it she would say he couldn't or offer up some other haphazard excuse; I don't recall them all, nor do I want to. Paranoia. Question: Was she unhappy because he didn't love her as much as she thought, because the words he used in demarcating his love were not united with his actions? Or was she unhappy simply because they couldn't be together all the time, and he was to blame? Answer: Excuses for such things make no sense. If you love somebody, really love them, you blow up your life with them. You want to be with them as much as time would permit. You want your beloved to be happy regardless of any other circumstance. There should not be a world that does not permit two people who love each other to be together, and if two people aren't together, does that mean one of them doesn't love the other as much as they thought? Probably.

There must've been other men, probably when both of us were away. Hindsight is 20/20. The way she looked at me; the way she looked at him. No man could refuse such a gaze. Her fixed stare intensified once when I was writing; it was so focused and warm that I felt it everywhere. All my muscles and skin and half-bit nails contracted and tensed, ready to fall away and illuminate the cold marble of my skeleton for her to chisel herself into. Without either of one of us realizing it, she was chiselling her way through my marrow. Ironic that I found happiness without even searching for it and how quickly it flees from me now as I try, ever feebly to hold onto those moments. It was my own fault for thinking happiness was anything more than a fleeting chemical reaction. I couldn't blame my body and my flesh and skin and bone and joints for demanding their fair share of those happy moments.

Now it all made sense, her coldness while I was away, her responses to my poems and the incoming frigid season. She was driving me crazy. Well, crazier than I already was.

At the party I had two suspicions: that he wasn't simply acting rude to appear unsociable and dominant as all mundane men are bound to act, but that he was simply rude and had no idea. Secondly I suspected that we were not the only men in her life.

What happens to those moments where our noses tapped each other's, those moments on long sandy beaches where our toes touched for a second, those tight hugs that made me think I'd be stupid to let go? That moment when we savoured on each other's lips the port we drank and the bread she'd baked. They're all lost now, like snowflakes in a blizzard. Still this would've hardly been an issue if she had simply been honest with me. I would've forgiven her. Angels know no morality. The fact of its concealment, the fact that she thought it was necessary to hide such things from me was insulting to my intelligence and undermined our feelings for each other. Maybe due to clogged rush-hour traffic, certain roads turn one-way.

"I read your short story Raphael. It was so sinister and devilish and dark and I was in awe of your vocabulary," Katja batted her eyelashes and hiccupped.

"I'm glad you enjoyed it," I watched the mist of my Davidoff Churchill rise to the mural on the ceiling. A painting of Joseph asking God *why* he'd been chosen to give up his wife.

Neil looked at his own cigar, stale and lying dormant between his index and middle fingers. He put it between other fingers toying with the idea of how Raphael would smoke and hold his.

"What story? *I* haven't heard it," Sophie tugged closer to her boyfriend while insinuating that she had a monopoly on my sentences.

"He wrote a story about me. But I could only see the first two parts. Where's part three Raphael? …" she took a sip of schnapps, "*Where* oh where is part three?"

"Here," I tapped my chest, "And here," and then my temple.

"What's it going to be about?" Sophie interrupted and intertwined her fingers with her boyfriend who was talking to another woman on his opposite side.

"About the man. Part one was about *you*," I looked at Katja but my words echoed into Sophie, "The second was about the machinations that pulled them together…"

On cue Sophie cuddled closer to her boyfriend and vied for his attention that never came.

"… And the third will be about…" I hadn't written it yet so I had to come up with a name, "Tommaso. How he got roped into and fell for a woman that would devour him and toss him to the side simply because she acquired some entertainment from it. And yet, contradictory, how would he retain the moments that have passed? What happens to them long after? All of them are lost in eternity like a wave over the Riviera."

Neil flipped back a few pages to find the quote about moments being snowflakes.

That was the only time her boyfriend acknowledged that there were other men in the room other than him. Turning to Benson who was himself confabulating with Josephine, he talked about some haphazard project he'd fumbled into and now had gotten in way over his head. I lit another Davidoff and watched the scene unfold with divine amusement. How predictable people are; how predictable and boring. He was fighting for the attention of the other women using Benson. Ending my conversation with Katja and Sophie, and his with Josephine; Sophie squeezed his hand the whole time, and he continued talking about how he was an incredibly gifted man who is deserving of every reward while simultaneously brushing off any failure as an injustice of celestial magnitude. A true romantic from the Renaissance he was. Brilliantly average. Astutely commonplace. The whole time I was also thinking about the way she kept crossing her other hand over her opposite shoulder. Why? What did she have to hide? Finally the oscillating waves of the coast settled into the subsiding beats of my heart's love for her and I *knew*. When? I walked by a café called *Muse* and could hardly contain my laughter. The cosmic joke that a 40€ burger is somehow invoking the treasure of the muses. How, that is the more important question than when. Because dearest reader of the journal that carries my soul, everything you just read and have been reading is hogwash. Who in the whole world could *read her*? I knew because I was connected to her in a way that no one, including her, thought was possible. All this talk of body language and predicting behaviour and being able to read her had nothing to do with my ability to know the truth. That was just the hubris of my writing talent seeping through the phrases I try to chisel into people. Sophie laid deeper than that. We were connected in such an unbelievable way that when I focused my thoughts on her, I would see, hear, and even smell the vanilla shampoo she preferred. She was so unmoved and so untouched by the past that we'd had that I applauded her ability to detach. It would only take a few minutes for me to feel like I was next to her. In waking dreams I would hear her calling my name and sometimes I would call hers and hear a response. I could picture and feel what she was thinking and feeling and whom she was with. It was as if we never left each other despite the infinite distance that now separated us. My grandpa used to say "Give everything to a woman and more. If she's as smart as she looks, you'll graze happiness and you know you did the right thing." "What if she's not?" I always asked. "Then my son, at least you gave everything you had and you're clear on where you stand." He'd read too many of those American noir bestsellers only sold at airports. The ones that were always about itinerant geniuses who would either wander into bacchanals of alcohol, drugs, and orgies; or stray and contemplate things in the rain, always in the rain; or wait in train stations and airports for their unrequited loves that *never* showed up.

I waited for the other shoe to drop. Now that I *knew,* she should've told me. Should've told me because I wouldn't have cared one iota. That's what it means to love someone; to give everything and more. The '*and more*' is the critical part. It took me 25 years to understand that. Yet the fact of her concealment only meant that she didn't care enough, that she insulted my intelligence and our connection by thinking I wouldn't notice a difference in the intricate movements of her body and thoughts. There are no secrets between the blade and the hilt. We were a katana.

The other shoe never dropped. She said nothing and did nothing. Canadian winters are Riviera summers. But I waited nonetheless in hope that for the first time in my life Virgil was right: love conquers all.

Epic and profound literature are too symbolic and often ignore the banal facets of daily minutiae. Alexei Alexandrovich Karenin's ears grow in proportion to Anna's dissatisfaction with her marriage. Raskolnikov's room shrinks in proportion to his guilt. Scrooge's greed and misery is inversely proportional to the hindsight gifted to him by the Ghost of Christmas Yet to Come, who shines a light in the faint glimmer of hope present in his heart.

There are too many motifs and metaphors and symbols; everyday details such as waiting are ignored unless they are representative of something more. We spend the entirety of our lives waiting. Waiting for trains, waiting for airplane delays to clear, waiting to grow up, waiting for our next birthday, waiting to love, to marry, to be *happy*; we're always waiting. Even in the end when we grow old or if we have enough time to face our mortality, we wait for death.

That's enough for one night. Having returned after a bout of drinking, I noticed my laptop was not where I'd left it. The wind knocked on the window. I thought I had closed it before heading out. … Where did I put the printout of the WBCT trustee list? And the GeoTex office list in third-world nations? It should be right… *here*. But when I shuffled the pages the sheet was gone. I probably lost it. Or maybe I never printed it? Did I print it? Of course I did!

"Reception."

"*Bonsoir*. This is Adler. Has someone been inside my room?"

"No, sir. Your room is still marked for cleaning. They should be there soon."

"And no one else has been inside?"

"No, sir. Is everything okay?"

"Yeah…." I hung up the phone and sat on the bed. I was being gaslit, which meant I was definitely onto something big.

When I got sick of waiting, got sick of hope, and got sick of the indecisive movements of her hands; I drank too much and reread some of my previous entries. How dare you hope? How dare you be so stupid? Before I passed out I tore out the hopeful and glinting pages along with my research about Maurus and GeoTex and the WBCT and hid them between the panels of my suite at the Fairmont. It'll make for a nice surprise when they renovate. Full of hope and agony and disdain. What was I *really* waiting for? …

Neil closed and tapped his nails on the notebook, tracing the word *happy* over and over again in a randomized rhythmic beat on its green cover. What *is* he waiting for? His marriage to suddenly take a better turn? For his understanding of the world to expand over the horizons of his newfound gloom? Would he forget Nora with time or will she be static in the momentary abstractions that had made up the experiences of his life? If the possibility of forgetting her was real, then the profound moments that he shared with her were just as important and complicated as a moment where he ate a sandwich or wrote an email reserving a table at Caina. How could he reconcile the idea that the infinitude of moments he'd lived that had not only made him the person he was, but that these moments can be interchanged or omitted from the pool of his memories and nothing would change. Either way the final purpose must be happiness or Zen; whatever the world calls it now. But to be happy consists of very particular and specific moments that accumulate over the course of an existence. We don't suddenly wake up and realize our lives are filled with despair. Further, despair is a necessity to glimpse elation, just as we know someone is *tall* when we have had the experience of someone shorter than them. Now would it not be frightening to accept this idea in relation to love? That we may only love or experience love when we've drank and savoured vile hate? We know this is untrue. We can hate without ever having been in love and we can love without ever having hated anyone. Why then, do we link happiness to strife and despair, and say things like suffering begets character, or that objects cannot make us happy. Is this not why most religions preach that serenity comes from within? How morbid and exclusive that seems. Is the boy born on Fifth Avenue any more or less deserving of elation? He didn't choose to be comfortable any more than the favela boy chose to be born into poverty. To scratch the surface of happiness requires *materials* as well as strife. Only then does the playing field reach equilibrium. How does a person attain happiness? Considering profound moments where moments of elation are kept *static*? We must then experience elating moments that do not change from one moment to the next. But this is impossible… thus we are fated to despair unless happiness is impermanent. How then, would an impermanent happiness differ from any other benign illusion? The abstract moments used to mark such rapture must be stored in a perfect memory bank where moments of strife and despair are in flux and change but moments of elation are kept static. Paradox: It's a negative trait for a person to be static. Imagine a 40-year-old who behaves as a child. We need not imagine but simply open any newspaper to the politics section for an example of stubborn invariability. Conclusion: What would happiness matter if everyone is either permanently unhappy or only impermanently happy?

The blinking light of his office line snapped him back to the shadowy lines covering the office through the blinds. The setting sun had turned the room orange. Neil hit the speakerphone and walked to turn the light on.

"Are we *ever* going to get some rain here?"

"Sir?"

"Apologies. What is it, Sophie?"

"I have Xavier d'Aramitz on the line. He comes highly recommended. Very discreet as well sir. He worked with Prime Minister Austin himself."

"Excellent. Thank you, Sophie. Patch him through."

"Hello, Mister d'Aramitz, you're on the line with Mister Meyollner."

"Good evening, sir."

"Thank you, Sophie," Neil waited for the click that meant Sophie had hung up. "Hello, Mister d'Aramitz, please call me Neil."

"Sure, Neil. What can I do for you?" His French pronunciation fit the stereotype.

"Mister d'Aramitz, I have a problem."

"You're in luck, Neil. My CV has 'Problem-Solver' as an ability right at the top."

Neil chuckled.

"What can I do for you?"

"I need one thing—no," he paused, "*Two* things from you."

"Are they related?"

"Not at all."

"We'll take them one at a time then."

Neil knew just how professional he was when he used the word *we*, only real leaders use the word we when they're really talking about a task. If it succeeds everyone gets the credit, if it fails they take the blame.

"That's my thinking too," Neil paced around the office and looked through the blinds at the orange dusk over the water.

"… Mister Meyollner? What's the first task?"

"I need you to find someone."

"Someone specific or will any woman do?"

Neil laughed again, "What makes you think it's a woman?"

"Men only want women found or lost."

"And the specific person quip. That's you being funny right?"

"Not as funny as you think. Sometimes men of your stature call looking for a mistress they haven't met yet."

"Interesting line of work," Neil thought how far and interconnected the oldest human professions had come: usury and prostitution. "I need you to find my best friend's wife."

"The relationship isn't important. I only need her name and contact info. Sometimes last known whereabouts help."

"Very well. Her name is Holly Vuotare-Voclain."

"There's a dash between the names right? She kept her maiden name because she's well known."

"Yes…" Neil paused, "I'll email you her address and contact information. She was last seen in… my office," he waited for Xavier's insinuations and gauged for a reaction.

"Excellent. You have a lot of data. Response time will be 96 hours," Xavier didn't react. Neil heard a lighter flick open and a sizzling sound. "Sometimes even sooner if they're in a major city in Europe. 104 if they're outside."

"You work quickly."

"Time is always the enemy and forever will be."

Neil ignored that line, "I don't know. You do what you have to do to find her. I understand you have a 20,000€ up front fee and a 10,000€ deposit on retainer. I'll sign over 55,000€ in trust over to you. You find her. Let nothing delay you."

"I know who you are, Mister Meyollner. I won't let you down. Not even Time himself would delay me," he exhaled and said in a quick breath.

"Excellent," Neil looked around his office and listened to the silence, "And another 10,000 for the second job."

"Who do you want me to find?"

Neil hesitated. He could've simply said 'Raphael Adler. He lived or is living in Copenhagen. He's Canadian.' And in 96 hours known everything there was to know about Raphael, but something held him back from saying that. He didn't want to *meet* Raphael. He wanted to *know* and *understand* him; that's rarely done in meeting someone. "It's not a person found. It's where a person stayed when they visited the Riviera. I need all the locations."

"Do you know the resorts or hotels?"

"The Fairmont Monte Carlo for sure, but I don't know the hotels in Portofino or Saint-Tropez or Nice, even Monaco. This task sounds harder than the other one. I have no *real* information to give you."

"No task is harder than another. It won't be a problem. Name?"

"Raphael Adler," a bird knocked and flapped away from the window and blinds shook and swung away from the glass where more light shined through.

"Done. This'll take half an hour. Stay by your inbox. Don't worry about the 10 grand. I like you."

"You are a strange man, Xavier."

"It's been said," the line went dead.

Neil looked at the receiver and pulled the cord that lifted the blinds. The purpling sky descended below the water in the horizon but Neil still felt feverish.

"Sophie?" he pressed the speaker button.

"Sir? The line got disconnected. Do you want me to get him back?"

"No. Everything went well. Thank you, Sophie. Get Edwin on the line please."

While Neil waited and waited he thought about all the other times he'd waited. *Damn,* he thought, he's right. He spun around on his chair and forwarded Holly's information to Xavier and took her letter to Edwin and held it. Writing letters seemed so childish to him. So old. And yet his opinion had changed since she'd confessed her love to Neil, and his opinion of Raphael, though ever-changing, had never been negative. Edwin didn't deserve to know. He didn't deserve her. Neil looked at his pending transfer to Xavier. 50 grand. That's more than what someone makes in a year. Holly should be fine because she has a joint account with Edwin. She'll be fine, he told himself, but she wasn't. Edwin had kept her on a leash and had wrapped a tight knot around her finances. Holly wouldn't survive with her lifestyle without him and had nowhere to go until her father died. She'd vowed never to speak to him again after he disapproved of her marriage. Had Neil known, he would've financed her any which way to wherever she pleased. In the time it took him to authorize the 50,000, one of Sousa's investments matured and Neil had personally made 225,000. What good is money? Like time it comes and goes with no in between. We can buy everything with it except what we really want: more time. More time to do things over again and fix mistakes. But there are no refunds on the past. No exchanges on decisions made.

"Sir?"

"Yes, Sophie."

"I can't get hold of him. It goes straight to voicemail. I've put a 911 call-back."

"Thank you, Sophie. He'll find me," Neil hung up and walked over to his Clearaudio Concept turntable. Coltrane's *Sunship* played out of two Magneplanar 1.7s speakers in either corner of the office.

Rain. Why is there always that foreboding rain with its constant sound and teary aroma? Wouldn't it make more sense to have despair along the sizzling cement of the Riviera in August? That monochromatic introspection and rain coupled with the hot sun is sure to make confident people sweat with dismay and dissatisfaction.

The frowning faces and wrinkled bodies were lit only by disturbing fluorescent lights at the Salle Blanche, and the smiles… the smiles were so fleeting. Elongated happiness because the ball had rolled to their number or the cards had fallen in front of them. There were no clocks in here, and the lack of time coupled with the steady supply of booze by the hands of well-dressed and refined women meant we were all losers. A casino is like a woman; the house always wins. The only priceless thing in a place like this is the price a soul sells itself. The most interesting encounter I had was with an older man in one of the private rooms. He was no more than 45 years old and was impeccably dressed in a navy Hugo Boss suit and Church's brogues. He sat down at the English roulette table, where the rules are the same as regular roulette but everyone has their own custom chips whose values only they know, and lit a cigar. Everyone stopped for a second to watch him. Even the croupier seemed to want an insight into his system. That's the thing about casinos, everyone has a foolproof system for winning, even after they've lost everything. A man who was either his assistant or a casino host walked over with a tray of custom black chips. With a wave of his cigar hand towards the table his assistant placed all the chips on *Manque*, a low bet that wins if the ball chooses any number between 1 and 18. Though no one here would miss a meal or need a Black Friday Macy's sale to buy a TV, a small crowd gathered to watch this man. The croupier spun the wheel and everyone backed away from the table. A waitress in a mid-length maroon dress came over and was curious about what I was writing. She thought I was a reporter and she smiled when I told her I wasn't and that the man had captivated me with his movements at the table.

"Everyone has a system," she said and hovered above me for a second in search of something between the lines I was writing. I looked up but before I could say something one of the honchos called her over and she excused herself.

The ball spun and clicked louder than the ambient chatter of the place. The man puffed his cigar, not even watching the wheel but instead focusing his gaze on a marble column in the corner of the room. The ball stopped on 18. The ooohs and awwws were a normal reaction to the masterful theatre work employed by the gentleman.

But the man neither budged nor acknowledged his winnings. His only movement was to point to the middle column on the table with his other hand. Now that he'd doubled his bet, I got up from my seat and moved towards the table to get a better look at him.

"No more bets."

The ball rolled and spun for what seemed to be forever. My phone vibrated in my pocket. Benson, Simonetta, and Sophie had sent me a picture someone had taken of them at our favourite bar: Moonshiners. There was a smile on Sophie's lips that made me wonder whether she missed me. I yearned for her. Her smile made me think she didn't. She looked so content with those chiselled cheekbones rosy from too much rosé.

"No more bets."

I'd missed the payout, but judging from the mountainous pile of black chips on 33 black I'd wager a poem he'd won and was now tripling down on 33.

He puffed a little quicker now. The ball popped and cracked through the numbers and the wheel stopped spinning with the ball on—

"Sir?"

"Not right now, Sophie."

The wheel stopped spinning with the ball on 15. Then I saw something that I doubt I will ever see again. Everyone who had lost and everyone who had gathered and was invested in the man's success grimaced with disappointment but it was the rain that dampened my spirits. The house always wins. But the man, the man ever so faintly and subtly, doused his cigar on the ashtray next to him and *smiled*. Then he got up and left.

* * *

"Still writing?" the waitress in the maroon dress queried.

"Always," I closed my book and looked at her for the first time. She had long wavy blonde hair and eyes as blue as the Mediterranean Sea, but I knew that behind those delicate feminine movements was cold calculation. Her senses were aroused. All women want, even if their capricious satiations may result in future pain. Behind those flickering eyelashes to draw attention to those gorgeous blue eyes was methodical precision, no doubt acquired after long hours of reflection on her womanhood after leaving this place where no one wins anything but despair. I didn't care. I wanted to get to know her, *really* know her from each wave of her hair to the ocean of her eyes to the toned thighs where her maroon dress contrasted her ivory skin. "Is your shift over?"

She looked at the watch she was wearing, "An hour ago."

"Have you been standing there the whole time?" I stood up.

"I didn't want to disturb you," she smiled.

"I hope you're joking. Allow me to take you out for drinks at the *Côté Jardin*," I pointed to the casino wall where I thought the Hotel de Paris would be if they'd let me tear these walls down.

"Is that your hangout? Is that where all the artists go?"

"I've never been. I wanted to try it. Who said anything about being an artist?"

"Don't play games. I can spot your type from the top of the Eiffel."

A crowd near the tables clapped and rejoiced. "I don't think many artists come here anymore."

"Let's go," she held out her hand. I was reluctant to grab it. It was a betrayal to Sophie. But she was happy back in Copenhagen, and *she* would be visiting her boyfriend soon, so it was okay. Was it? No. Excuses. Rationalizations.

"Sure," I grabbed her hand.

She was friendly. She liked what she did.

"See that?" she lifted the sleeve of her trench coat to reveal a Bvlgari bracelet, "Some tycoon bought that for me. Said I was a good luck charm. He won 2 million in one night."

We walked inside and were guided to our table.

"He was right."

"No..." she looked outside trying to shut out the ambient music and gibber-jabber of Arabic, Mandarin, and Turkish around us, "He lost something like 7 over the course of the week he was here."

"The house always wins..." I followed her gaze outside where raindrops sloshed the pavement.

"Yeah...," she looked back at me, "Exactly! Exactly, people have the weirdest systems and superstitions when they walk in. Atheists find God. Cynics court Lady Luck. Believers lose faith."

"It's because beliefs are timed. Time doesn't exist in there."

"No clocks."

"Yes."

The waiter came and took our drink order. "We have a rather fine 2000 Bordeaux from Château Jean de Gué."

"What do you think?" she asked.

"We'll take it."

"*Merci*," the waiter walked away.

"My knowledge of wine is not sufficient enough to know if we just ordered something nice or not."

"I'm sure we did."

"I don't even know your name," she moved her napkin closer to her left side.

"I'm serious. You should come in there and write about the casino. About the people that come and go and their systems."

"I think it's already been written."

"By whom?"

"Dostoyevsky." A man a few tables over looked over at us.

"Everything's been written before. It's not what you say; it's *how* you say it. Isn't it?"

"You're absolutely right," I watched each of her movements carefully.

"My name's Lara."

I drifted off, "Old flames. Sweethearts..."

"Pardon?"

"I said that out loud?"

She smiled, "Yes."

"Lara is a person in *Doctor Zhivago*. She … it doesn't matter. It's a wonderful name."

"You are well-read."

"Not particularly."

"No. I can tell. I have an eye for these things. But don't you mean she's a *character*?"

"Characters are caricatures. Aren't there people in books or movies?"

"That's exacting and pedantic," she changed the subject, "I don't know your name either."

"Raphael."

"I don't know any fictional people named Raphael."

"Now you know me."

"I said fictional," she put her hand across the table but that I couldn't do. She retracted her hand and smiled again, "When I got off shift, I looked into that guy for you."

"Which guy?"

"The guy at the table. With the cigar! The guy! The one who didn't watch the wheel but looked at the wall."

"Oh. What about him?"

"Each of his chips were worth 50 grand. On that last bet he had over 480,000 on that square," she threw an agitated glance at someone over my shoulder. When I looked back I noticed a sheik ogling her.

That smile had cost him nearly 500,000 euros. And if I could ask him, I bet he would say it was worth every cent. "Don't worry about him."

When she went to the bathroom I stood, like you're supposed to upon a lady's entrance and exit. I hope you're creative dear reader, because now *you* have to imagine my colossal surprise when that same man's son, in a green and gold custom designer suit, turned to me as if to reveal the secret truth to the universe, and whispered, "Habibi. Why you bring her *here*? Take her to café where is stronger and less expensive alcohol. Let her ride in passenger seat of good car. But these infidels habibi; give an arm, and they take body."

"I am one of those infidels," I don't know why he thought I was an Arab or a Muslim or this or that. We are so judgmental as a species that we look for the most benign and obscure markers simply in order to judge.

I stood when she returned and though I am not fluent in Arabic by any means, I knew him and his bizarrely dressed friends and father were having a laugh at my expense. What a world. Where being born in a country that has stagnated since the Middle Ages, and a culture responsible for every manmade atrocity and calamity since Vietnam, means you are able to dine with your enemies, buy their daughters, and bed their wives at no extra cost to their souls.

The downpour was now a drizzle. The stillness and even rain of those summer evenings, especially when contrasted with streets or seasons that seethe throughout the day were permeating my longing. Pattering drizzles along the Riviera on a June night for example, on *Avenue des Beaux-Arts* or *Princess Charlotte Boulevard*. The curving *Avenue de Monte-Carlo* that turns into *Allées des Boulingrins* where you can wander into the *Jardins de la Petite Afrique* and still have the sea right behind you. Question: Why do these comforts fill me with a lonely dread, especially on a night like this where a chance encounter might turn into a sincere human connection? By day I am among the thousands of faces that traverse along these streets, lost in the ocean of unseeing eyes and ears that hear nothing past what they're already prone to agree to. But by night the probability for these chance encounters increase and I can be more like myself. Sometimes during these languorous nights I can sense a deeper awareness of myself. That everything I feel and think is mine alone but then it can be also something outside of me and outside my control. I don't control my dreams or desires or feelings or even loves. How incomplete most interactions and connections are, like hearing people hurrying to get under shelter around the corner ahead of us or the sound of a sports car being revved with a naïve or knowing woman in the passenger seat. How many of our interactions are simply due to chance and how many submerge the surface to venture deeper into human understanding and into the deepest part of another's soul? Answer: Once, if we're lucky. in the entirety of a life.

We walked not to the glinting lights of the yachts in the distance but to the *Garden of Little Africa* where the raindrops were landing on little ponds with big lily pads on them.

"There's something so romantic about rain. It's so calm," Lara twirled and extended her hands towards the sky to feel each drop. Her hair and lips were dampened and lit up by the moon who winked at me whenever the clouds parted.

I tried to light a cigar but she flicked it out of my mouth, "That's a filthy habit."

"It is. I apologize."

"It's true."

"What is?"

"The politeness of Canadians."

"Only some of us," I recalled our conversation, "I never told you I was from Canada."

"You have to show ID when you come in right? I just asked Nick, the guy who let you in."

"Clever girl."

"Hmm," she moved closer and touched my cheek with her wet hands but it did not warm me. I felt shivers all over my spine; Canada had followed me here. I couldn't get Sophie's smile out of my head. Our lips grazed but I pulled away. Once I start doing stupid things I start a streak and nothing can stop me. "What's wrong?" her lips trembled as a raindrop fell from her cheek.

"Nothing. I'm sorry. I can't… do this," I was being an idiot.

"I understand. There's someone else right? People like you are never available."

"Ye—no. Don't be ridiculous," I took her hand, "Let me take you home."

She crept her hand away, "No. I'll go for a walk. It's nice out," she pecked me on the cheek and disappeared into the rain towards *Moulins Boulevard.*

The rain. Always the rain. Why is it always raining? I'm on the goddamn Riviera and haven't seen Sophie, I mean the sun, for a second! I sat in it on a bench somewhere and wallowed.

Neil looked up at the windowpane that was too hot to touch.

Took the chopper to Portofino with Edwin. I <3 you!

N.

'I <3 you,' Neil couldn't remember the last time she'd sent him a letter or note that had said *I love you*. She loved a lot of things. She loved Hermès and Bottega Veneta and passionate, feral, and wild sex and flying first class but Neil was always kind and gentle and driven and great. She had never *loved* Neil. She had never even said it. She *'less than threed'* Neil.

"Damn you, Raphael," he muttered as one of the *Sunship* pieces came to a close and he stopped the record.

"Sophie?"

"Yes, sir?"

"Have Alec bring the car around please."

"Right away, sir."

"Thank you, Sophie."

The stairway was hot. Too damp and hot to breathe; beads of sweat ran down his back and cuddled his shoulder blades. He moved through the hall like a zombie; having to think consciously about putting one foot in front of another not to fall.

"Take me home—no. Not *home*. The hotel. Take me to the hotel, Alec," Neil could see heat mirages in the distant horizon.

"I guess home is the hotel now isn't it, sir?" he slighted left onto *Avenue des Hellènes.*

His phone vibrated. He was exhausted and wanted to rest if only time would permit him.

"Sir I have Mister d'Aramitz on the line."

"Put him through."

"Mister MEY-OLL-NERRR! The master puppet! The shadowed figure. The man behind the veil."

"How are you, Xavier?" Neil saw the man with the cane sitting on the bench and looking out towards the sea. He tapped his window with his ring even though the Bentley had already turned down Avenue du Trois Septembre.

"Easiest 65,000 I ever made. I'm not kidding. Neither of them were hiding. Your Holly Vuotare-Voclain is in Malmö. She takes the train into Copenhagen every morning, walks to the Illum rooftop for a coffee and a Danish; which are actually *French* by the way, it was *discovered* for the rest of the world by a Dane. Then…"

Neil heard some paper shuffling.

"… Then then then… she walks down to the SMK, the National Gallery of Denmark, looks at a Matisse on the second floor. …Good taste. She takes her lunch in the museum café: an open faced Danish sandwich on the weekdays and the special brunch on the weekends. Afterwards she walks towards Nørreport station where it's a straight shot to the Central Station that takes her back to Malmö. Before bed she orders a carrot juice from room service and finally goes to sleep.

"Mister d'Aramitz," Neil had absorbed the information, "Not to sound mistrusting but I emailed you the info less than," he looked at his watch, "… Less than 8 hours ago. Now you're telling me what she's been having for lunch. How do you have all this information?"

"Every move is recorded. Every action is catalogued somewhere. You just have to find somewhere and you're there."

*Some*where is *there*. That sounds like something Raphael would say, "You are a strange man."

"It's been said…," he shuffled a page, "Your boy: Raphael Adler. He's a writer. Stayed at the Fairmont in Monaco in June. Suite number 412. Before and after that it was a suite at the Belmond Hotel Splendido in Portofino. I don't have the suite number for this hotel yet."

"I only needed the Fairmont room number. I am impressed. And believe me that is no easy feat, d'Aramitz."

"We're here, sir," the car slowed to a halt in front of the Grand-Hotel.

"Call me Xavier," he said over the phone.

Neil furrowed his brows, "I'll be down in 20, Alec."

"Yes, sir… I know I know. Call you Neil."

"Thank you," Neil walked inside and into the elevator.

"You're welcome," Xavier turned a page over the phone.

"I didn't mean… I meant— Thank you, Xavier."

"You're welcome. And because this was the easiest job I've ever done, I've left word at the Fairmont. Tell them you're Álvaro de Campos. You are looking for Margarida's earrings. Margarida is your wife."

"A strange man. And should the receptionist be Portuguese or a Pessoa scholar?"

Xavier chuckled, "You're too smart to be a banker."

"It's been said," Neil walked into his room.

"Don't worry. She's neither," the line went dead.

VI
The Triumph of Galatea

The first thing Neil did was look at the chessboard. The next move had been played. She'd moved her king's knight just ahead of the bishop to C3. He thought about his next move when he stepped into the shower. It was cold but again he didn't feel cool and smelled cedar and tangerines. The dry cleaner had hung his grey Brooks Brothers suit outside his closet. He took it out of its garment bag and placed it on the bed to wear and folded three more suits and six shirts into his black Tom Ford holdall. Where's *La Danse des Tigres*? He looked through his ties, running back and forth between the closets. Then he remembered he'd ruined it and that meant Nora had either thrown it out or was having it dry cleaned. He wasn't going to take his document holder so the journal sat comfortably between his Burberry and Hermès shirts.

On the chessboard he reunited his knight's pawn with his master beside him to G6.

"To the Fairmont, Alec," Neil sat back down in the Bentley with steam rising from his face.

"We'll be there momentarily, sir."

They were waved through a police checkpoint looking for the murderers from the apartment complex. "Horrible what happened isn't it, sir?"

"Yes it is." Neil booked three tickets to Copenhagen from his phone. For himself, Christina, and Karina.

Karina's number went to voicemail, "Hello, Karina. I've bought you a ticket to Copenhagen if the invitation to be my tour guide is still open. We can also meet your clients in Malmø as well. The flight is later today. You can get your ticket from the booth. Call me back or email me."

Next was his email to Christina. He hadn't understood or appreciated what Raphael had done until that moment. Reading the words laboriously line after line is easier than writing them letter by letter. He had to be surgical with them. But how? What would Raphael say?

Dearest Christina,

I have a lead on our friend in Copenhagen. I want to sit where he sat, to see what he saw. I want to hear what he heard. In case you're interested, I've purchased a ticket in your name at the Ticket Booth for tonight's departure from Nice. I hope you will make it.

Yours,

Neil.

"The Fairmont, sir," Alec turned back.

"Thank you, Alec," Neil got out and it felt like boiling sands were spread all over his body until he walked through the lobby, and even then, there was hardly any air.

"Welcome, sir," a lissom auburn-haired woman smiled at him.

"Good afternoon," Neil looked at his watch. He had to be at the airport in two hours. There's enough time.

"How may I help you, sir. Checking in?" her smile was nothing compared to Karina's.

"No. My name is Álvaro de Campos. My wife Margarida left her earrings in room 412. She sent me to pick them up."

"Of course, sir. I've been expecting you. Your assistant has already organized everything. I have your key. But since it's currently a vacant room housekeeping will enter once they begin making their rounds."

"Maybe they'll help me," Neil felt his jaw tighten.

"They will do their best, sir," she handed him the key card.

"I'll just be a few moments," Neil walked towards the lift.

"Hello, sir."

"Good afternoon. You don't know Raphael do you?" Neil asked the elevator attendant.

"The painter?" the man chuckled.

"No. He was a guest back in June."

"A lot of people come through here, sir."

"He's my friend and I'm trying to find him. He's a writer."

"What's he look like?" the elevator jerked, "Sorry sir. Happens sometimes when it's too hot. The wires burn. We're getting it fixed."

"It's not a problem," Neil froze with the elevator. He still had no idea what Raphael looked like.

"What's he look like?" the attendant repeated when the elevator moved again.

"I… don't know," he tried to recall dialogues and descriptions in the journal. "He looks at things… differently. He's a writer."

"You already said that, sir. He's your friend but you don't know what he looks like?" the elevator doors opened.

"It's complicated," Neil got out.

"I'll think about it. But giving out guest information is prohibited anyway, sir."

"I know. I figure I'd give it a try. I'd love to reconnect with him."

The man nodded as the elevator doors closed.

Neil followed the '*Rooms 409-412*' and an arrow pointing to the right plaque. He was nervous and had no idea why. Since when had he cared so much about what other people had written about themselves? He'd always turned down *Wall Street Journal* interviews, rejected *Forbes*'s profile. The housekeeper was inside room 409. Neil walked to the corner room where 412 stared back at him. He inserted the key card and the light turned green. There was no breeze when he walked in. It only felt that way. Neil sat on the bed and eyed the room; European elegance all the way through with its wooden-designed closets and parquet floors and the lonely Persian rug in the middle who people walk all over and it never says nothing but spreads its designs all across the floor, designs that contrast the banal lines of the parquet and the systematic patterns of the wallpaper. The lonely rug, the unique rug, the lonely rug. He smiled and slid the rug to the side and dislodged the parquet panel under it to find pages and sketches that matched the notebook's. He even recognized the penmanship and wondered whether there was any data that would reveal someone's personality and appearance based on their penmanship.

The pages stared back at him. They were so at home and so hidden. Why didn't he want anyone to read them? Are thoughts that fleeting that sometimes we don't even want to infringe on our *own* privacy? Was Neil infringing on another man's privacy who had the right to write down his thoughts and simultaneously demand that no one read them? Privacy doesn't exist in the modern world. *Everything is catalogued*, Xavier had said, and Neil wondered what it would be like if someone had been pursuing his life from afar.

On the bed he looked at a sketch on one of the the pages, a study of a woman whose eyes matched the sky in the background and whose yellow hair was dancing with the movement of the wind, which was represented by cutting white lines through the blue sky. On the back page read: *Portrait of Divinity; or Sophie's Eyes.* The next page was the Valentine's Day entry Neil had been looking for: page 37.

Happiness and despair are both silent dripping poisons. The symphony in the museum had forced Sophie's boyfriend…

He heard a knock, "Housekeeping."

Neil got up and looked at the removed parquet panel and rug, "One second," he stomped the panel back in place and moved the rug over it. Stopping for a second to look outside at the cloudless sky, he tried to remember that vicious rainstorm they had last summer. That summer that had finally permitted Nora to boast her new Burberry and Hermès umbrellas.

The door opened and the maid was startled when she saw Neil frozen outside the door, "OH! So sorry, sir!"

"Not at all. I'm done in here. Thanks," and he tipped her 50€.

In the elevator the attendant smiled, "Hey, chief?"

"Yes," Neil looked up at him but kept thinking about the pages in his pocket.

"There *was* a guy who stood out."

"How so?"

"He was young. In his 20s I'd guess. But it wasn't daddy's money if you catch my drift. He always sat down for breakfast by himself and always outside on the terrace, even though it rained most of the time, and drank his triple espresso. He was friendly. Told me he was from…" the attendant looked up to remember.

"—Canada?" Neil jumped in.

"Yep! That's him. The Canadian! I remember because he said they sometimes say *bienvenue* colloquially for *you're welcome* while we say *de rien.* Peculiar, isn't it?"

"That sounds like him," the elevator got to the lobby but Neil held the close button, "Tell me about him."

"I can't, sir."

Neil took out his chequebook, "100,000€. I *need* to know."

The man's teal irises lit up and dimmed, "It's not a matter of money, sir. I can't tell you anything… I simply don't know. He wasn't… *open* to conversation," and he forced the door open.

Neil shoved the cheque into the man's hands.

"Sir, I can't accept this."

"Then don't deposit it," he walked by reception.

"Mister de Campos?" the receptionist asked with her banal smile. "Did you find the earring?"

"Yes, I did," Neil tapped his pocket where the pages were and heard something scratch them, "Here it is," and pulled out the earring he'd forgotten about since the Ovid lecture.

"That is a nice earring. I'm glad, sir. Thank you for staying with us."

"Good day…" Neil held the earring up to the light and examined it; its stub refracting the sunlight onto the elevator doors or the lobby floor or the receptionist's desk at the turn of his wrist. *Portrait of Divinity.*

"To Nice airport, Alec."

"Right away, sir," he pulled out of the Fairmont towards Nice.

Neil reached for the pages now tucked with the rest of the notebook in his holdall. He squared them and placed them where they belong.

The symphony in the museum had forced Sophie's boyfriend into an envious act of Kantian self-worth. Hastening to violate her autonomy and infringe upon her experiences…

His phone chimed. "You *must* be joking…" he squeezed his fists and closed the book. The sun came through the tinted windows of his car.

"Sir?"

"Nothing Alec. … Wait. Turn the A/C up to maximum please."

Alec looked at the controls, "Mine is already at maximum, sir. You have your own control as well."

"It's already maxed out."

"Oh. Then we're maxed out, sir."

"It's too hot."

"But it's cooler than yesterday. Are you ill sir? We can stop by the doctor's office," he passed the toll and turned onto A8 highway.

"No, it's all right. I'm okay. It just doesn't feel cooler," his phone chimed again, "One second, Alec."

"Of course, sir."

"Neil Meyollner."

"Sir, it's Sophie. A man named Marco Capello left a package for you. For your eyes only. I am to get it to you ASAP. Can you come back to the office or would you like me to come to you?"

Neil looked at his watch, "Alec, let's drop back by the office." Opening the back of the journal where he'd put Marco's note, he unfolded it and read it: *We can't talk here. Be at your office. I will have a package delivered.* Followed by his phone number.

"Right away, sir," he waited and changed lanes and merged into the exit ramp."

"I'll be right there, Sophie."

"Excellent. Thank you, sir."

* * *

The walk from the car to the office was dry and sticky.

"Sophie."

She looked up, "Please hold," and pressed a button, "Hello, sir. Here's the package. He delivered it personally and made sure to mention twice that I'm supposed to hand it to *you* personally, ASAP. He said you were supposed to be in. That he'd talked to you. And he asked me all sort of personal questions, sir. May I ask who he was?"

Neil took the long envelope, "He's an investigator, Sophie. What was he asking about exactly?"

"He asked about Edwin and the new guy."

"The new guy? … Calvin?"

"Yes. And about me. How long I've been here and so forth. It made me uncomfortable."

"Making you uncomfortable is what makes him excel at his job, Sophie. Thank you for your help."

"With Edwin here, sir, it takes a lot more than that to make me uncomfortable."

"Oh Sophie, remind me to give you a raise when I'm back."

"When will that be?" she joked.

"I don't know yet," Neil turned around to walk out when he bumped into Calvin.

"Sir, may I thank you for the opportunity?"

"No. It's not necessary. We're a team."

"I'm making real headway with some old clients. They want to merge their portfolio with our firm."

"That's excellent. Do a thorough background and authorize it."

"Thank you, sir."

"Again, not necessary," Neil looked at his watch, "I'm late. *À plus tard,* Calvin."

"Yes, sir. See you soon."

Neil exhaled and unbuttoned his shirt in the car to let the A/C in. "Now to the airport, Alec."

Alec nodded and turned onto Avenue du Trois Septembre.

Neil unsealed the envelope from Marco and read the accompanying post-its on each page.

For your eyes only, Mr. Meyollner.

We are interested in accounts whose trades route through the WBCT executed on behalf of Mr. Wilbert Schermer by two members of your firm and one outlier. Mr. Edwin Voclain and Mr. Calvin Wechsler. These are the only trades we need. The transaction IDs and usernames associated with those trades are enclosed.

Neil scanned the page. *Born2Rule* was Edwin's ID, that ridiculous man. "Using your name is caving to the establishment. That's junk! I want *this* ID!" What a buffoon. Neil let his thoughts stray to Edwin's hands around his wife's waist. Exchanging glances at brunch or interlacing their fingers together.

CalvinWechsler had executed some stable trades here and there for varying firms across Europe and the Americas and three trades in Africa.

GMaurus. Neil moved the page closer. Why did that name look so familiar? Where had he seen that name before? Who *is* GMaurus? — Neil reached for Raphael's notebook in his bag and leafed through he pages until he found it.

Giltbert Maurus was found shot in his black Mercedes sedan in Midtown Toronto well past midnight…

Disbelief sunk him deeper into the custom Italian leather of his Bentley. "Do you believe in fate, Alec?"

"Sir?"

"Fate. Do you believe in it?"

"I'm not religious, sir," the sign for the airport was up ahead.

"I didn't ask if you were religious. I asked if you believe in fate."

"No, sir."

"Why?"

"Because I don't like the idea that I'm not the one making my own choices. It makes me lazy and lets me blame all of my failures and shortcomings on fate."

"Yeah… you're right. Do what you can. When you do it. Take responsibility."

"That's over my head, sir. … Which terminal?"

"Huh? … Oh. I'm flying SAS."

"Got it," Alec merged into the Departures Passenger Drop-Off.

Maurus. Neil looked at his trades. All routed through Schermer's Dutch firm across a multitude of capitals. He had to make sure he was dead. Was it the same guy that'd been killed? It couldn't be. This one had never been to Toronto. Neil ran his fingers down the routed WBCT trades: TSX, TSX, TSX, TSX.

Neil highlighted every Maurus transaction number and sent an email to Marco: *who is GMaurus?*

"We're here, sir," Alec pointed to the check-in through the entrance.

"Thank you, Alec. I'll see you later."

"Would you like me to carry your bag?"

"No. I've got just the one," Neil walked through the doors and looked at the Ticket Pick-Up booth in search of Tina. He saw and heard no one.

What an imbecile he'd been. To believe in meaningful words and gestures that meant something to him but something else to the other. It was childish to believe there was something more than reasonable rates of return and smiles that could be more than simple muscle contortions of the face. Raphael was a child, an aberrant and isolated man who didn't live in the real world. How could he think his words carried any meaning? How could he hope that Sophie understood him for who and what he was rather than what he could give her of himself? Everyone is selfish. Wisdom is never unity.

"Passport or ID, sir."

"How are you?" Neil handed her the passport, "Is the seat next to me taken?"

"It is…" she typed, "Not, but it's bought for and on hold for…"

"Me."

"That's right. But for a different person."

"Yes. I just wanted to check if she's picked up her ticket."

She put his passport back on the counter, "No. But for continental flights not that much is required. You can go through security now. And if you check in online and print your boarding pass next time you don't even have to stop by the counter. Since you don't have any luggage you can go straight to security."

"I know... I wanted to say hi."

She gave him a quizzical look as if he was hitting on her, "Have a nice flight, sir."

Every middle-eastern looking man was randomly searched but Neil breezed through the priority security line. Then a straight shot into the lounge with his access card.

"Scotch and soda," Neil sat down.

The man pointed behind him.

Neil turned around expecting to see someone he knew but instead he saw the *Scotch & Soda* boutique. "It's over there."

"No. I meant a drink. With scotch. And soda."

"OH!" the man jerked back, "I apologize profusely. Coming right up, sir. ... Coming right up!"

An announcement went through the airport. *Do not leave your bags unattended. Unattended bags will be seized by security.* ...

Neil watched the people shuffling in and out of the duty-free designer boutiques. Watches, suits, shawls, bracelets, cigarettes, booze; existing.

This is an update on the flight board. SAS 794 direct to Copenhagen has been delayed. We apologize for the inconvenience.

Neil felt the sun on his nape; he looked outside at clouds approaching in the distance. He had ample time to wallow now. "Always. Every time," Nora had objected when they were delayed on their flight to Vaduz. "We should fly private next time." Neil had agreed. Now he had the Eurocopter and wondered how easy it would be to charter a jet. He ordered another round just as the gates next to his were called. Everyone huddled and cramped into the spaces even when their rows weren't called.

"May I join you?" a voice sounded him.

Neil turned around and saw Christina standing above him.

"Of course," he smiled. "I'm glad you made it."

"Me too. I wasn't sure. If I was coming I mean. I didn't want... I'm sorry about what happened that night."

"Don't be."

"It looks like we're delayed."

"Yes. It's horrendous," he watched the planes outside taxi and go across the airfield.

"Not really. Gives us enough time to catch up. Made any progress on our mystery man?"

At the Ruby Bar I saw a man and a woman talking and getting close to each other under the table. Their legs tangoing and tapping the marrow under their skin. Is it even possible for two people to be close to each other? For humans with vastly different experiences and vastly different definitions of words that make the meaning of a life to find similarities and attain intimacy?

Their conversation was so predictable and uninteresting. They chattered about out-of-body experiences and where the mind was located. How many times had each of them had this conversation and with how many other people?

One of them asked, "What is a concept to you?" These words, now trapped in the marble designer backdrop of this dimly-lit cocktail bar made me wonder the banality of man. Man, not woman. How many dark and dim bars, with only the orange and yellow of the candlelight shining in her eyes like shooting stars over a blue sky were homes to men like the man that sits not three feet away from me. "I watch French Cinema so…" as if those words denoted something deeper other than the condescending critique of exclusive or genre-defining art forms.

The singing sparrows, having grown stronger now and fluttering their little wings, the shushing whispers of the fields through my window, my neighbour's barking dog, and the mumbling, incoherent conversations I'd hear through the wall echoed off the walls. Persistent noises that emanate in the background of a life, noises we all hear but let dwindle and fall, noises that would be unrelated, irregular, and steadily irksome if we listened to them. Noises that tread over the abyss of existence, those enigmatic tidings that the ear puts together simply to remind us we're alive. They always seem to yearn to harmonize but are held back until one-by-one those harmonies fall into the night and there is only silence. With her the sounds harmonized and the silence was not a reminder that there was, ahead of each of us, a bottomless abyss, but that each sound carried a natural jocundity.

I cringed when the man's hands crept towards the woman's fingertips. Her red lipstick turned blood-red because of the candle… I had lived this scene. Is this what it looked like from the outside? Question: Does everyone look and behave the same when they attempt to grasp in vain these fleeting illusions? Suspiration. Beating hearts. Aging. Death. Do the universals of human experience include love? Follow-up: Is the behaviour of heartbreak universal too? To cringe at the sight of others getting closer to each other? Me, now, at this moment, how average and universal was my reaction? It is an absurd vileness in behaving as if private torments transcend another's painful experience and are universal tragedies.

"Give it time. It'll blow over," a man touched my shoulder.

"Time… everything exists in time!"

"Exactly," he swayed and used my shoulder as a support beam, "Time is awesome."

"But how can the eternal exist in time? And when we brush it, how can we accept that it was timed and must come to an end?"

"Yeah! How can it?" he roared.

The woman moved through the candlelight and kissed the man whose lips had landed on red 18.

I smelled lemon sage and tasted vanilla and had to leave.

On the gloomy streets the nocturnal tranquility of the city pushed me deeper and deeper into golden silent stanzas. I had lost count of the number of poems I had written for her. An entire red notebook filled with idylls, cantos, sonnets, prose, and rhymes for the celestial Sophie. All poems are about love except love poems. … Even its colour, like the 18, was selected before time had caught up to my present. I bought it before I'd met her and had never used it until the day we'd met. I still remember the date, the time, the headlines, even the weather.

The silent steps of lovers walking hand-in-hand on Danish, impossible-to-pronounce streets resound through me. Their voices drone through the night in strange volumes under those little planted trees and pass like the incomprehensible gibberish of a forgotten dream. I am exhausted, fatigued at the mere prospect of an existence without her. I wish she were here despite simultaneously being aware of my own absurdity. Rising before me, with the unwanted lure of someone standing in front of the abyss, an unknown pang settled into me, more violent and pronounced than any other pain I had ever experienced. I listen to the echoes for a sign, listening to myself think and imagine myself…. But all that echoes back is silence.

"Imagine himself what? What's he talking about?" Tina wrapped her hands around her tumbler.

"I don't know. The sentence just *ends*," Neil flipped back and forth between the pages as if the sentences he was looking for would be any different from the ones he was reading and would jump out at him.

I just reread that last sentence and chuckled. Her infidelity to me! Me me me! HA! The difference with loving someone because it's convenient, and loving someone because of the inevitable fusion of souls, is judgment. Would her boyfriend forgive her? Would she forgive herself? Loving someone is never judging them. That's when I knew I loved her; on that dark, desolate, dreary street during a lonely night with only the Vartov Church as my witness and this creaky bench as my only ally. I judged nothing she had said and judged nothing she had done. That's why love is impossible. Humans are so prone to judge each other that we'd rather live an entire life without love than simply refuse to judge.

Where was it Simonetta had searched for love and failed if not inside a judgmental heart that demanded of itself and the other what she thought love was and how to fulfill it. How easy it was for her to judge and criticize anyone who might even graze the potential of loving someone else. Only *she* was allowed to be *in* love. Only she was allowed to love. Only she had experienced happiness. She she she! There was always a thin veil of envy underneath that narcissism; an envy that guaranteed she would never find love or happiness, or accept any of her friends' pursuit as noble or praiseworthy. Yet she was herself only one person. One person of many, and in her average existence how many more were like her? Judging others and being led by their judgments to make questionable decisions based neither in reason nor in heartfelt emotions.

The beginnings of relationships and loves are preferred since feelings are sincere and ungoverned by judgments and self-denial. With time we judge our friends and lovers because we have preconceived notions about people and their habits, the predefined concepts of friendship and love, thus we judge them if they do not fit that mould. Yet most people wouldn't consider themselves judgmental and would say with passionate disdain how much they detest judgmental people. But time makes us become the thing we hate most. The best we can hope for is to die before that happens.

"Some of the pages were missing," he showed her the torn edges of the notebook, "But I got them."

"That's weird. Why would he tear them out?"

"I don't know, Tina. I've given up trying to get into his head."

The delay for flight SAS 794 to Copenhagen has now cleared. We are now ready for boarding. Please proceed to your gate.

"That's us! See? *Tempus fugit.*"

"Yes," Neil watched her movements but couldn't read her. Nothing about her was obvious. Nothing on her hair made her personality discernible. No item of clothing made it easier to read between the lines of her character. No smile made her thoughts transparent. How time flies and makes us become the thing we hate most: judgmental.

Question: Is united wisdom the negation of judgment? Answer: Yes. When we refuse to judge we find that the people we had previously judged are not as we saw them or would've liked to see them. They are more as they see themselves. More accurate depictions of character are possible when people are permitted to be themselves. This is why when people wear physical masks to hide themselves, they act more like themselves with impunity. The apprehension from judgment has disappeared.

Now that he'd left the city only lit up by neon lights and excess and the jungle where prey eats smaller prey and no real predator exists he would finally be able to breathe. So he hoped.

Once they took their seats Christina yawned and crossed her legs. "Neil please bill me for the flight and the room I assume you booked at a luxurious hotel."

"Nonsense."

"Yeah! Nonsense lady! Wonderful women like you should not pay for anything," a man with square, thin-rimmed glasses looked over.

Neil chuckled, "We agree," and turned to Christina, "I won't have it."

The attendant walked by and apologized for the delay.

Tina yawned again, then so did the man. "I'm going to take a nap Neil. I've had trouble sleeping the past week."

"Sure," Neil gave her the armrest and heaved for air.

"Would you like anything before take-off?" the attendant walked by again.

"Politiken," the man with the glasses raised his index finger.

"Sure," the attendant shuffled through her papers and handed him the *Politiken*. Neil saw an ø in a headline and turned to the man, "Are you Danish?"

"Yes. I'm glad you didn't mistake me for a Swede."

"I have a Dane working at my firm. I knew the o with the line through it is Danish and the o with the umlaut is Swedish."

"Smart man," he pointed to Tina.

"She's Swedish."

"Well… no one is perfect…" he tucked the paper into the seat pocket in front of him.

Neil laughed and extended his hand, "Neil Meyollner."

"Everything must be a nail to you," the man extended his strong and muscular hands, hands that had never been idle, hands as coarse as the fields he'd ploughed and razed all his life, and the crinkling corner of his eyes behind those square glasses, eyes that had seen both despair and elation, eyes that dilated behind his glib charm of friendliness; they looked into Neil's soft skin and unwrinkled forehead, "Niff Nesluop."

"It's a pleasure. Any place I should visit?"

Niff's voice carried through the pressurized cabin as the attendant lectured on the safety measures. But slowly and without any surreal resignation Tina's head had found its way onto Neil's shoulder. The plane was taxiing and Niff was listing off one-by-one the hotspots of the city. Neil was already flying.

He heard her breathing in sync with the wind outside, heard the shuffling of her legs towards the wall of the plane; he looked at the food trays open to his right with people playing games or listening to music or reading the paper. She exhaled and Neil watched her reflection in the plane's window with a cloud in the distance complementing the blue sky when he realized all at once that she was the most beautiful woman he'd ever seen. The stars glinted in her eyes and her hair was rays of the golden sun. *What are you doing Neil?* He thought to himself. He had a wife, a life.... A person walking up the aisle looked at him and he felt vainglorious. There was a beautiful woman sleeping on his shoulder and though *he* knew it, everyone else did too. Nora had always intimidated men with her gaze and loathsome preference of luxury brands.

Christina slept through take-off and Neil's elation made him forget for those two hours his unfaithful wife, his disloyal friend, and even the unread pages of Raphael's journal. Pages he would read soon enough to better comprehend why the blank lines between Raphael's sentences, though white, were filled with darkening despair. Nor did he know that at that moment, Nora was actually talking to another man in the seductive vile way women do when they want something. He would never see the shade of the red lipstick his wife was wearing, or her lightly applied green eyeshadow. Not even God can help you when a woman decides she wants something. No apple is safe. Surely no man. Time and circumstance hadn't caught up to Neil yet. That's what he would never understand, the pragmatist. And that's what Raphael didn't understand either, the idealist. That happiness was neither a state of mind one achieves once that lasts for eternity; that is sophistical philosophy and religious dogmatism, nor is it a sequence of events that line up in the way you expect in the contemplative and fleeting moments of experience that sum up a life in a particular way. No, happiness is ignorance. Is there such a thing as a happy genius? A charming naiveté exudes from a soul who smiles that his bank account increases while being poor, whose marriage is perfect though his wife is unfaithful, whose belly is full when he is starved of something more. Neil only felt that elation, that blissful paradisiacal moment *because* he had forgotten his bank account, his wife's betrayal, and his famine.

"This is your captain speaking. We apologize for having to reroute and circle around for a while. But we've made up for lost time and should arrive shortly. We're now flying over Leiden. If you look outside you can see the wonderful Rhine River and the city's gorgeous canals."

Of all the cities he could've announced why did he have to announce that one?

Neil jerked back into reality. The moment was gone; the problem with living in those moments is that if they're not eternal, reality hits you all at once. That's why some people die from shock.

Tina woke and yawned and stretched. Looking at Neil's wrinkled jacket where her head had been, she blushed. "Oh. I'm sorry."

"Don't be," Neil smiled.

"Ladies and gentlemen we're in luck. We're having a longer Danish summer than usual. It's 20 degrees outside and only a little cloud in the distance so it must feel like home."

"Great…" Neil pulled his collar from his shirt. The air had been thick and even in the north it would be the same.

"Isn't it?" Christina clapped.

"But… it's supposed to be fall." Neil saw her smiling and wanted to immortalize the moment. Why do people love the sun? That unruly and temperamental old fool! Always calling on us lest lovers are bound to his glowing presence thus! Whose beams and burning brightness is of a wench who chides lovers in the night wanting to immortalize their moments. That scorching Ulysses of the sky, should leave those ocean waves and tides, if it left pain would be absent.

All love is alike, knowing no season, sun, or clime, but that damn sun does represent lovers' ever-changing time. Why does it rise to show lovers nothing lasts? Does it not see those lovers and think, 'I can eclipse and darken them with a wink. I could kill all love by rising and sending them to their forlorn pasts. I can make them for each other pine, and wait and wait as I rise and set. HA! Buffoons, they are all mine. And every time I shine they owe me a debt.'

Damned sun! It shines and burns everyone but many people adore it. They worship it like the ancient Egyptians, vacationing where it shines most and where it tyrannizes the clouds and the sky. We look into it even when we know it will burn us. Maybe we like to be burned. From the fire's perspective, it's the absence of the enflamed who burn. We all burn and there's nothing we can do but enjoy it. Enjoying it bothers the sun, that conniving, divine, and wicked star.

Neil began to enjoy the heat and the pain. The awareness that no moment can last past a wink of the sun, past the present belief that love could last longer than the elation powered by the sun before it sets, or the passion fuelled by the night before it rises to take everything.

Their flight landed on time at Kastrup. Niff said goodbye and pointed to the metro escalator connected at the end of the wooden terminal floor.

"The hotel hired us a car," he turned to Tina.

"Okay," she looked out towards the sun who Neil imagined thought about winking.

When they loaded their bag into the car something nagged at him, "Do you want to take the metro?" he looked at her through the back seat.

"Sure!" she reached for her bag.

"No. Leave it." He closed the door, "Sir will you please take our bags to the hotel? We're going to take the metro and then walk around for a bit."

"It's not a problem. I'll take good care of them," he smiled and got back into the car.

They ascended the escalator and watched the Danes and Swedes walking to and from the metro. *Check-in Stations* beeped when people flashed their travel cards in front of it.

"We should buy a Journey Card Neil. It makes things easier."

"That sounds like a great idea. Where?"

"That booth I think. We have them in Sweden. Only buy one though. We can have multiple people travelling at once on one card."

Neil came back to Tina bathing in the harsh afternoon sun and she tapped the card against the blue-bubble where a beep and "CHECK IN OK" appeared.

The unmanned metro whirred towards the city. Neil looked at the transit map and pointed to *Kongens Nytorv*, "That's our stop."

Tina nodded. The sun hid behind a building for a moment and a deep blue submerged the train. Neil enjoyed the idea that Raphael had been where he was standing. Something separated the suite at the Fairmont from the train. Where had Raphael stood on that train? *How* would he stand? Was Raphael on that train right then? Neil walked up and down and pointed out to Tina that it was unmanned. The spiralling of the leaves outside when the train sped by. The whisperings of the rain he hadn't heard in so long. The silence of sunlight screaming in his ear. They reveal nature to the unnatural. But even the unnatural is replicated through nature.

When the metro passed *Øresund* station and then stopped at *Amager Strand*, people with beach towels and sandals walked on. Neil looked out towards the strait.

Having water so close and around a city had a solemn tranquilizing effect on its inhabitants. They were so civilized and ordered in their movements. The Nordic designs of the newer buildings, the old, carved, classic architecture with Danish or Latin phrases that were cozy apartments, fancy start-ups, and bars all at once. How was Kierkegaard so anxious living as a native of this city? The cyclists behaved as cars, obeying every traffic symbol and were so unpretentious and quiet.

They got out at Kongens Nytorv station where everyone lined up behind the *Check-out Stations* and one-by-one the machine beeped them on their way. Outside the station, they took a detour towards the *Storkespringsvandet* fountain. Neil watched them; the delivery boys looked like interning museum curators, the waiters and waitresses were artists searching for a glimpse of glee in this city. Now he knew why they ranked first in the Happiness Index. Why hadn't he moved to Denmark yet? Tina fit in so well; her serenity and throbbing calm was a sunlit fusion with the city itself and with everyone else. There was no one, no I, only a unity of identities and bodies curving back and forth through bizarre sounding streets.

They walked along when Neil stopped in front of a store and tried to pronounce the street name: "Strøget, Østergade."

Tina chuckled, "It's a difficult language." She made an attempt in her Swedish accent and eventually gave up and pronounced it in Swedish: "Östergate."

"Quite glottal. Swedish sounds different."

"Yep! We like to tease and poke fun at each other. There's an old rivalry between Denmark and Sweden. They have something here they call *hygge*. It's one of those untranslatable words."

"What does it mean?"

"It would be difficult to translate into English or French. It means 'a coziness' or 'at home-ness.' Like having fun, or even a nice atmosphere. For example, lighting candles and and hanging out with friends or a loved one is *hygge*."

"Why? … The candles I mean. That seems like almost necessary."

"Maybe because there's not as much sun in the North. I don't know. The Dutch have it too. They call it *Gezelligheid*."

"What do you," he interrupted himself, "The Swedish call it?"

"We call it *mysig.* "

"They're first in the Happiness Index," Neil looked up and saw the *Illum* rooftop terrace and thought about Raphael, Edwin and Holly, and Marco's investigation. He was envious of Raphael's quick and swift forgiveness of treachery. He hadn't even flinched. What is that like? To forgive? And not only to forgive, but to do it so readily with an acute awareness that the treachery may occur again.

He felt loathing for Raphael because of it and felt cheated out of the bliss he wanted to share with Tina. He was supposed to be happy! *This* was supposed to make him happy!

"No small thanks for *hygge,*" Christina turned back and pointed down the street, "Our hotel is down that street. Do you want to keep walking or check in?"

Neil thought about Marco and Maurus and the investigation. "Let's check in. I do have to catch up on some work."

"Welcome to the Hotel d'Angleterre," this woman had the same smile as the one at the Fairmont. The twitching of her jawline and the extension of her lips meant to wrinkle her dimples. It was *exactly* the same.

"Good evening. My name is Neil Meyollner. I've reserved two suites."

"Of course, sir. The driver brought your bags. Was there an issue?"

"Not at all. We wanted to take in some of the sights."

"Oh excellent. Here are your keys. You sir, are in the Deluxe Suite, and Miss Lindström is in our famous *The D'Angleterre Suite*."

Tina started chatting to the receptionist in Swedish or Danish, Neil couldn't tell but the up and down harmonies of the sentences lingered in his ear. He tried to transfer it to his audiotape of Ovid or the slant rhymes of Yeats's poetry. What did Raphael think of Danish or Swedish?

"I'm telling her to switch our rooms. You stay in the suite."

"I won't have it. I do have a suite."

The concierge handed them their key cards.

In the elevator Christina turned to Neil with her key card in hand, "Please switch with me. I wouldn't feel comfortable."

"Don't be ridiculous. I booked that suite for you!" and when the doors opened to Neil's floor he turned to the buttons, "Thanks—" and chuckled.

Tina laughed, "You're not in Monaco anymore."

"Apparently not," the doors closed.

Neil's suite was about 60-70 meters-squared with a separate living room and bedroom. He felt somnolent after arriving and collapsed on the bed, reaching for the journal in his bag just out of reach of his fingertips.

There was an email from Marco waiting in his inbox.

Re: G. Maurus.

Neil ran a bath instead. Marco and Maurus and Edwin and Nora could wait.

He could hardly believe, replaying the past two to three weeks of his life, how heavy it'd suddenly gotten. Why? He could nap before his bath. Ripping off his pants and loosening his shirt, he threw himself onto the bed, where the immaculate Nordic duvet kissed his legs, and he simply surrendered his body to the exhaustion. He had the perfect life. He would return to his wife and that dormant part of him that had awakened would lull itself back to sleep. How relaxed he felt in that minimalist room; there was so much sun and so much air and so much light. Neil would've shaken himself awake in blissful pleasure if he weren't exhausted. Mindfulness, Nora's meditation or yoga instructor had repeated over and over again. *Will it to be* and so the universe shall hear you and it will be. Neil had laughed later to himself that night. What an idiot… but it was *he* and Nora who had been the idiots, paying 450€ an hour to be told that anything is possible. What a fascination the Western World has with sophistical Eastern Philosophy. A month in India or Tibet or China or Japan and everyone is enlightened and can teach it to you at a bargain rate. *Will it to be*, or will it away, he thought. He can put his mind off the investigation and Raphael and will himself to fall in love with Nora again. In unity and in happiness. She was an angel; she'd stuck by him despite the highs and lows of CAM and his insecurities about her wealthy and affluent family. Then he was overcome by arrogance; what was wrong with him? Nora *should* stick by him; he was a great man, an ambitious man, a resilient man. He felt a single tear falling through the grooves of his stubble and cheekbone like rapids along a river. Looking over at the window there was Nora walking towards him now. Nora! Her tight, muscular shoulders with a birthmark on the left that looked like a teardrop, and her long legs that were deceiving because she never wore heels, they weren't touching the ground. She floated to him. What a woman. Will it to be; will it away. Will away Tina, will away the investigation, will away Edwin, will away Raphael; Raphael, the journal…

The symphony in the museum had forced Sophie's boyfriend into an envious act of Kantian self-worth. Hastening to violate her autonomy and infringe upon her experiences, he thought he would imprudently infract her apperceptive "I." How romantic to cage a leopardess. But if my conversation with her had in fact aroused his envy, the wonderful Sophie Vildegrube was herself simply aroused. All week my words orchestrated and played the coarse strings of her heart, where the trailing E of love was struck vibrant and swung the sharp F of fate like a pendulum. She was flattered. I had written her in an angelic light, unlike the practiced mask of smiling but cold uprightness that reflected back to her from her professors, other friends, former lovers, and her boyfriend who could utter no such remarks. She would see herself in the mirror of a bar and blush but then berate herself for the gender-based indulgence. She was an independent woman who needed no man.... Still, the fantasies were sure to rise, and when they did she let them traverse the jungle of her thoughts, let them rest on her tongue like sweet desserts, or the savoury breakfast shortbread from her youth when her desires were new and unrestrained. Desire. Longing. Tingle. Intrigue. Intimacy. How expected the fusion of romantic Swedish vocabulary with the emotional paradoxes that now so easily described the palpitations of her heart.

I walked by Hermès on my way to see her. I wanted to buy her something for Valentine's Day. Luís said I was insane. The window was magnificent. Shawls shaped like manta rays spread behind the glass. The word 'Manta' comes from the Spanish for *cloak* or *shawl* and in Dhivehi mantas are known as *madi*, which translates to 'small fish eating ray.' Whoever the designer of that window was, they deserved a raise.

There was an orange, white, and beige one with four horses weaving and knotting around the borders of the 70 cm square. A vintage silk scarf called *Quadrige Costumé*. She'd told me she loved horses and I felt compelled to purchase it. She wasn't the materialist type but I could afford it; I had three poems and a short story shortlisted for publication next month.

"Is it a gift?" the employee asked.

"Yes."

"For Valentine's Day?"

"Not exactly."

On my way towards the café a black Rover slowed before turning and it looked like he watched me cross the street, watched me *personally*.

"He doesn't want me to see you anymore," she was on the verge of tears on the one day it wasn't rainy.

A man walking by shook his head as if I was breaking up with her on February 13. But even if I was, would that be any different from any other day? Why do we perpetuate already failed relationships and dead friendships? Isn't it better to end them the day we realize their failures and deaths?

"I can't do it, Raphael. I can't *not* see you. I can't do it. But he said he'd leave me."

"Take a deep breath. Come sit," I took her hand and guided her to a couch near us in the lounge. "We won't see each other anymore then. Your relationship is more important. I want you to be happy. I don't want to get in the way of that," I pushed the orange Hermès box deeper into my leather shoulder bag.

She sank lower in the seat and put her head on my shoulder, "No… that's not what I want."

"What *do* you want?"

She got up and paced up and down in front of me, turning in weaving movements and retracing her steps like an infinity symbol. "I don't know," she clenched and unclenched her fists. Her hands… how delicate and slender and strong they were. I could write an entire novel just about those hands. The way they displaced the air when they moved, the way they outlined my jawline when she was feeling seductive, the way they moved quickly in large bubbly shapes when she was sketching something. The way they covered her face when she wanted to conceal her emotions. …

"Say something," she put her left hand on her thigh and reached over with her right to grab mine.

"I don't know."

They were shaking. "Say anything then." How surreal and incredulous it was to hold a hand like that. The Graces must've invoked the Muses before moulding those hands. Like a spring meadow they stood still.

Near us some people were playing table tennis and the irregular bouncing of the ball on the floor and emulating trash talk seemed to unnerve her. The sound of the bouncing ball on the ground, that seemed to last an eternity every time, and the tapping and popping sound of the racket slashing the ball, always followed by an "Ooohh!" and some ceremonial ribbing, hovered through and seated itself atop the sounds Sophie was hearing. And its regular monotonous sound was as soothing as the sound of waves landing on the sand again… and again… and again, until her breathing slowed.

Her thoughts repeated over and over again like the chorus of a pop song, "I want him. I love him." But in waking moments, abruptly and precipitously when her thoughts roamed from the realities of her life, they had no greater meaning. Like ghostly drums in old cultures that resonate through the natural jungle unnaturally, awareness made her thoughts of the rising tides of her soul wash away the islands of her personality. Moment after moment tiding across her past, present, and future like a tricoloured rainbow. That sound of the waves inside her, the sound concealed by the bouncing ball echoed through the hallow caverns of her heart and made her look at me with fright and horror. Never had I seen more doleful eyes. Two clouds held hands, there was a raindrop. It landed on the window. Rain has no choice; it has to fall. Looking at her, what else was there behind the splendour of her refined beauty?

If I walked in front of my morning train, or if that chance event hadn't brought me to this city, would I not be I but someone else? And would someone else be sitting here next to her? Some earlier lover perhaps, or a future one. Nothing but the incomparable splendour of her hands' movements could conceal her inability to control how she felt. Those stories of her former lovers still in love with her, of her curiosity in my past, or her creative ambition thwarted always by circumstance. Most of the time her cleverness and charm permitted her to let the silence speak. The quiet always told me what I needed to know. Her not speaking was among the most poetical experiences of my life. Like the time I dropped her off at the train station and the sound of the closing doors made her blurt out, "Come give me a kiss," when in reality what the words had *meant* was, "I love you," and the sounds of the wheels creaking along the tracks away from me made me think of her. I never believed her. No matter how many times she said it or made me feel it I didn't believe her. She didn't love me. Otherwise she'd leave her so-called paramour and actualize that love. Love has to be more than a word; it has to be an action, a moment, a belief, a hope, a thought… everything. It's impossible to love two people at the same time. Yet every time she said it I wanted to hear it just once more even if I wouldn't believe it. There is something about us: humans. We covet to hear those three words even if we possess the foreknowledge that behind them is another: disappointment.

The ball fell again and bounced across the floor, stopping at my feet.

"Hey, man. Pass that?' one of the players called.

But I didn't want to move; there was something incredulous in the serenity of her face. Her face that was either sexy, friendly, flirtatious, or cold; but now it seemed to be none of those things. It seemed to be more itself. If it was merely her sex appeal, her warmth, or her following of a stereotype, I was simultaneously conscripted to contemplate her unified being, her complexities as a woman, and the understanding that her vision of the world differed from mine.

The man took the ball from beside my boot and watched us. Shaking his head he said something to his friend in Danish.

To think of her as only a woman was to deny her existence as a unification of nature and femininity. It bored her. All beautiful women are alike in their nature, but every woman is natural in her own way.

Question: What *did* she want? Follow-up: Could I give it to her? Answer indescribable. First question abandoned. Second answer in the affirmative regardless of the first.

When someone suddenly walked by she moved her hand away and left mine hovering over the air like a raindrop on a tree branch that refuses to fall. When we walked up the stairs she lingered. "Carry me Raphael. I'm paralyzed."

"To the ends of the…" I realized that my words would have an effect so I abrogated them and let the silence reign. But silence has an effect too. "Take a deep breath Sophie. It will all work out. Trust me."

She smiled and ascended the stairs where she stood beside the sun and they merged. Loathing the words I used; stock phrases used by everyone from the Wall Street banker to the Pope, phrases we say that have no meaning and carry no meaning. In Copenhagen, something can be true at dawn but false once the sun sets. The problem with this city, rather than Florence or Johannesburg, where the sun rises and sets pursuant to a logic of sunrises and sunsets, is that the sun rises between 4-8 but no one can predict when it will set.

She glided towards the window sipping her coffee and smiling. What I would do for that smile alone. Its crimson shade beguiling and warming me straight to the bone.

Why is it, when we make ourselves a conduit for words that write themselves, they only write of the darkness of the sky in midnight moonlight? Why do muses always form as lustre for sunlight in the day rather than the day itself? Why do we need to know *when* the sun will rise to bask in its glorious light?

This is not only necessary but a quality of the protagonist. Having some unquantifiable despair in his heart as he stands in silent nobility under a leafless tree, waiting for the moment when his lips touch those of his muse, if he should be lucky, drives him forward. The kiss, withheld by the muse for an immeasurable amount of time, is then well received, but that moment now past can never be relived and thus becomes an impossible standard.

Yet even with this thought and acceptance of its impossibility, the protagonist's heart twirls upon the movements of his muse like a buoy in the middle of the ocean. Why can he see her urges but do nothing about them? Why does he feel as if he's heard this tale before? Do voices within him speak to him in silence about her fine dress catching bits of the drizzle in the night and her scarf waving tall and high towards the sky like a flag of his heart? There is an ambition to his soul in times of darkness, one that yearns for an outlet that never comes. That is how all tales end.

She shook my shoulder, "Come back to me."

"I never left."

"You did. You weren't here," she leaned in and I felt those ruby lips warm my soul.

The sun started to set.

VII
Saint George and the Dragon

Neil put his navy suit on the following morning. He left a message at reception apologizing to Tina for being unable to join her to breakfast and lunch. Outside his window ravens had perched on an electrical wire above the fountain. He made an afternoon reservation for coffee at the *Café Norden* just down the street before having a breakfast basket brought to his wife in their Monaco suite.

Hoping to intercept Holly at the SMK he walked into the French Gallery and sat across *Portrait of Madame Matisse*, (The Green Line) from 1905. The longer he stared at it, the more the colours contrasted and complemented the background wall. The lime green down the centre of her face. The blue weaving in her hair, and her pink blouse turning orange, turning red from left to right. The simple geometric shapes fusing and yet keeping the colours separate, a minimal spatial modulation where shadows were broken down not into shades but hues of colour. What resplendence contained in a mere half metre canvas.

On my birthday she insisted on joining me at a bar where I was drinking alone. My headaches have been getting worse. At the counter a man flirted with her and ogled her and she savoured every second of it. When she blew him a kiss I knew what I had asked earlier about hurting me wasn't what I had inquired. Looking at her she said, "You're making me nervous. Look over there," and pointed to the wall blotched with rotting wood. Real pain is never physical. The nature of love is not to influence your lover, but to alter the way you love.

Of the people you know, how many have ventured to know you the way you sought to know yourself when you were younger? And of these people, whether they were former lovers or friends or family, how many wanted to know you at no benefit to themselves? We know ourselves when our relationships are only at great cost to our souls. When we value our past friendships and relationships this way, we find that none of our lists are exhaustive. Former friends, current friends, acquaintances, lovers past, present, and future; we find that we can count on one hand the glimpse of true companionship and intimacy despite a world connected pocket-by-pocket, minute-to-minute. With blurry ideations of nation states if no global sports tournaments are in place, we see that no two people are truly connected. In fact, we sometimes find that if people had made their desires known from the start we would've done our best to curtail them, or if we could, satiate them completely. But most people are not themselves but a thick veiling mask of what they think they ought to be, thus it is too much to seek to know another behind their mask, let alone coming across another who seeks to know us the same way. How could we know another that does not know themselves first? How could we love them? Thus we know no one, feel nothing, and fall in love with only the masks presented to us by cultivated personae of feigned honour, courage, beauty, and elation. All unhappy, never satisfied.

Sometime back in April we were walking along those confusing and curling streets when at a florist I saw a rain dampened purple peony with a lobe deeper set than usual. She walked ahead and paused in between all the flowers. I thought about ending it. My memory never fails but I think I omitted the last word of that thought. *All.* I'd left her and got lost looking for the route home. The clouds slid away and the high sun cast my shadow below me. Then I *felt* the presence of someone behind me. Someone long dead. A former lover or a grandparent. There was no one there. My shadow disappeared into the circular abyss cast by the rotunda at the end of the street. We'd spent the previous night at my place in the country. The horses had danced and the linseed oil fields had whispered. It was hot and breathless. I held her shaking body next to mine. I wasn't there. Like an onlooker or a dancing leaf in those fields, I had no influence. I was never there. I couldn't sleep but didn't move. I wanted to lie there forever, to die at that moment. It would always be like that. A dream where I wouldn't be able to move until it becomes a nightmare. When she got up to get a glass of water, one of the horses, probably the black one with white blotches, my favourite, chortled and neighed.

When I got home she'd sent a note to my computer: *My question. My knife.*

It was the kind of note you never forget even if you have no active memory. I could tell by the air and by the sudden exhaustion of my laptop fan as if a jet were taking off. Maybe it was just intuition. If it was a physical letter the ink would've ran and blurred as if it had sat in the rain. Carrying it with me across my synced devices I thought about it all day and night. I always had it with me but I never read it. I thought about ending it.

"Jesus Christ," Neil looked up and there was another woman in the gallery who looked at him in disdain for his splenetic outburst. He exhaled and held the notebook tighter. He put the journal back into his pocket and heard something crumble. It was Holly's letter to Edwin. Why did he still have it with him? Providence or stupidity?

Then he saw a woman with a familiar figure sitting in the opposite gallery in front of Matisse's *the Green Blouse.* She had her hand on her stomach. It couldn't be her. Where was her Bvlgari ring? Her Hermès shawl? Her Tod's boots or her Cartier earrings? She didn't notice when he got closer; Holly's gaze was elsewhere, looking *into* the complementary red and green in between the fauvist wooden chair.

"Matisse was poor when he was young," Neil whispered but she didn't look up, "The expensive tableware you see in *the Dinner Table*, even that red cloth in that painting in front of you, was borrowed from friends or family, but mixed oddly well with the simplicity of the middle-class figures."

"Really?" she focused her gaze on the red.

"Yes. He and Pissarro bought fruit or flowers they could ill afford just so they could paint summer colours and summer fruits and flowers during those frigid Paris winters. To make the fruit last longer, Matisse worked in overcoats and gloves and kept the studio unheated. His style was so unique that everyone who saw him working on the painting in his studio, from his friends Pissarro and Huklenbrok to the most progressive Evenepoel, thought it stood no chance of sale or promotion."

"Starvation breeds character."

"Could *we* say that? … Holly?"

Finally she looked up, "Neil! What are you doing— did *he* send you? He couldn't even come himself could he?"

A year ago Neil would've told her that Edwin hadn't even noticed she was gone. A few months ago Neil would've convinced her to come back because it was detrimental to CAM that she'd left. A leader and co-founder who can't keep his wife surely can't keep millions of euros of other people's hard-earned money. A few weeks ago Neil was someone else.

"He misses you. He loves you. He just wants one more chance. You should give it to him."

She let her stare fall on the painting in the corner of the room, a landscape with a pink sky and a single female figure walking through a green garden. "You used to be a much better liar. You could've convinced me if you really wanted to, I imagine."

"No one can convince a woman of anything she isn't already convinced of."

"I'm not going back."

"I'm not asking you to come back, Holly," he reached into his pocket and took out the letter, "I took this. I'm sorry. I'm giving it to you. I don't know what's in it or even if he deserves to know. But I think now that you have a clearer head you can decide whether you want to send it to him or not."

She took it and slipped it into her purse; Neil couldn't guess the brand.

"Thank you, Neil. You always were the gentleman no one appreciated. And this society turned you into a shark."

"No. I was always a shark, my dear. Just a well-read one who liked different prey."

With her hand now on his, she squeezed the top of his knuckles, "Are things okay with you and Nora?"

"I haven't talked to her in a long while. Or maybe it just feels that way. We're playing chess again so that's something, I guess."

"Yeah… it is. You came all this way to give me this letter?"

"No. I wanted to see you. I wanted to see if you're okay."

"I am. Did you know Danes are apparently the happiest people on the planet? You wouldn't guess it looking at them though."

"Yes, I did actually," Neil followed the wooden design across the floor and through the window where the sun reflected its yellow light from a pond into the gallery.

"How long are you here?" she let go of his hand.

"I don't know yet. I'm looking for someone."

"What'll you do when you find them?"

"I don't know yet." A woman's shoes echoed across the gallery.

"What *do* you know?" In the silence they could hear each other breathe.

"That I'm looking for someone, or some*thing*."

"That's not a lot."

"No… it isn't."

Neil's phone chimed.

"Get it."

"It can wait."

Holly got up holding her stomach, "No. Get it. I'm going to have lunch and then I have to get back."

Neil got up and their noses grazed for a moment before he hugged her. "Let me know if you need anything."

"Thank you, Neil. I mean that," she squeezed him for a moment before letting go.

"You're welcome. I'll see you later."

Her footsteps echoed out of the gallery. Neil sat back down on the chair.

Neil. I caught an early flight to Copenhagen. We must speak of such matters in person. Never by phone or over email. I've left word at your hotel. Find me. Marco.

It wasn't cold in the museum. It just felt that way.

Every second without her was like an ember landing on my body. There was a desolate despair and a powerful pang in my inability to express neither in words nor by emotions, the bleeding of that corner of my soul reserved for her. I could see it in front of me and hear it ahead of me; I could touch it if I reached out, but I dare not try to put into words what I went through over the course of my acquaintance with her.

At the University of Toronto I won a writing award as an undergrad. Something to do with prose and style. There was a dinner at the banquet hall of my college and then a reception at the Intercontinental nearby. There was applause when I arrived and I had to converse with the donors and professors and elder writers who knew too much to listen to me. When I found a moment to myself I walked through the garden, where the first woman I thought I could love was listening to a man boast of his dated accomplishments and his important colleagues. She listened and listened with that smile she had. She looked through him for a second and saw me but her face didn't show it.

I would meet Simonetta years later, Simonetta, whose wailing dark-brown eyes would whimper and ask where love is located. Where does it come from, its source where everything is and would be flows? It must be a hidden, secret place inside a soul's most innermost chest. And from inside that chest such love could flow. No matter how much we penetrate within ourselves we may never find this place. The source eludes us until we begin to wonder if it exists at all.

I'd had too much to drink and walked down Devonshire towards the Hart House for some fresh air. It'd rained, or was still raining. My shoes squished in the muddy fields but I could finally breathe. In the windy silence I heard the grass whisper something about love. It took a few seconds but I realized it was two people talking. Two people who had a lot to drink too. As always there was a girl, and as always there was a boy on his knees in front of her, sinking in the mud beneath her feet in adoration. He was bleeding just above his chest near his shoulder blade. Then with a little knife she did the same, cutting herself deeply on the opposite shoulder. I could see the maroon blood in the dark descending into the earth. I had my phone ready for an ambulance, but then they leaned into each other and closed their eyes. They were weeping but not of sadness or happiness; it was something else. I couldn't recognize their expressions and still don't. There were no adjectives or modifiers sufficient to adequately capture their rapture. I suddenly became woefully inadequate as a person and aware of my limits as a writer. I have to this day, never seen someone unmask themselves to such an extent, to nakedly exist in front of another. Most of us are masked even to ourselves. I remember walking back to the reception in a furious haze with the foreknowledge that every relationship is bound to be masked and everyone always clothed. Confronted with this realization, how else ought we feel other than betrayed by existence and exploited by being? Never naked, always masked. Our lives are a Venetian festival.

He walked through the museum garden back to the hotel where the receptionist handed him a note card.

Illum Rooftop Terrace.

M.C.

"When was this delivered?" Neil asked.

"A few moments ago, sir."

"Thank you." Neil navigated the mazing streets towards the rooftop bar, where the chatter of happy Danes in full view of the sun filled his ears with nothing but dread.

Marco was sitting in the Bar Jacobsen on the terrace outside. Neil wondered if Holly ever came back to the Illum Rooftop in the afternoon and kept looking over his shoulder.

"Do not email anything like that to me again. With names. There's a reason why I sent you the package by hand," he whispered the last bit and stopped talking when the waiter came over.

"What can I get you?" he asked Neil.

"Ardbeg."

"Single or double?"

"Single."

"Straight?"

"Always."

"Very well, sir."

"Thank you," and when the waiter walked away he turned to Marco, "What's the matter with you? You seem fidgety."

Marco leaned in. "I don't know how many people they have or in what cities. Denmark is safe for now. Sweden isn't. That's why I came. Why were you asking about Maurus?"

"Who is he?" Neil followed a church steeple to the horizon.

"He was an arms dealer turned banker turned arms dealer," Marco looked around and tapped the table.

"You're not making sense. Calm down."

"What do you know about GeoTex?" He looked over the railing towards the street.

"Who? … What are you looking for?"

"Black Land Rovers. Tinted windows. What is it you think these guys do? He was killed. There was suspicion of foul play. But we have to play it like Al Capone and get them on the financial crimes. How do we do that when they control all the financial markets?"

"Since when has anyone gone to jail for financial crime anyway? … Except maybe in Iceland."

"Their routing banks are different. They don't abide by our rules. That's why they were punished. We can't prove the WBCT was involved in anyway. But we know. There's an absence of evidence where the evidence that would've pointed to them should be."

"You're talking in riddles."

"Who wants to go up against them?" Marco waited until the waiter put down Neil's drink.

"Is that all, gentlemen?"

"Yes. Thank you. …You *really* are paranoid."

"You weren't there. You're *not* there. They've infiltrated every aspect of government. Why you do think Maurus was bumped off? He was trying to make it out on his own."

"Why should I trust you? If they're as connected as you say they are, they've infiltrated the Justice Department too, and the SEC. So you could be one of *them*," Neil sipped his drink.

"Look up an article in *the Times* from a few months ago. You'll find something about a young intern who was killed in a car accident alongside her boss, the CFO of a major Dutch bank. That intern was my niece. You're the only person who knows. I know they found something. They definitely found something they shouldn't have."

"Did you access her files? I keep everything digital now."

"Purged. They're too smart for that. It won't matter anyway. We're not enforcement only intelligence and inform."

"So you know all this and do nothing?"

"Obviously. Aren't you listening? Nothing would change anyway. Who would we go to? When you own the governments and most of the media and the companies what are you going to do?'

"People deserve to know don't they?"

"You're in danger of becoming human… and you're out of practice," he got up to leave. "I'm leaving tomorrow. I'll be at Nimb. Let me know what you decide. … By the way, Maurus was trying to topple some dictator in the Middle East by giving weapons to the rebels. Problem was, we put that dictator in place. Which banks do you think all these leaders deposit and wash their money in? Where do you think they invest?"

Neil was contemplating the thousands of investments his firm had made on behalf of his clients. Of course he knew most of them, the ones with the best returns and the shifty deals were not exactly the kind of business he preferred to do, but Nora wanted for things. He did what he had to do. Rationalization. Justification. Given enough space and a sufficient vocabulary, any action can be justified and rationalized. The truth was and always will be: Neil was smart enough to know too much money came into and out of his accounts through suspicious routing numbers; there might be laundering, gambling, drugs, or firearms involved. Why else would an African start-up invest 2.3 million U.S. dollars into an app that was designed to find the nearest dry-cleaner's? Controlling the flow of money, the flow of weapons, the flow of information, and concealing the fact of that flow will always be part of human society. How else have Western countries become so wealthy without even half of the resources of their competitors? Control.

"Hello?" he answered his phone.

"Hi, honey!" Nora blew him a kiss.

"Good afternoon, my love. How are you?"

"I'm good. Thanks for the basket! Where are you? Are you at home?"

Home. "… No. I had to fly to Copenhagen for a few days. I'll be back this weekend."

"Copenhagen? I've always wanted to go! Is it happy there?"

"Not particularly. It's better in France and Switzerland."

"So I shouldn't come up there?"

"It's up to you but business will constantly tie me up. And the luxury isn't the same here. There's an Hermès and a Bottega Veneta but the restaurants aren't the same, not as luxurious and nice, I mean. The service is questionable."

"All right. I'll see you when you're back then!"

VIII
Sistine Madonna

Our culture has brazenly accepted the illusion of time. Chest beating like proud apes, present moments are felt as nothing more but an invisible thread being pulled by a causative past and an unforeseeable future. A cognizant tug-of-war between nostalgia and expectations and lacking the awareness and reality that there is nothing except the present, reality becomes surreal. The world and our experiences therein simply become what's described with words, measured by numbers, or feelings of failing expectations and fallen memories. The average person is diseased with the morbid fascination that words and numbers and feelings are actually useful tools in unpacking the world as an absolute reality even though those tools are best for unpacking a relative concept. Words are our only tools. Question: What is the difference between the relative and the absolute? Is it the same as the difference between full and empty or between alive and dead? A mere word, or is the difference something more than words could express? Answer unknown. Words change from one temporal moment to the next as unstable and unreliable as the wind over the waves as if they were whispers lost in the air.

The other day I decided to leave. To leave her to her lovers and relationships and friendships. Isn't that really wanting another's true happiness? Sacrifice? As Kierkegaard would say, and what better place to say it than in his city, that the greatest act of love is to leave your beloved to *freedom*.

The weather forecast reported rain but the sky was too clear to hope. It was hot enough to make even the ice-hearted bubble.

Rain is eternal. Unity is a fusion of happiness and love. But love is impossible in loneliness and thus so is unity. Alone the best we might be is happy, but even that happiness would be a superficial happiness that doesn't equal fused unity. Alone, happiness is tied to space and the objects it contains. A flower may remind us of someone in superficial happiness as if the agglomeration of beating hearts begets unity. Peonies were her favourites but I didn't like them, they're like orchards. They carry with them the aroma of sweet innocent humans. All flowers wilt. A tree reminds us of particular experiences tied to time and space. Trees have roots yet they are not unified. And what else do poems remind us of other than past lovers and potential future bets on happiness? Never in the present, we breathe as images of our former selves and who we might be later in life. Therefore we are never ourselves but someone else. I'm so tired of the rain; it's been pouring all week and no chance of it clearing. The forecast is wrong. On Rådhuspladsen I visited Hans Christen Andersen's study and listened to him through the speakers talking about travel and his personal life.

I visualized never returning. Time would pass regardless. I would be liberated from that long walk from Nørreport station down Frederiksborggade bending into Købmagergade, where the baker with his thinning blonde hair always smiles behind his tall moustache; where the street florist with a light windbreaker and high-riding toque above his bald head inquires every day whether I'd like a peony for my beautiful girlfriend; and the barista who sees me finishing my cigar outside the Lagkagehuset and has my double espresso at the ready when I enter and take a number, who asks in her wonderful English what I've read or written lately when the café isn't too busy. The cold waters of the Øresund strait, mixing the Baltic Sea with the Atlantic Ocean were only remnants of the momentary alacrity I'd had with her, the apogee of which climaxed on a lachrymose evening at Moonshiners where she flaunted a puerile *friend* in my face. He burbled his name and shook my hand over Luís, and the hand that shook mine would wrap around her waist moments later, causing a splenetic reaction from both Luís and Benson when she left with him and Simonetta to a party. She left for a moment and came back wearing red lipstick. It was the first time I'd seen that shade on those lips. Lips he would touch with the same hands that shook mine. Who knows? Maybe I was being paranoid. Yes... I was being paranoid. Yet what bothers me to this day is that I forgave her the second it happened. The ones that make it hardest to love them are the only ones worth loving. Nothing she did could propitiate what my mind refuses to forget. In front of that rutilant strait I wondered what parts of myself I would forsake by departing. Not a paucity of experience by any means. The no doubt amicable torpor of those interactions with the old baker, the romantic florist, the kind barista, and that vile lover of hers, had all become a part of my life whether I liked it or not. To separate myself from those interactions would be to lose future moments and experiences. "She's using you Raphael!" she would scream at me under her world map where I'd found myself and love as an islet being washed over with every wave on its shore. But life uses us all cyclically. Does the universe not use God, and God not use angels who use humans who use their demons to justify their wickedness and resentments and past mistakes? Angels know no morality. The stars are indifferent in their vastness. To be used knowingly and willingly was to combat that indifference. Now I understood why that man in the casino had bet everything on 33 if only for that momentary smile. He'd beaten the house.

The Maurus case was getting to me. I couldn't solve it. Facts are always obvious posterior. I was no cop or detective. Still I had a hunch the WBCT was involved. The Internet makes things easier and harder on all of us. Every time the flow of weapons increases in certain, let's say "developing" regions of the globe, their quarterly returns shoot up. There is too *much* information sometimes, saturated and useless bits of meaningless knowledge and data. Red herrings. Notwithstanding large investments—there is a threshold that denotes whether an investment is small or large—and trades by the WBCT and their consultants are a matter of public record. However, the data on the larger investments lies at the middle of a maze in a smoky strip club owned by a mirror factory. The ones I found were routed through Swiss or Monaco or Dutch consulting firms and brokerage houses. I called some of them. These guys are a different game; they hide behind privacy laws. Private marriages and court cases are a matter of public record but a bank's investment portfolio is protected by privacy laws? I wonder who writes these laws. Laws that legally permit the government to read my emails and have a list of my favourite books and films and my registered voting preferences; I am naked in front of every camera and under every streetlamp but it is prohibited of me, the voter and citizen, to access private bank records linking exponential quarterly profits with subtle violent increases and settled power struggles in forever destabilized regions? "We need more evidence… this isn't enough," Martin said over the phone. "It's *illegal* to get more evidence," I screamed back. And evidence acquired illegally, or evidence that exists but shouldn't exist, ceases to exist in a court of *law*. How convenient. When Martin's sergeant found out he was livid and Martin was ordered off the case. "Relax Raphael. It was a needle in the haystack anyway." He told me to drop it. He was paranoid too.

Why is it getting to me? It'd always been this way. Thieves steal, murderers kill, lovers starve; why would the modern world be any different or better? Why should change mean something *now*? The house always wins. I would never solve that case. I would never be with her.

I was drowning. Gasping for air I heaved and panted like a dog whenever she was near me. She was so sexual; her movements were methodical, designed to invoke the deepest desires of my soul. That's what everyone kept saying; Simonetta's ramblings about her ability to feign intimacy and manipulate men, and our classmate's begrudging sentences sculpted to con me into surrendering because he thought he had a chance with her. The concept of a femme fatale was discovered to portray her. They thought me obsessed, saying I was *compelled* to love her inside an irresistible impulse for adulation. It wasn't like that. I chose her. Her specifically, and with every sunrise I could stop loving her. This dawn wouldn't be that sunrise, and tomorrow's won't be either.

They were all wrong. It was vain to love anybody else. Futile to ask *'why her.'* We love the people we love because they simply are what and who they are. Their being spills like sand grains on a windy shore. Their mere existence becomes a necessity in the future of the universe. Simple tasks like eating dinner or getting out of bed no longer represent *another day* but *another day with her in in. …* She was that *universe*. A woman, a being of indefinable substance, the detective of lost souls, a person whose light warmed the resting ice shaking my bones. Then the possibility of not being in love with her sets in, and eating alone and getting out of bed in a world that jails one person for killing another but awards medals to mass murderers gestates; and the universe implodes back into its indifferent insignificance.

By then it was obvious to everyone but me that nothing would break her image or corrupt the podium she stood behind day after day. Humans aren't complicated. We think in terms of good or bad. Is he or she a good person or a bad person without any definitions of what these concepts mean to us and what might they mean to the other. Everyone is good and everyone is bad. We just have to find that the good outweighs the bad and the bad outweighs the good.

A sparrow flew by my window in front of the sun setting earlier than expected, and the light of the city turned towards the distant horizon where there was only silence. All I had was words. The house always wins. Near the train station a group of people were smiling and laughing, tourists exhilarated by the organized movements and storefronts on Copenhagen's airy bike-lanes. I was irked by the glee that filled the streets; there must've been joy in overcoming violent or cunning struggles and coming out on top.

Neil ran his fingers over "Swiss or *Monaco*… consulting films."

Morning Sophie. I need a record of all incoming calls for the last 3 months.

Thanks. Neil M.

The dictator of Zimbabwe was rich. Neil knew that. The question is not how someone *acquires* wealth but how they keep it. Zimbabwean currency isn't worth anything so where does this leader keep his wealth? His money? With *me*? He thought. And what is the trade-off when this man gives me his money to invest somewhere and I take a percentage? What makes him select a particular consultant or bank? There has to be something in it for him. More power. The elongation of control. More wealth. More more more!

On my walk I sat on the side of the grass and drifted through the air. The ending was getting closer and closer and part of me didn't want to write it. I heard a bird approach from the trees behind me and opened my eyes. There he was: the hawk, perched just ahead of me on a long, fallen branch that extended up towards and sky and curved. It looked at me, tilted its neck, and flapped away.

"There's an excellent museum here you should see," Tina walked to his breakfast table from behind.

"Good morning," Neil stood up, "The SMK? I had to drop in yesterday."

"No. The New Carlsberg Museum. It's near the Central Station."

Neil knew exactly which sculpture he wanted to see, "Sure. Let's go."

Of course Neil couldn't understand a word of Danish, but the front page of the *Politiken* had a picture of an African village with its young people holding up AK47s.

"What's that say?" he turned to Tina.

She skimmed the page up and down, "They've scored a major victory for the rebel forces. One of the villages was taken by the local warlord but they've got it back now."

"That's interesting."

"It's good news."

"I guess you're right."

* * *

"Where's the French Sculpture section?" Neil asked the first man in a green jacket when they walked into the garden.

"To your right, sir," the man pointed up some stairs to a blue room.

"Have you been here before, Neil?" Tina asked.

"No. I read about it." His phone chimed.

AAHH! Neil! We made 120 last night! Calvin had word on a future through Schermer and it came through. :):) I'm about to have a heart attack.

Keep on winnin'! EDWINNING I should say! HA!

120 million euros without lifting a finger. He was in Copenhagen thinking about Tina and Nora and unity and happiness and somewhere else someone was clicking buttons on a computer and now he has an extra 120 million euros for his firm.

There it was. In front of him.

"You like it? It's called..." Tina looked at the plaque, "*Adoration.*"

"*One* right? Adoration One. By Stephan Sinding."

"You've seen it before?"

"I've read about him. He was originally Norwegian. Many of his sculptures are credited to realism, yet Hansen Jacobsen and Sinding could both be considered as part of the symbolism movement. The meanings beneath the layers, the raw emotions, the multi-faceted projections of man and death and life."

"You are a peculiar man."

"Yeah..." Neil said but then immediately regretted it. *It's been said* would've been perfect but he wasn't quick enough on the draw. "I'm ready to leave whenever you are. We should take our espressos at the café before we leave though."

"They have Degas and van Gogh paintings here too. Wait... did you come here to see *this* sculpture?"

"Yes, I did."

"Fair enough."

After espressos Neil separated from Tina to work back at the hotel. There, he printed all the files in the Media Room and sent them by personal courier to Marco's room at Nimb Hotel. These were misnomers. None of it mattered. He had enough put away to buy most of the countries in the free world.

Evening Mr. Meyollner,

Attached is the incoming call list for the last three months.

Have a good night!

Sophie.

He opened the PDF and scanned the page. Nothing jumped out. He had no idea what he was looking for.

Thank you, Sophie. Please forward me all incoming calls for the last six months.

Neil Meyollner.

Then he sank into a reverie, imagining the high and low tides of the Riviera and wondering how cold or hot the water would be if he walked in and never stopped.... The people walking below him on those small streets towards the fountain, they would be whales and sharks and fishes, where clouds would come and go over that vast ocean. He held his palm against the sun and created those desolate and lonely shadows that happen in places where the sun sets too early. Pretending to isolate the thousands of people walking gaily beneath him and in anger he thrust his hand away and bathed in the sunlight. He looked across where he thought Sweden would be and imagined the sand along the shores of the Øresund. There is no logic to sand, it spirals towards the wind and dances for the air and lets the water wash it whenever it pleases. Sand adheres to nothing; it knows no time, there are no geometrical shapes on the shore; it knows no math, there are only tiny mounds that appear large to others, smaller mountains of untimed sand. There were no fjords or mountain lines across the Danish horizon. How did these people appease their ambition? How did they understand one another? Letting his eyes rest on that long distant horizon, the foamy line of the waves across those questionably designed Scandinavian buildings with their sharp edges and dark-coloured shingles contrasted the golden arches of their churches and its clocks. Withdrawn through the thin line of those buildings standing in front of the hypnotising Øresund, one of the church bells in the distance begin to ring 12 times to signify 45 minutes past the hour. Now the reverie that had taken him from the Riviera through the hills and mountains of the Alps had brought him back to the Øresund. The water was cold.

Those waves... they've been there before the clattering champagne glasses and meaningless conversations and they will be there long after everyone has become a grain of sand on its shore. Who made him? Neil thought. He wasn't made by anyone, had he made himself? No, he was made by no one. Was it God or chance or fate? When he was made, what was there other than the thing that had made him? That thing that was a non-thing that was meant to be, meant to be Neil Meyollner. It made him the way it wanted. It didn't ask him nor did it ask his other self if he wanted to be; there he was, suddenly and without warning he had begun his existence. He was of the formless sand and his creation was under the sky but above an ocean that had to be; now he was under the sky and above the ocean without an ability to swim or fly. He wasn't loved or thought of before then. How was he made? Was he moulded and shaped? Nothing had asked him *how* he wanted to be made or if he even wanted to be. Now there he was, growing tall through the summers, winters, springs, and falls, and when his eyes were dimmed that non-thing had given him colour, and until then there had been no difference between the dust and him before his soul had entered his body. He saw no angel in white with thin, indelible fingertips forming and straightening and chiselling his now rounded nose.

What are the chances of existing? It's an infinitude of possibilities among crackling leaves and dried trees in the desert of existence. None of those things had crafted his body with a sharpened, exact, and quick brush. It had made him as it wanted and not anything else. He was not a seed to be planted that would bear the fruits of a poet nor a being that would eventually rue. It would will him to be a private banker. He looked, he listened, and heard the flight of those seeds that were poets and engineers and doctors through the air. He had no wings to carry him back through time to that non-thing where it would fulfill his wishes and desires. There were no familiar faces or loved ones staring back with the foreknowledge that they would search these jungles for the best wild heart that would fit him. When the possibilities narrowed in the sculpting of his soul, nothing had handed this thing what would become Neil's soul and said, "This one." Nothing roamed among the souls of lost poets, writers, angels, artists, or bankers for him. Things appear predestined by the divine or chaotic by luck, but eventually it fell to him to choose among the infinitude of faces and bodies and souls to live. As time progressed, Neil had picked all of those things himself.

A couple stopped and Neil espied them through the curtains. The woman spun around and threw herself into the arms of the man and they hugged and squeezed each other for what felt like hours. It is not power or knowledge we desire. The purest form of humanity: a child, knows neither power nor knowledge. It knows only love and unity. Neither love nor unity can come from power or knowledge. Quite the contrary, power is hatred and war, and knowledge is pain.

Here are the incoming calls from the last year, Mr. Meyollner.

Sophie.

That was quick, Neil thought. How long had he been in there? He opened the PDF again and scanned down the pages of various caller IDs and names. Mundane names and random integers that meant nothing and only did something. Average calls from other brokerage firms poaching for clients and various people thinking this was another— Bill Faulkner? Neil laughed and followed the number. It was Denmark's area code. He dialled and hoped. A woman's voice said something in Danish that he didn't understand and the call was disconnected.

He forwarded the information to Sophie to check whether there were any other interactions, either by email or telephone, that were from this name or number. Did she remember talking to him? Sophie would respond in just under 20 minutes that she hadn't taken the call. It was the other temp, the one before her, and would tell Neil the number had called only once.

He rubbed his temples to will away his migraine.

It was only after the eighth or ninth ring that he realized, lying on the bed and exhaling, his phone was ringing.

"Howdy," his southern accent slipped through while he tried to keep his voice even. He tried.

"Neil, *mon ami*, I like you. You didn't say it; I don't know why, but I found that writer fellow you were looking for: *Adler*."

Neil's migraine faded and he listened to every word. Jumping out of bed and looking out at the window towards the colourful buildings across the street, he scanned all the faces while his eyes darted back and forth.

"Don't run to the window or wander through those narrow streets yet. He's not in Denmark."

"You're too smart to be a private eye, Xavier."

"We get good at things throughout our lives, old friend. Not being wary at the thing we're good at, that's when we lose ourselves… like you and those rates of return I imagine."

"Where do you live, Xavier? We could be good friends."

"That is a horrible idea. I'm not a great friend at all."

I had no ending. That's not true. I knew the ending but I didn't want to write it. There is always an ending, even if it's one we hope never comes. Having left her I was afraid of the sentences. I didn't know, no, I didn't *want* to close certain arcs and write a climax that only confirmed the tribulations of my soul and the truth that our being together was impossible. Yet there was something about her; she lit me up from the inside… if she was the light in the corners of my mind, what was I over here *in* it?

There were four people ahead of me at the Kastrup Air Canada counter. She didn't even know I was leaving but for some reason I still expected her there.

In my bag I had my goodbye letter to her. She'd never see it. I wrote it a month ago because I had a feeling… that night was so windy and it was raining in slanting drops as if the window was talking in splashes of ecstasy. It seems like so long ago now. Sixteen months. How long is sixteen months? And along those months she would whisper "I love you," and those hugs from behind while she was kneading dough for the bread she would bake. She was so fearless, so unafraid, so wild. What would happen to that fearless woman, the wilderness of her golden hair like trees in the beginning of fall, with that strand of hair that always sought its liberation in the wind? Four people became three. Those mornings where by some miracle I could sleep and wake with her next to me; that smell of lemon sage and the sound of her breathing so close to me I could feel it. There was a couple amongst the three. And that aroma of fresh coffee when I would emerge from the shower, filling the kitchen with the wooden floor bathing in the sun. She would grind it and even heat the cup and wait for me before manually pressing it. Then there was just me. I checked my bag and the letter. She would *never* show up.

I'm so tired… so tired. I hope she never reads this… goodbye.

"Where is he, X?" Neil closed the book. Only one written page remained.

"X… I like that. It's enigmatic. He's up north somewhere. In a cabin."

"Alive?"

"As of this morning, yes. This guy is odd. He called your firm once. And consulted on a murder case in Toronto for a case that connects to the client you just took."

"How do you know—never mind. Did they catch the guy in that murder case?" Neil pushed the curtain to the side and watched the sky. The sun was setting.

"It was an important case."

"Is that a no?"

"It always is. I won't ask if you want the address because you might say *no*. My well-read financial friend, your writer friend is a recluse. He's in north Ontario in a cabin. I have his routine here. I'll send you the information."

Neil felt a shock. He didn't know what to do. He flipped through the book to the Valentine's Day post. "Is Sophie Vildegrube alive? … Would you be able to find her?"

"Spell it for me. Or email it to me."

Someone knocked at the door. "I'll call you back, X," Neil opened the door. Christina walked through; Neil didn't want to visit Raphael. The man is always inferior to his image. He didn't want to meet him.

"Are you okay, Neil?" she didn't step all the way in.

"I haven't been good company. I'm sorry, Tina."

"Don't be. I like it when you call me Tina." She smiled.

He returned her smile, "You know what's funny about belief?"

"What?" she looked through him to the outside window where the curtains were drawn and no sunlight could get in.

"We believe what we want."

"What do you mean?"

"I'll give you an example. One time a client had gone to see a Cézanne at Paul Rosenberg's Gallery. He stood paralyzed in front of this one painting. Eventually Paul Rosenberg came and asked him what he thought. The client turned over his shoulder and said he admired and respected the splendour of the landscape. Rosenberg had chuckled and retorted, 'But sir! This isn't a landscape. It's a *cathedral.*'"

"He was just misunderstood to others. Other artists adored him. Renoir thought he was a genius. Gauguin and Monet both owned a lot of Cézannes. Gauguin used to take a particular Cézanne to a nearby restaurant to study it further and show its brilliance. You know the museum we went to had Cézannes right? … But you only wanted to see the sculpture." she was wearing a V-neck t-shirt for the first time. Neil followed her shoulders down her forearm and saw the wings of her tattoo in the light.

"I know. I just like that story," he followed the wings back up to her shoulders and her now purpling eyes, "That is a nice tattoo."

"Thanks," she turned her forearm under the light where its wings flapped in circular threads, "It's an archangel."

IX
La Disputa del Sacramento

Sunlight was shining in squares through the window when Neil woke. Opening his eyes with the birds fluttering across the sun, the feeling of love flooded through his entire body as if a dam had opened in his soul. Seeing for a moment, before he was fully awake, the world through unity, he understood Nora and Tina and Edwin and Sophie and Benson. The sky became them and the sparrows sang to them. He *felt*, imagining the people biking down the street outside one-by-one, the sun floating across the sky and the trees dancing under the music of the stars. Life is made up of separate moments lived one at a time, then it becomes a wave that rises and falls at the same time and kisses the sand.

Neil expected them to be together. What sort of world would it be when two people loving each other wasn't enough? The kind of world where young lovers don't end up together, is that a world we want for generations to come? His momentary rapture was shackled by his age, by his indifference, and the dance of the tigers surrounding him. But for him to look out into the city as Raphael was sure to have done was an ecstasy unknown to him. It was love, he thought, and both of them had squandered it. Idiotic young people! He clenched his fists and slammed the curtains open and shut them to block out the sun. A love that despite all attempts at unification had never clutched its object, how rare was it? What were the odds? Where would he place all his chips if he were standing at the roulette table in Monte Carlo? What was unity other than the love between mathematicians and their operators, writers and their words, and poets and their verses? Raphael could've been anyone; he would think and connect the same with Raphael as any other man's journal he'd picked up, like his team back at CAM, even like his wife. The people in his life were all interchangeable. Was that the kind of unity that becomes the world and the world becomes? Why did the sight of the city fill him with the same effect and exaltation as an investment that returns an exquisite profit? He mused the height of that ecstasy, that the water should rise and fall like the moments of a life and a love forever unfulfilled.

He could will away the pain if he only tried. Sitting on the bed he thought about his life on the Riviera. Willing himself to be happy and becoming the man he had always been.

If I were to watch home movies predating my existence I would notice that little has changed. My mother looks the same, my father the same, the staircase that leads to the dining room and the décor of the condo has been aptly prepared for the arrival of a new human being. Presented with the sheer terror of pre-existence as time approaches the very moment my soul was imprisoned into a perishable body, I could've only understood existence when both as a child and an adult I had begun to realize how alike coffins and cribs were. The circle of existence begins and ends with non-existence.

The plane taxied and took off, everyone, her among them, shrank to the size of ants. She became smaller and smaller in the distance on the ground below me but grew larger and larger than my heart and soul could possibly endure.

So unsure when our hands had crept across the table and touched that first time, the despairing goodbyes on Nybrogade or the ambient silence inside the Ruby bar will be lost in time. How could I reach for another's hand now? It would be easy to pretend but that would only perpetuate disunity and court guilt. Ignorance is so gentle with its subjects; truth is always so painful. All those careless words that whispered through the air and thrashed the shores of my heart and mind. The silence that night was so loud; now that things ended this way, and all those words we should've said to each other every night and every day. The thought of being together in that silence forever…

It would be *her* hands I reach for until I die, or for eternity, whichever comes first. My journal reads like a best seller! It's all a joke.

The last line was crossed out. That was the last entry in the journal; the rest of the pages were blank.

Birds hovered in the wind before jerking in the opposite direction and cruising between the buildings.

A decrepit leaf had rotted on the cement but was still alive somehow. It was red. Neil walked by it and then turned back and walked by it again. Between the cracks of the pavement, a plant was growing under it above the dirt.

On the train towards the airport Neil checked the accounts. Calvin and Edwin had made trades on Schermer's portfolio routed through the Netherlands and then Lichtenstein. Final investments were made in real estate properties in Harare. It was backdated the day before the coup d'état.

The waves of the Øresund kissed the shore and receded down into the horizon. Surprised that his flight wasn't delayed, Neil looked at the departures board. The announcement not to leave bags unattended paralyzed him under all those cities that weren't Nice. We put up with delays all our lives and get used to them. Eventually we delay our own lives in the placating belief that there will always be time to board the next flight to happiness when we're ready.

"Sir?' an airport employee walked up to him.

"Hello daisy," his Southern accent propped up again, "I mean, hello ma'am," he looked at the exhaustive list of cities. Why were there so many?

"Where are you headed?" the woman was standing under the huge '2' designating the departure terminal just ahead.

"My ticket is for Nice but I haven't decided yet…." The *'attend to your bags announcement'* echoed in him again. Neil fixed his gaze on one of the cities on the board.

"Okayyyy," she phrased it almost as a question, "When you do decide, the Air France counter is over there," she pointed behind her, "Past the Air Canada counter."

Neil's eyes shot across the board. *'Toronto. On time. Departure: 11:45.'*

"Unless you're flying SAS, which is *this* way," she pointed away from the Air France kiosk.

"Just there?" he pointed to the Air Canada counter.

"Yes. Past that maple leaf."

"Thank you," he was way past Air France now. He passed it as if he hadn't planned to get on it and fly back to Nice. He walked by as if he hadn't imagined walking up to Nora and hugging her and kissing her and telling her he loved her more than anything else. That would be too expected. Too cheesy and too sentimental. "Hello! Do you have any space for me? It's a spur of the moment thing. I don't have a reservation."

The lady behind the counter looked at him, "Sure. Let me check," and typed as fast as his heartbeat.

Despite being a banker he had led a rather anodyne life, except for Nora's parents who preferred her to marry the son of their oldest family friend he had never been wild or done things on a whim. Now he hoped he could find the acrimonious Raphael. He was angry with him. He was going to tell him what he thought. He was going to beat some sense into him if he wouldn't listen. Then he was going to give him money, enough to live on for a long time but on the condition that he not squander his talent and his love. That was Neil's flaw: his Romeo-like unawareness of himself. He thought he could buy anything, even people. Those that demand from life only the material see meaning in only the material. But meaning sits outside itself, and in its personification and exemplification of momentary experiences realized. In pursuit of transcendental meaning people exist, but their existence never transcends the material. Trapped to meaninglessness we find only the material, forced into an existence we never wanted or desired.

"There is a first class ticket available, but there might not be a first class meal. Is that all right?"

"It's perfect," there was a plant in the foreground of the counter that made the Air Canada logo look like it was growing out of a little tree.

The people under him grew smaller and smaller and Neil beheld the imaginative power of those sentences in the notebook. Soon he would have his answers.

* * *

The plane was on time when it landed at Pearson International. Everyone had to tread the long walk because the moving walkways towards customs were both out of order. Toronto felt different than he'd imagined. It was hotter and drier, like an urban desert.

Where are you? <3

Nora.

She had signed her full name. She'd never done that before. Neil considered for a moment the insanity of what he'd done. What others would call insanity. Why do we need insane asylums when the world is itself one? … Xavier's email had Raphael's address plain as day.

In Toronto.

I'll see you when I get back.

When Neil showed the airport limo driver the address of Raphael's place, he looked at him and cross-referenced the price with a map in a little pocketbook.

"You sure you want to go here?"

Neil wasn't sure, "Yes. Is there a problem?"

"It's pretty far. Over four hours. We have flat rates fees based on postal codes. I can take you there but it'd be around $550."

Without hesitating Neil nodded and dropped 700€ into his lap, "That's more than enough. Now take me to my friend's place please."

"You're the boss," the Chrysler 300 pulled out of the taxi lane and left Airport Road. Merging onto the Ontario 401 East highway, Neil watched the cars weaving in and out of traffic like ants. He saw a plane take off above them in the distance and smiled.

Neil wondered when he'd started to think about himself in the third person, remembering those old conscious moments when he had to play the persona of Neil Meyollner the husband when he first married Nora, and Neil Meyollner the banker when he'd opened CAM with Edwin. He signed papers N. M. over and over again with swift resolve without giving it much thought. What does it mean, and *which* name would appear on his tombstone? Would it be Neil the husband, Neil the co-founder of CAM, or Neil the man? The city misted and blurred under the sun. When was the first time? More importantly, when had he become aware of the multiple personae he'd cultivated over the course of his life? It had to be sometime at Caina; maybe the time he'd sat with Nora's parents just before Christmas when her father had asked whether Neil paid his own way through school or whether he was there on a scholarship. He'd felt such disdain. Maybe it was the time Edwin had berated the waitress for bringing him a double espresso instead of his usual cappuccino. So many unsettling disappointments overshadowed by day trips to Saint-Tropez or Nice or Vaduz. It was the chronic headaches and the more recent pain in his shoulder that portended his descent. We go to doctors for our physical ails. Who do we go to for mental ills? How often he'd thought how different his life would've been if he had never married Nora, if he hadn't opened CAM, if he hadn't come across Raphael's journal. There was no wind, no sound of any kind except the roaring engines of the cars speeding to their destinations on that highway. That highway to… even his marriage to Nora; the ceremony, paid for by her parents because he had no real money of his own, and her father, that so-called Pulitzer-winning journalist and modern artist telling him at the reception that he'd opened up a trust for the children, the children Neil would never have. It was at her parents' estate but they were in their winter home on the Riviera and arrived by chopper only hours before the ceremony. It was on their honeymoon in Nassau and then Florence that he'd discovered Nora's parents had bought them a vacation home in Barcelona. He's never been.

He looked outside at store after store after factory after warehouse on the highway that seemed to have no end. Neil knew he should tap the driver on the shoulder and tell him to turn back to the airport. He knew he had to return to CAM, to Nora, to his life. Instead his eye fell on the highway that led into the sky in the horizon, submerging himself to the truth that the shadowless roads were only signifying the light. He read the green exit signs across boards roll calling the material: Yorkdale Shopping Mall, Vaughan Mills Shopping Centre, Tangers Factory Outlet. To the right the Toronto skyline stood tall, the SkyDome they'd renamed the Rogers Centre; Rogers, the major telecommunications and borderline monopoly of Canadian cell phone providers and cable TV, the CN Tower with its pointed tip kissing and displacing the clear sky. That was where Raphael had lived once, the city that was a metropolis but safer than other urban squalors of the United States.

"Oh honey you work too hard!" he heard Nora's voice in his head. Those words had meant something to him then; that repeated sentence every time he had to cancel a plan or reject an invitation. That sentence had defined his life from the moment of his nativity to just before the moment he opened the journal for the first time. The stopwatches that started the laps of his future tied to rounds in the boxing ring, to opening market rates, and to the countdown of his marriage. The past, everyone wishes they could go back and do things differently but Time grants resets to nothing, not even God. Existence is a generational fiction tied to time. Why should Neil feel any different? What right did he have to feel different than Nora, than her father, and her grandfather, and her forefathers before him? All those highways leading places unseen by everyone, all that logistical management of free markets shackled by corruption and cyclical materialism. His teeth chattered; how does he define, and what does it even mean to experience loss? A sense his forefathers had felt upon whenever there were crises of religion, divine wrath, or even blessings. There was a rational, albeit spiritual rationale to the end of an existence or a crisis of it. Those old biblical stories of faith being rewarded and tales of the prospect of happiness like Job and David.

Neil had failed himself not by anyone's standards but his own. It was his world vision that demanded he defend his failings to himself. In fact, by nearly anyone else's standards he had been a great success. He found himself whispering *Christina Lindström* into the Canadian air, hazing through time and finding a way to bridge a gap between him and the refined, intelligent, respected professor of Ancient Literature. She pronounced his name *Rafayello*, the way it was meant to be pronounced. Nora used to be like that. When had she lost it? What does time do to women like that, women who inspire *This, This Rude Knocking*, *the Countess Cathleen*, *to Vittoria Colonna,* and the *entirety* of Nabokov's authorship. Women past the material substance of what a man should be? He knew what. His heart rose above his body through his fading materiality as if he were lost. He recalled the state of the art air conditioning system he'd put into CAM's offices. Remembering fondly Edwin's advice he'd learned in school, to offer the contractors only 70% of the agreed-upon price or refuse to pay them, he winced at having considered it if only to save some money. Hiring his secretaries from a temp agency as if to allay fears that an affair was possible because there were so many of them on a rotation. A temp agency that meant they could not unionize and demand benefits from CAM. Society has come a long way but how gendered the role of a secretary remained. She got paid simply to screen his calls and greet people from behind the front desk. Nora's movements were so different, affectionately pronouncing certain vowels and hiding her accent behind others. She stopped as much as she could, no matter where they were, in front of creeping sunlight through the blinds or curtains before zooming back to the greying methodical calculation that came from her understanding of men's minds. He could smell her perfume and lotion in that taxi. He had retained his personal existence and remained an undeniable presence in her mind just as she was in his. Sometimes she would say something and shift across the room where he was working and rearrange the last thing she'd said, was it because of him?

Thinking of Florence Neil suddenly remembered Raphael's travel journals bookmarked on his uPhone.

He clicked on Florence.

Hello darlin'. I'll be back from Toronto later this week. I saw the clear sky in the distant horizon and remembered one of our walks around that little bridge in Florence. What did you feel when we visited Florence? I've been thinking about it.

Neil.

The next few minutes were agonizing. This was his wife! Why was her response so important to him? A particular response meant to—

Yes I remember Florence. It was great. I don't remember the little bridge though. The '98 Masseto we found was wonderful wasn't it? And that cute little yellow dress I picked up from Cavalli. That was a fun trip. I can't believe you remember all that. ;) We should go again. Maybe fly private? Take the chopper to the airfield? I love that thing!

Nora.

The sands along the shore rose into helixes touching the sky. A woman sat in it. She stood and walked through it as Neil approached. He couldn't see who it was.

"Hey. We're here man," the driver looked back.

Neil woke and looked around, "Huh? Thanks," and cleared his throat. The area was so remote. He heard a little bird flutter away through the trees. "Is this the place?"

"Yeah. There's the house," he pointed to the house. "I can't drive up."

Neil looked ahead where the road turned into a walking path.

"You going to be all right?"

"I'll be fine."

"Is your friend expecting you? There's nothing around here bud."

"No. But it'll be fine. I'll call a car. Cars come out here right?"

The driver chuckled, "Yeah… you can call a local cab."

"Thanks."

The Chrysler snapped wood and threw rocks up on the forest road. When it turned and disappeared from view there was only silence.

X

Self-Portrait with a Friend

Canada is seasonal and Neil felt chilly in his light suit jacket. It was the threshold between autumn and winter. The sun was out in full swing through the trees, brightening their greens and the yellows and the reds of the leaves that tumbled across the sky at the wind's behest. Light snowflakes began to fall in floating movements among the dancing trees. Neil paced himself and approached the house slowly. He'd had so much time to think but he still didn't know what he was going to say.

On the path there was a bench. Neil sat down and smoked a cigar. Ascending the creaky wooden steps Neil exhaled and knocked on the door. There was no answer. He knocked again. No answer.

In the silence the wind picked up and Neil put his ear up to the door. He could hear mumblings and whispering from inside the house. Walking around he came across the cedar terrace and looked through the screen door and window. There was a man smoking and typing in the main room. Neil tried sliding the screen door and it opened. There was nothing in the room except a coffee table and a desk where the man was working. The scent of wood filled his nostrils when he sat down on the only other chair in the place: an old leather single-seat couch in between two cedar bookshelves that covered the entirety of the back wall.

The man didn't even look up. Typing with his cigar in the ashtray fogging up the room he simply started talking, "There's a theory in subatomic particle physics: Schrödinger's cat theorem, that postulates the existence of all alternate histories and futures. Alternate histories," his voice was deep and glottal as if he hadn't talked in weeks. "Meaning every time we make a choice, the universe adjusts to that choice. We continue living our life, and in the other universe where we didn't make that choice another us is created. Imagine billions of people making trillions of choices. That is an infinitude of worlds. An infinite number of yous, an infinite number of Is. There's a Copenhagen Interpretation that allows you to predict the probabilities of certain events. When one event occurs, it becomes reality and other alternative possibilities are discounted. Things not observed in those realms might as well have not happened."

"That's a lot to think about," Neil calmed down.

"The question is, if there's an infinite number of each of us in infinite worlds, how do we know which one of us is the real us and which were created simply because a choice that wasn't supposed to be made was made?" he took his cigar and leaned back in his chair.

"So there is a world where you and Sophie are together? Hmmm, that's why you're still alive then," he wanted to see how he'd react to personal attacks. That's the true test of a man's limits.

For the first time in this surreal interaction, the man stopped typing and looked up with his eyes fixed on Neil's pupils. Neil noticed what everyone had been talking about, that wild, focused stare into the distance, the introspective reverie that dances like waves of the sea. He was frightened but not because of the stare. No. What terrified him was around the eyes; he'd seen it before, the crinkling movements of those unblinking, large eyelashes… he reminded Neil of himself. How does a man lose that stare? That purpose, that drive, *when* does a man lose it?

He even looked familiar but Neil couldn't place him. A sparrow flew by the window and stopped on the stoop just outside the screen door. Thunder sounded and rain tapped on the glass. The silence was uncomfortable. Neil reached into his bag and brought out the journal. "Don't look at me like I did something. Here," he put the Moleskine beside a stack of manuscript pages wrapped in an Hermès shawl with four horses on the table, "I assume you're Raphael."

"I don't know you Monaco-Man," Raphael leaned back for a moment and stretched.

"But I feel like I know you—wait, how'd you know I live in Monaco?" the clouds parted and sunlight lit up the trees.

"We've walked by each other a couple of times on the Riviera."

Neil stopped and recollected the faces on the streets of Monaco desperately wanting to remember Raphael, "Anyway, I came to return that journal of yours," he sat back down.

Raphael's movements were controlled and flowing; cigar smoke had created clouds above them and lingered just below the ceiling. "Keep it. I know what I wrote."

Neil followed the shelves of books across the wall. His eye caught a red Moleskine hardcover journal in the top left corner, "May I read what you've written?" he pointed to it.

The typewriter stopped, Raphael creaked on the wooden chair, "You *read* it? … You now have my attention Banker-Man." The rain came and went as it pleased.

"Yes, I read it. I know I shouldn't have but I did. I feel like I know you."

Raphael puffed his cigar and started typing again, "That makes one of us," a wind blew in and howled against the window.

"You're all alone out here?" Neil looked at the manuscript pages lying under the notebook.

"No…" Raphael kept typing with one hand but with the other pointed to the shelves."

"Ahhhh," Neil exhaled, "Of course."

"You're a peculiar man. Why did you come here?"

"I came to return your journal."

"I gave it away myself… Neil."

"How do you know my name?"

Raphael smirked in the silence. A mystical air thickened the room, "I read your email."

"Oh, of course. And you called my office. Bill Faulkner? That's risky. Even for you. He's a Nobel prize winner."

"How many private banker's receptionists do you know that read? *Really* read?"

"You're right," Neil paced towards and away from the shelves, "Did you ever find an ending for that novel you were writing?"

"Just about," the typewriter needled through the page.

"How did it end?"

"How all finite things end."

"Are you purposefully vague, or do you make sense to yourself?"

"Both," Raphael looked outside for a moment and followed a bird through the branches.

Neil stopped pacing in front of a *Madame Bovary* hardcover, "I think my wife is having an affair with my friend. That's a cliché isn't it?"

"Is that why you're here? You're running away from confrontation? I thought you used to be a boxer. … Don't you have a duty to yourself to be happy?" he asked.

"But what if your happiness is tied to someone else?" Neil sat down but got up immediately and started pacing again.

"That seems like superficial unity. An excuse to justify being pushed around because you're afraid of change. Everyone needs to find their own happiness," the typewriter's needle banged against the page.

"Happiness isn't personal, it's unifying," Neil lit a cigar and sat down, a light bulb went off in his head.

Raphael doused his own cigar and stopped typing. The sparrow landed outside the window again and in the silence they heard it calling for something, "Happiness is a hawk. Pursue it and it will either attack you or fly away, but stay still and it will nest in your heart."

"My happiness could go to hell!" Neil tapped his shoe on the wooden floor.

"I didn't know you could be so… funny. … Or reactive." Suddenly his eyes glazed over and he began typing faster. The needle burned through the page and little black chasms opened up shaped like letters on the white pages Raphael threw to the side.

"I'm not a character. Don't make me into one," Neil pointed to the white page being blackened by the ink.

"No one is a character unless they are caricatures of themselves. You're a *person*."

Neil had no response. He wasn't sure whether he was a person or not. "To be honest, I came because I wanted to see if you were still alive. I wasn't expecting you to be."

"Sorry to disappoint."

"It would've been selfish. You would've pained the person you claimed to love. I know you know your Goethe. If you love the person you want the beloved to be happy right?" … When Raphael didn't respond and just kept typing Neil went on, "You want them to be happy being themselves while you suffer in silence. That's rather romantic isn't it? But you *do not* negate your existence."

"Weren't you listening? There are infinite decisions and versions of us. In one world somewhere I did do it."

"But not this one! That's the easy way out! The selfish way because you're making it about you! Love is one-way. It always has been. It cannot be conveyed in temporal sentences or spatial inadequacies. It expands past the universe and extends past the tenses of time. And what is love but the fusion of temporality to eternity, and space to infinity? What else would it be, if not love, that exists before the past and after everything is gone? Real love, the ones we read about, can never sustain in an imperfect world. And maybe there is a perfect love in one of those worlds of yours."

"Who are you trying to convince?"

"I don't know. I want to leave my wife."

"Why don't you? Are you your own worst enemy?"

"I don't know how to love anyone else…" Neil sighed and looked outside for a hawk.

"Live in the past and the future. It's a safe bet. Good return. Never the present. It's risky. Hedged. The only thing stopping you from making the decision that would make you happy is *fear* of your present, and the fear of having to live in the *now*. When things become real, when they become the present, we flee," he nodded to a bird outside with outstretched arms. "Why? Because we fear the present and the *real*. We'd rather bet on a better future contingent to a worse past that we'll perpetually improve into the future."

"I'm going to make myself a cup of coffee."

Raphael pointed behind him to the kitchen.

There was nothing but bananas, apples, and a loaf of bread in Raphael's fridge when Neil opened it. Neil turned the kettle on. Its cool air kindled something in him and he wept. It was only for a second but the loss of purpose and his inability to articulate his love for Christina froze him. Most of the time when we cry we don't really know why.

He poured himself the Twinings English Breakfast from the pantry. When he walked back into the studio, the studio… or was it a study? It could've also been a library because of all the shelves and books. It was also where Raphael was writing and presumably had written, was it a writing room? Writers must read in order to write, the reading room perhaps? But reading what? The Shakespeare room? You see, dear reader, we may descend the hierarchy of words into absurdity: the Shakespeare

Room, the Blogging Room, the Word Room. Like people, words have their own classes and power structures. Therein why they have no meaning. What is the most important word? The most meaningful verb or turn of phrase?

Infinite worlds being created every second. It doesn't matter what choice he makes because in another just-as-real world he's already made the opposite. What matters is the *now*, the existential unity abiding and pushing forward his being. Neil looked outside behind Raphael, where he imagined his love for Tina lit up the stars that glinted across a sky that had begun with darkness.

When he approached the table through the cigar smoke he stole a glance at the first sentence of the manuscript sitting next to Raphael: YACHTS SWAY ABOVE THE DEEP BLUE WAVES OF THE FRENCH RIVIERA.

ACKNOWLEDGEMENTS

I am indebted to Mads Leonard Jensen for his poetic translations in Danish.

This novel would not be possible without the assistance and advice of my editor: Christopher Veri.

My gracious thanks to my sister Mohabat, and my mother Farahnaz for their never-ending support.

www.ingramcontent.com/pod-product-compliance
Ingram Content Group UK Ltd.
Pitfield, Milton Keynes, MK11 3LW, UK
UKHW041630190726
13854UKWH00006B/2401